American Shadows

Lora Moore and Julie Zuehlke

To Tom,

    Enjoy this little

adventure !

Cover Photography by Lora Moore
Cover Design by Jen Naumann

ACKNOWLEDGMENTS

We would like to thank our husbands, children and families for giving us the time, space and understanding to create our stories. Without your support, this would all be impossible.

Thanks to our editor, Janelle Hawkridge, who consistently offers honest guidance throughout this process. We greatly appreciate her wisdom.

This project wouldn't be complete without the candid advice from fellow writers and readers. Huge thanks to John Pfaffinger, Charlie Moore, and Sue Vogelsang for the helpful feedback. Once again, thanks to Jen Naumann for her guidance throughout the final construction of the front and back covers.

And finally, a very special thanks to our sources who must remain anonymous due to their careers keeping this country safe. There are truly extraordinary men and woman working tirelessly for our freedom, and for that we are grateful.

Chapter One

Alzira, Spain

"Bless me Father, for I have sinned."

"Go on, my son," Father Carlos Aznar Sanchez answered, curious as to who was sitting on the other side of the curtain. The soft male voice spoke broken English, dominated by a heavy Spanish accent.

The parish of Saint Mary's Catholic Church was small, the congregation rarely exceeding twenty loyal members. Father Sanchez knew his parishioners well; by name and by voice, as they all regularly attended confession. Sanchez glanced down at his wristwatch before he could stop himself. He had a long afternoon of confessions and impatience had no place in his line of work. Besides, what else did he have to do? Nothing much, other than finishing up his preparations for the sermon he would give tomorrow at Mass.

"My last confession was...." the unfamiliar voice paused, before finally saying, "a long time ago."

"It's alright," Father Sanchez commented, noting an odd undercurrent to the man's voice, almost as if the man was carefully selecting his words. "What's important is that you are here now," the priest added, deducing that the man was most likely nervous, or at least uncomfortable sitting in a confessional after what he admitted was "a long time ago."

"Is it?"

Father Sanchez leaned forward on his elbows, his prior sense of unease quickly upgraded into something more troubling. He had spent countless hours listening to confessions of all types, people who came from all walks of life. The majority of those who sat in his confessional could be easily grouped into three different categories: the deeply sorry, the tired and defeated, or most often, the dutiful atoner of sins who felt the need to confess regularly.

The stranger sitting across from him didn't fit into one of those categories. His soft controlled voice, even though hesitant, didn't hold even a hint of remorse or nervousness.

"Of course it is, my son," Father replied. "Please, let me help you with what's burdening your heart." Father waited in silence, feeling his own heart quickening.

"I believe the burdens on my heart will have to

wait for another day, Father."

"Pardon me?"

"Today, I'm more interested in you," the voice proclaimed, still soft and controlled but now completely devoid of the Spanish accent.

"Who are you?"

"The answer to that question isn't nearly as important as knowing *what* I am."

Father Sanchez peeked through the small gap between the curtains draped across the narrow door of the confessional. He spotted a handful of his faithful followers sitting in the pews awaiting their turn. "And so, what are you?" he asked, trying to keep his nerves calm in order to remain clear-headed.

"If you do what I say and cooperate, you will never have to find out."

The voice had transformed. The broken English was now spoken perfectly, with an American accent. His words had lost the soft smoothness and now held a dangerous edge.

"What do you want? What do you need from me?" Father asked as his left hand eased toward the small shelf that held a handful of prayer booklets.

"Domino."

"What? I don't understand." Father's heart was beginning to pound and the small confessional walls were closing in on him. He felt a surge of adrenalin just as his fingers reached the cool metal of the

9mm fastened underneath the shelf.

Suddenly, the flimsy shaded screen separating himself from the confessor was shoved aside. Father Sanchez found himself staring into a pair of cold bluish-gray eyes that seemed to bore right through him. The man's face, although young, portrayed no innocence. His fair skin was stretched tightly over his prominent jaw and strong cheekbones. The man appeared to be thin, gaunt almost, but nowhere near weak. Actually, if the priest had to guess, his visitor was in peak fighting condition.

"By the time your hand wraps around that gun you're reaching for, you'll be dead," the man said calmly. "Hands where I can see them, Father."

Sanchez slowly placed both hands on his lap.

"Dominique Rodriquez Sanchez, aka, Domino. Your little brother. Ring a bell?"

"I, uh, I haven't heard from him in years," the priest stuttered.

The stranger smiled slowly, revealing a perfect set of white teeth. His smile, however, did nothing to warm the ice in his eyes. "Now, Father, shame on you," he stated smoothly. "Lying so blatantly in a church, in the confessional, no less. Care to confess your sins?"

Sanchez felt the sweat beading up on his forehead. He looked down at his hands, angry that he wasn't able to retrieve his gun quicker and take control of the situation. There had been a time, many years ago, when he might have been able to out-maneuver this threat.

He looked up and met the American's penetrating stare. Sanchez immediately changed his mind. Even in his prime, he would not have been able to match the lethality that the stranger's cold eyes promised.

Father Sanchez had hoped and prayed this day would never come, but he had known it would. He knew in his heart that he would one day be forced to face the dark side of his family.

He had once vowed to always look after his younger brother, to make sure no harm came to him. He had promised to keep danger from knocking on his door. Those promises were made a long time ago, in a different time and a different place. Life had warped and reshaped any semblance of who he and his brother had been and what they had become.

While his brother had been blessed with brilliance, charm and the strength to lead people, Dominique had chosen a path full of vengeance and anger. Unfortunately, his leadership was wrought with death and destruction.

Carlos had chosen a different life. He chose to lead people as well, but in prayer and in peace. He would always love Dominique, but he attempted to put as much distance between himself and his brother's dark, dangerous world as possible.

Unfortunately, Dominique never allowed much time and distance to separate them. Father Sanchez did his best to keep his small corner of the world safe, but apparently, his best was not good enough. He would no longer be able to keep danger from knocking down the door.

Now, danger was at the door staring at him with a pair of steely eyes.

"What is your business with my brother?" the priest asked quietly, unable to quell the tones of betrayal from his voice.

"Your brother is responsible for the deaths of thousands of innocent people. He is planning to kill thousands more. Domino, *your* brother, is an international terrorist. My job is to find him and kill him. You're going to help me."

Father stared at the face of the American across from him. The man's voice remained calm, almost soothing, yet his words spoke of murdering his brother! He couldn't possibly be expected to help this assassin hunt down and kill his own brother, could he? Father Sanchez struggled to find the words to respond. When he started to speak, the American suddenly held up his hand, motioning for him to stay silent. Father watched as he pulled aside the curtain and glanced out into the congregation, where people were patiently awaiting their turn in the confessional.

"You need to come with me," the man

demanded as he shoved aside the small screen separating the two of them. "We can't talk here."

The priest looked up at the tall man and replied, "I'm not going anywhere with you."

The American sighed and pulled out a silenced handgun from behind his back. "Yes, Father, you are coming with me. I'm not gonna kill you, but I could make this rather painful for you. I'll do what I've gotta do. Capish?"

Father Sanchez, no stranger to weapons himself, quickly recognized the casual comfort with which this American handled his gun. The gun itself also spoke volumes about the man holding it. From his best assessment, the weapon appeared to be a custom 1911 pistol. This sort of weapon was common among Special Forces and the military. However, the weapon in this American's hands hinted at several carefully constructed modifications in the sight and trigger. What caught Sanchez's eye the most was the intricate etching of two stars and two dice on the flat side of the slide. One star was tinted blue, one a deep red and both of them were partially hidden behind the dice. He could only imagine the significance of that image to the man holding the gun, but to Sanchez, it was obvious that the weapon currently aimed in his direction would not be found in the hands of an amateur. This American was a professional killer. There was no doubt that this man would indeed do "whatever it took".

"Who are you?" the priest asked as he stood up, noticing that at his full height, his own eyes were at the same level as the man's broad shoulders. He figured the man had to be at least six-four.

"Not here," the man answered. "We need to go now."

"Why?"

"Something's not right out there," the man spoke softly. "Look," he demanded. "Look out there and tell me if there is anyone you don't recognize."

The priest cautiously peeked out the curtain. He studied the familiar faces of his parishioners. All were elderly women, but one. The lone exception was a troubled teenage boy who came regularly to confess his dilemmas. Father was about to release the curtain and inform the American that nothing seemed out of sorts, when the sanctuary doors opened and two men walked in. They were dressed like the locals, in loose-fitting linen pants and flowery button-down shirts. The way they moved, however, told a different story. They appeared uncomfortable, eyes darting quickly around their surroundings. They walked slowly, trying to take everything in. They seemed to be looking for something, or someone.

"There's two men, in the back. I don't know them. They look like they're lost or looking for someone, perhaps?"

The American quickly yanked the priest's 9mm gun out from beneath the shelf and looked at the gun in surprise. It was the sort of pistol issued only to military, Special Forces or law enforcement.

"A USP Compact," he stated as he checked the weapons for bullets. Finding the gun fully loaded, he added, "not the kind of gun I'd expect a priest to have." Then the American began scanning the walls of the confessional. "Is there any other way out of this thing?" he asked.

"No. Maybe if we just go out there and ask—"

"If we go out there, we're dead. Those two men are looking for you. Probably me, too. We need to get the hell out of here. Now."

The American stuffed both his gun and the priest's gun into his belt and began exploring the walls with his hands. Feeling nothing but solid brick and wood, his eyes looked up. His plan formed the instant he saw a vent and a false ceiling.

"Okay, Father, looks like we're moving up in the world."

The American clambered up onto the same small shelf that had hidden Sanchez's gun. He began sliding away the ceiling panels and vent cover. Quickly the small escape hole was revealed. He hopped down and said, "You first."

"You can't be serious."

"I hardly ever lie in church," the man replied. "Now go. I'll be right behind you."

The priest carefully squeezed up into the vent shaft and crawled slowly into the dusty darkness. He heard the American stifle a sneeze right behind him.

"Kick it into high gear, Father. This isn't the time to slow down and smell the roses…and the dust. Shit, doesn't this place use air filters, for Christ's sake," he added, stifling yet another sneeze.

As they scurried along in the ventilation system, they heard increasing commotion from the sanctuary below. At one point they heard a woman scream, bringing them to a momentary halt in their climbing. The American, however, quickly pushed on.

"What are they doing down there?" Father asked, feeling panic well up in his chest.

"Don't think, Father. Crawl."

Finally, a shaft of light filtered down upon them and when they saw the large metal grate that led to the outdoors, they both felt a sense of relief. That is, until they saw that it was bolted firmly in place.

"I don't suppose you have any tools tucked away in your pockets?" the American asked sarcastically.

The priest said nothing, feeling zero sense of humor about this predicament.

"Well then, maybe start praying. You have a direct line to the Big Guy, right?"

"I've been praying since the minute I laid eyes

on you," the priest answered seriously.

"Good. Thanks. I need all the help I can get," the man answered lightly as he fidgeted with something in his pocket. "Goddamn tight spaces," he mumbled before suddenly realizing what he had said. "Sorry. I'm just a little claustrophobic. Tends to make me swear. I'm sure it will happen again. I apologize in advance."

The priest felt his breathing slow a bit and his curiosity rise. This man crowded beside him, whose first impression was deadly and intimidating, was somehow not as scary anymore. Father Sanchez wasn't completely convinced that the man wouldn't kill him if he deemed it necessary, but he was feeling a glimmer of hope that the American wasn't as cold as his eyes first indicated.

The American mumbled a few more swear words before he pulled out a black steel utility knife. He flipped open the small wrench triumphantly. He adjusted the wrench to fit onto the bolt and twisted.

"Good God," he uttered when the bolt didn't budge. He put forth another massive effort into the wrench with the same result. He glanced at the priest and said, "Are you still praying? Maybe you could amp it up a bit, Father, because if I can't get this grate open, we're screwed."

The man adjusted his body and gripped the wrench with determination. He pushed down as hard as he could and finally, the bolt groaned as it twisted. Just a little. A few more stubborn turns of the wrench, and the bolt was loose. The American quickly focused on the next bolt, seemingly oblivious to the increased screaming in the sanctuary below them.

"Are those men killing everyone down there?" the priest whispered loudly, already knowing the answer in his heart.

The American only focused on loosening the remaining bolt. Sweat dripped down the man's face, and he grit his teeth as twisted the wrench one last time.

"There," he said and folded up his knife. He pushed on the grate. It didn't move. The man repositioned himself while grumbling about "everything being so difficult." He pressed his back against the vent shaft and used his legs to kick at the vent. After two solid kicks, the grate finally gave way and tumbled to the ground below. The American stuck his head out and stated dryly, "Well, I've got some good news and some bad news."

"What?"

"The good news is there's a possibility we might live through this."

"And the bad news?"

"The bad news is that we have an equal possibility of *not* living through this."

Father Carlos only stared at the American.

"Well, let's think positive, eh?" the American stated with a smile. "We're two stories up. Guess we'll just have to "tuck-n-roll" our landing. You first. I don't want you chickening out on me."

The American shifted so the priest could get to the opening. Father Sanchez peaked out and hesitated. Suddenly, the sounds of screams below were covered up by the loud booms of explosions.

"No time, Father! Out you go!" the American shouted as he shoved Father Carlos out of the small opening.

The American immediately squeezed through the hole and prepared himself for the hard landing. He truly did "tuck-n-roll" as he protected his knees and head from serious damage. Still, the impact jarred his bones. He didn't take time to evaluate as he quickly grabbed the priest and dragged him along toward the wooded grove near the cemetery.

Before the two men could reach the safety of the trees, the small explosions gave way to an eardrum-shattering, intensely hot, blast that left the once sturdy little stone and brick church, a pile of rocks and rubble. Ironically, the only part that remained intact was the steeple that housed the bells. Despite the chaos and destruction, the bells chimed beautifully as the sunshine was slowly blocked out by the black billowing smoke.

$$* * *$$

Father Sanchez forced his eyelids open. His ears were ringing and his head throbbed. He wasn't sure what had happened. He only remembered being pushed out of the second story escape hole. Everything after that was a bit murky. Did the American make it out?

The priest softly felt his head to search for any outward signs of injury. He tried to take a deep breath but the weight on his chest made it nearly impossible. Slowly, ever so slowly, his senses were returning. He smelled smoke and saw shafts of light filtering through the tall evergreen trees. The cool damp earth felt as though it was trying to swallow him whole. He tried to lift his head to see why he couldn't move. Had the blast rendered him paralyzed? Maybe a tree had fallen on him. Trees? He remembered running toward the trees when everything went black. The explosion must have propelled him into the grove.

He lifted his head slightly and looked at his chest. There, lying on top of him, bleeding and unconscious, was the American.

Father Carlos slowly and carefully shimmied his body out from under the man's significant weight. True to the priest's first assessment of him, even though thin, the man was built like an elite athlete. Nothing but knotty, lean muscle.

The priest sat up slowly and inhaled a few careful, deep breaths. He looked back at what remained of the church: Stones, broken bricks and plumes of black smoke. Then he looked down at the unconscious man lying next to him. He had a nasty gash above his right eye that was the source of most of the blood. However, he had several smaller cuts and abrasions that were adding to his blood loss.

He reached for the man's wrist to find a pulse. The slow strong beat was easy to find. Father Sanchez couldn't help but notice the odd shaped scars scattered along the man's forearm. This obviously wasn't the man's first time in a detrimental situation. Father Sanchez wondered if he should try to move the man and arrange his lanky body in a more comfortable position. As he studied the man, he noticed the two black handguns jutting out from his belt.

Quickly deciding that guns in his own possession was a far better situation than guns in the mysterious American's possession, the priest reached for them. Before he could lay a finger on the cold steel, a hand with a vice-like grip intercepted his reach.

The American had regained consciousness.

The priest met the piercing eyes that were staring up at him. He tried to pull back his hand, but the man only gripped tighter.

"Please, I, uh, I only wanted to protect myself,"

the priest stuttered. The American continued to stare at him. The priest noticed something flicker in his eyes. Confusion? Fear?

"Are you okay?" the priest asked, softening his tone.

The man released his hand and carefully sat up. He wiped at the blood streaming down the side of his face. After inhaling deeply, he glanced at what was left of the church. Then his eyes, once again, fell on the priest, whose face was black and sooty from the blast.

"What happened?" the man asked, his voice scratchy.

"They blew up the church," the priest answered. "Thank God you got us out of there or else we'd be dead."

The man rubbed his eyes and wiped again at the streaming blood. He appeared to be struggling with clearing his head.

"Are you sure you're okay? There's a clinic a few blocks from here," the priest stated, feeling more and more concerned about the American's state of mind.

The man leveled his eyes once more at the priest, and again, Father Sanchez caught a flash of something enigmatic in those strange eyes. The frosty distance was gone; however, a wary vulnerability that the priest would have never thought to be possible had taken its place.

"Can you walk? I'll take you to the clinic," the priest stated firmly, deciding there was something seriously wrong with this stranger.

"No. Wait," the man replied. He shook his head slowly then winced, as a fresh round of stabbing pain shot through his skull. He waited for his vision to clear once again, and then looked at the priest, "And who are you?"

Chapter Two

Langley, Virginia

Gabrielle O'Connor poured herself a third cup
of coffee this morning. She was accustomed to
working on little sleep, yet after three days of
working nearly non-stop, she was beginning to lose
her edge. She gazed out the window of the small
non-descript farmhouse, at the rolling hills dotted
with beautiful oak trees. The leaves were tinged
with colors that would erupt in only a few weeks.
Soon, those hills would be painted in golds, yellows
and reds as autumn descended onto the land. This
seemingly remote farm was conveniently located an
hour outside the city limits. The owner listed on the
deed of the house, Tom Warner, was an elderly
man, a third generation farmer who had also worked
part time as a Ford mechanic at a local dealership.
He was currently retired and resided in an assisted
living facility near his family in Georgia. Tom
Warner had lived a wonderful life and was now
enjoying his twilight years near his four children,

six grandchildren and two great grandchildren.

There was one more interesting fact regarding Tom Warner; He didn't actually exist, outside of papers, files and documents. Mr. Warner was a complete and total fabrication created in the minds at work in the secretive halls of the CIA. The truth of who really owned, and occasionally occupied, that small white farmhouse tucked in the hills of rural Virginia was known to only a handful of people, people with the highest of governmental security clearances. Miss Gabrielle O'Connor was one of those few people.

She watched as the dust swirled behind the speeding tires of the white Chevy pickup truck as it approached the house. The truck skidded to a stop and out stepped a long-legged, rangy cowboy with dark hair that would match his current mood. He quickly strode up to the door and entered without knocking.

The door slammed behind him as he shouted, "You better damn well have some good news for me, O'Connor!"

Gabrielle sighed and took one last sip of the coffee before she faced the angry man approaching her.

"Good to see you too, James," Gabrielle stated cordially.

James Hughes, his official title within Off Grid Operations (OGO), or simply The Team, was unclear. He was a skilled computer hacker, adept at unraveling complicated security systems and quite talented at conducting surveillance. He could also hold his own in field work. James was the ultimate utility player. The only thing that was crystal clear about James Hughes was that his employment with The Team was contingent on one thing – his brother. If it weren't for his brother's recruitment into the shadows of American security, James would still be running his cattle ranch and training Quarter Horses in Montana.

"Have you heard from him?" James asked impatiently.

"There are eye witnesses who claim to have seen two men escape from the second floor moments before the church exploded. We also have confirmation that he is not among the dead found in the church. Neither is Carlos Sanchez. I believe the two men that escaped before the explosion were Chance and Sanchez."

"Then why haven't we heard from him?" James demanded. "Even if he lost his phone, he would find a way to contact me."

Gabrielle handed a steaming cup of coffee to James. He grudgingly accepted it and took a slow sip.

"This has happened before, you know," Gabrielle stated calmly. "This is how he works."

"I *know* that. The difference is that I'm usually

out there working with him. I knew this sort of shit would happen if I left him out there. I should've stayed with him."

Gabrielle merely shrugged. "So, how is George doing?"

James shook his head. "The old fool is already trying to cut the damn cast off."

When he was notified last month that his lifelong friend, and the one person he trusted to run his beloved ranch, George Big Eagle, had been hospitalized after a bad wreck involving a young horse, an angry bull and a broken gate, James knew he had to get back to Montana to help. Even if it meant leaving his brother to operate on his own. This wasn't the first time James had stood on the sidelines as his brother worked the trenches. Regardless, James felt uneasy every time he wasn't able to watch his brother's back.

"He'll contact us when it's safe to do so. You know," Gabrielle added thoughtfully, "he could help us keep track of him better if he would just agree to get chipped."

"Not gonna happen," James shot back. He knew his brother was adamantly against having a GPS microchip imbedded into his body. James agreed with Chance completely. Their sanity relied heavily upon their ability to simply disappear at times. A microchip would completely take that ability away.

"So how long do we give him before I go and

find him?" James asked, feeling slightly calmer and controlled.

"Twenty-four hours. If we haven't heard from him by this time tomorrow, you'll be on the first flight to Spain.

James looked at Gabrielle in surprise. He didn't expect her to act so soon. Typically she gave her agents days, even weeks, to check in before taking aggressive action. Unless, of course, she suspected that her agents were in immediate danger or gravely injured.

"What aren't you telling me, O'Connor?" James asked, setting his coffee cup down. Suddenly, it didn't taste so good anymore. His stomach had tightened into a rock-hard knot.

Gabrielle fingered the handle on her coffee mug and gathered her thoughts. She was well aware of James' protective nature over his younger brother. She didn't want to risk triggering a brash, destructive response from James, but she also knew he was her best bet for getting her most valuable agent home in one piece.

"Officials responding to the explosion found a spot near the cemetery where they believe someone was hurt. They found a significant amount of blood."

"But no body?"

"Nothing. They found a few footprints leading away from the area, but they quickly lost the trail and can't find any more clues to where the injured person, or people, may be."

"That's Chance," James replied with certainty. "He wouldn't leave a trail. What about DNA? Are they going to test the blood? Can they figure out who he is?"

"They can test it all they want. All of Chance's records lead to a black hole. No one will ever figure out who he is. His identity is safe."

"So, he's hurt but on the move," James said quietly as he paced the floor. "I should get over there tonight. How long of a flight is it? About eight hours, right? I could get there by—"

"Just hold your horses, James," Gabrielle interrupted. "Let's give Chance a few hours to complete his mission. You going over there might put him in danger."

"But I could track him. I'd go to the church, find where his trail started and I can track him," James argued.

"If Chance thinks he has a tail and doesn't know it's you, he will completely disappear. Not to mention, you would be in danger, as well."

Gabrielle could see the worry etched in James' stubborn face. She had worked with him and his brother for the past six years. She always maintained a safe, emotional distance from her agents. She had to since she was responsible for sending them into deadly scenarios. The men and women working for her clearly understood that their lives were expendable, in order to maintain the safety of this country. Her agents knew that if Gabrielle were forced to decide between letting them perish at the hands of the enemy, or maintaining the security and safety of the United States of America, she would choose the U.S.A. For her own sanity, Gabrielle couldn't allow herself attachments in her business.

Still, somehow the Hughes brothers scratched their way past Gabrielle's carefully guarded walls and she found herself emotionally invested in their lives. They didn't do it on purpose. Matter of fact, both brothers were difficult, hardheaded men who had a tough time following orders. They certainly didn't make her job easy. However, she understood why James felt the compulsive need to protect his brother. Life had taken a traumatic turn early on for the Hughes family and James was the strong, grounding force that kept their shattered lives from completely falling apart. Possessing a flaring temper, James also had the ability to smile warmly, talk easily and disarm the most guarded of personalities. Gabrielle quickly learned that James' ability to make people feel comfortable and at ease, came in handy when gathering human Intel. People generally weren't threatened by James. When people weren't threatened, they tended to talk.

And then there was Chance. Chance was

undeniably intimidating, and he took no measures to try to make people feel at ease around him. Perhaps when he was much younger and less jaded, he was capable of being charming and amicable, but the path his life had taken him left him socially impaired. Despite that, Chance, with all of his deeply imbedded emotional scars and physical trauma that he had to overcome, had become like family to Gabrielle. She felt a need to mother him at times, most likely due to the fact that Chance had lost his mother at such an early, impressionable age.

Gabrielle's own son, Sean, idolized Chance as a hero, almost a super hero, really. And for reasons unknown to Gabrielle, Chance was incredibly gentle and kind to her son. Sean had never experienced having an involved father in his life, but he did have an ex-Marine sniper and America's top terrorism fighter around to teach him the basics of throwing a tight spiral, or a wicked curveball. Downtime was rare, but whenever Chance had a few days off, he'd make sure he visited Sean. Every time Chance returned from a mission, bruised, tired and spent, Sean's admiration grew ten-fold. The missions were always top secret. Sean would never know what Chance did in the shadows of civilization, but he knew that he felt safer because his hero was out there fighting the bad guys.

Oddly enough, Gabrielle felt the same way.

"Look," Gabrielle stated thoughtfully, "it's

probable that Chance wasn't the one who was injured. It could have been Sanchez and Chance is trying to stabilize him and finish his mission."

"When is the last time you had contact with him?" James asked.

"I don't have contact with him. You know that. My only contact is through you."

"I know that. But if he's in trouble and needs back-up or something, he would contact you, right?"

"If he gets himself in trouble, his only back-up is you, James. I can't help him. That's the cost of working completely off the grid."

James pressed his palms to his eyes and nodded. He understood. His brother didn't exist; therefore, nobody could come to his rescue. There was no cavalry to call.

"Look, he's never asked for help the past six years. I doubt he'll start now," Gabrielle said, trying to keep James from coming unraveled. She gazed back out the window and stated quietly, "Six years and he's never failed. He has a way of making it through just about anything. He'll come home this time too."

James' mind attempted to skim back over the traumatic events that had occurred throughout his and his brother's lives, but he quickly shut off the memories. Now he had to focus on the present and future. This wasn't the first time he had to worry and wonder about how to get his brother home. Unfortunately, for his nerves and increasing number of gray hairs, this probably wouldn't be the last time, either.

* * *

Alvira, Spain

"You don't know who I am?" Father Sanchez asked in surprise.

Chance rubbed his eyes in frustration and shook his head. His brain felt like it was pounding against the inside of his skull and his vision wavered. The rays of sunlight only made the pain worse. Obviously, the gash on his head was more than a flesh wound. Something had clocked him hard enough to fuzz up his brain. He glanced over at the man who stared at him with a mixture of trepidation and curiosity. Who was he? By his black attire and white collar, he appeared to be a priest or reverend of some sort. However, even though he didn't understand why, Chance refused to assume the man next to him was exactly what he appeared to be. Something deeply imbedded in his jumbled brain told him never to assume, to not trust appearances and to always be cautious.

For all he knew, the man that looked like a priest could've done this to him. That passing thought caused Chance to grab his gun and in a blink of an eye, aim his weapon at the priest.

"Who are you?" he asked again, this time with urgency.

Father Sanchez scrambled backwards, fell down and then held up his hands. "Carlos Sanchez!" he proclaimed. "You came looking for *me*. You *know* who I am!"

Chance lowered his gun, his scrambled brain desperately trying to connect the dots. He slowly stood up on shaky legs, but still firmly gripped his gun.

"Who are *you*?" the priest demanded.

The question felt like a dart shot into a deep, dark abyss. Chance suddenly felt a wave of panic as he realized he didn't have an answer. He had no idea who he was.

Father Sanchez watched as the American struggled with the question of his identity. Sanchez himself felt overwhelmed with the current situation, as well. He here was, alone with a man he could only assume was some sort of gun-for-hire, looking to kill his brother. But now, the mysterious man was injured, confused and angry, and obviously still dangerous. Sanchez looked back at the remains of his dearly beloved church where he had spent the past twenty years of his life. That part of his life was blatantly over. The next stage involved surviving long enough to get away from this assassin and finding another quiet place to go into hiding…hopefully for another twenty years.

Sanchez cautiously approached the American as he asked, "You have no idea who you are?"

The man only looked at him blankly.

"Your head injury is serious," the priest said. "I'll help you get to the clinic so you can get treatment."

Once again, the gun was pointed directly at the priest's face.

"Tell me who I am," the man demanded.

"I don't know."

"How did we end up here?"

The priest sighed and answered, "Put your gun down, please. And sit. You look like you're going to pass out."

Chance lowered his gun, hesitated a moment before realizing he really did feel himself approaching the edges of consciousness. He sat down.

"You came looking for me," the priest started. "You came into my confessional, looking to get information from me."

"What information?"

"We didn't get that far in our conversation," the priest lied, not wanting to bring up his brother.

"Why?"

"Two men came into the church. You said they were looking for me, I guess, although I have no idea why. Anyhow, they began shooting and attacking people. We escaped into a vent shaft. We ended up jumping from an opening on the second floor moments before the church blew up. That's how we ended up here."

The American was deep in thought, trying to dig up the memories.

"I never said who I was, or why I was looking for you?" he asked in frustration.

"No, but you made it clear you were doing a job and that job involved killing someone."

The American's eyes widened and then he looked down at his gun.

The gun did feel intimately comfortable in his hand, as if it was a part of him. He ran his thumb over the etching of the stars and dice on the slide. That image meant something to him, but he couldn't recall what it was. This weapon had been made for his hands only. Was he a hit man? A gun for hire? An assassin? A wave of nausea thrust through his gut, threatening to make him vomit. He leaned forward and took several deep breaths. His vision blurred and his head pounded mercilessly as scattered fragments of images began to race through his brain: a dingy, tomb-like cave, the cross hairs of a scope on a high-powered sniper rifle, nameless faces dropping from precisely placed bullets.

"No," he whispered to himself, trying to stop the violent memories.

Father Sanchez watched in fascination as he realized that the deadly, intimidating man he laid eyes upon less than an hour ago, was now someone completely different.

"You need medical atten—"Father Sanchez started.

"Stop," Chance interrupted. "Just stop and let me think a minute."

He started to take a closer look at his injuries and his surroundings. He stood, straightened to his full height and stretched his bruised muscles. He quickly checked the chamber of his weapon, saw that it was still fully loaded and stuffed it back into his belt. He pulled out and briefly studied Sanchez's USP compact.

Chance glanced at the priest before stating, "I'll be keeping this for the time being."

Walking in a small circle, Chance studied the ground. Something shiny caught his eye. He bent down and discovered a cell phone. It was no ordinary looking cell phone either. It was thinner and when he activated the screen, he noticed many options that a civilian would never need, or even understand. After checking for a signal, he activated the screen and realized the coded options made perfect sense to him. He scrolled through the "contacts" list and there were no names. Only abbreviations and numbers.

"Is this mine?" he asked the priest.

"Must be. It's not mine. Do you recognize it?"

"Kind of, I think," he answered, not sounding certain.

They both turned to look back at the church when they heard the approaching sirens and voices of the first responders nearing the smoldering scene.

"We need to get out of here," the American stated as he slipped the phone in his pocket.

"Why? Those people will help us. You're seriously injured."

"Where are the dudes that blew up the church?" the man asked as he looked back at the smoldering remains of the church.

"I, uh, I have no earthly idea."

"They were trying to kill us, not make a statement. I doubt they detonated themselves. That means they're still out there and once they figure out we didn't go boom, they'll be searching for us. We need to disappear."

"Who are they?" the priest asked.

"I'm not a fountain of useful information right at the moment," the man answered. "But I'm gonna trust my instincts until things start making sense. I needed you for some reason so I'm gonna stick with that plan. We need to get out of here and you're coming with me."

"Where are we going?"

"I'll let you know once we get there."

Chapter Three

Istanbul, Turkey

Rashad Jafari ordered another glass of Merlot as he struggled to appear interested in the conversation at his table. His tailored Bisse designer suit was beginning to feel hot and confining after this long evening. Typically, he would have been long tucked away in his modest, but comfortable home on the other side of the city. However, tonight was special. He was being awarded one of the highest honors in the field of medical science, the Wolf Prize of Medicine. His brilliance in the field of chemical reaction research had been utilized by his country, and lately, by the world, in order to discover new chemical cocktails that could be used in the war against cancer. His research had been successful in finding therapies with fewer side effects, while maintaining, or even increasing, the efficiencies in destroying cancer cells. Most of his life's work was aimed at saving the lives of others.

Most, but not all.

As a matter of fact, the flip side of Dr. Rashad Jafari's noble research to improve chemotherapy, was quite cruel. Catastrophically cruel.

A tall waitress approached the table once again, and this time Jafari only requested a glass of ice water. The waitress offered a small smile and a cool glass of water. Jafari sipped the water, watching the waitress walk away. Something about her seemed vaguely familiar, but he couldn't find anything specific. Nothing about her was striking, with her dark hair pulled back into a harsh bun, and her nothing-special brown eyes. Even her face seemed ambiguous, her features not unpleasant, yet not quite pretty. But, despite her frumpy uniform, he sensed an athleticism about her body. Maybe it was the confidence of her mannerisms. Something about her didn't match the outward act of a humble servant.

He took another sip of water, trying to shake the odd sensation that he knew the waitress. He almost smiled at himself and the ridiculousness of his random thoughts. Obviously, he had been working too hard. He needed a vacation.

Or, maybe he was just getting incredibly bored at this stuffy dinner and his busy brain couldn't help but entertain itself with paranoid thoughts about a waitress.

Suddenly, his thoughts of the waitress were erased. His mind quickly fogged over, his ears deafened by the buzzing of his own brain short-circuiting. Jafari desperately coughed and choked as he tried to fill his lungs with air, but the pain that shot through his chest like a lightning strike, prevented him from taking a breath. He had a fluttering, momentary thought of having been shot. But the pain in his chest wasn't the result of a bullet. The pain arose from the fact that his heart, that only moments ago was pumping a regular seventy-five beats per minute, stopped. Jafari dropped his glass of water with a shattered crash and clutched his chest. He gasped for air and his eyes bulged from fear and shock.

The large banquet room hushed. All eyes were focused on the man who was about to accept a prestigious award as he fell out of his chair. A fellow doctor was the first to break the shocked silence as he ran to Jafari's side. Seeing the dire nature of Jafari's condition, the doctor quickly demanded an emergency evacuation to the nearest hospital. With all the attention focused on Rashid Jafari dying on the floor, no one noticed as the tall, thin waitress, discreetly exited the room.

* * *

The waitress slipped behind the wheel of a rented Renault and drove at a steady speed away from the convention center. She met several emergency vehicles speeding in the opposite direction, no doubt on their way to try to save the life of Dr. Jafari. Too bad she couldn't save them the trouble and let them know that no matter how fast they drove, they would be too late. The amount of the alkaloid toxin, Aconite, he had ingested in those few sips of water virtually guaranteed a speedy, non-reversible trip to death. Even the most sophisticated toxicology tests wouldn't detect the poison. To everyone, with the exception of a small handful of people, Dr. Jafari had succumbed to a massive coronary infarction. A heart attack, plain and simple.

He got off easy, the waitress thought, as grotesque images flashed through her mind. She had seen first-hand the results of the good doctor's accomplishments. For all the horrible deaths he had inflicted upon countless innocent human beings, Dr. Jafari deserved a much more painful, prolonged trip to hell. However, he was a small part of a larger picture and she couldn't waste time inflicting proper punishment on a piece of shit like Jafari. The past five months in which she had to pretend to be his helpful assistant as she prepared various deadly chemical cocktails in Jafari's private lab, made his death even more satisfying for the woman.

After nearly an hour of careful driving, constantly monitoring the possibility of a tail, the waitress pulled over into the shadows of a dark, quiet side street. She sat another ten minutes, watching her mirrors and scanning for anything or anyone that posed a threat. Seeing none, she quickly began her transformation. The dark-haired wig was yanked off. The brown contacts popped out of her eyes. The prosthetic nose peeled from her face. The skin-darkening make-up scrubbed off her face.

She pulled down the sun visor to check her appearance in the mirror. Gone was the humble, plain, ambiguous Turkish waitress. Taking her place was a blond, blue-eyed, angel-faced killer.

She flipped up the mirror and the visor. She shimmied out of the black and white waitress uniform and into comfortable, sensible travel clothes. She strapped inconspicuous holsters on her belt and her ankle, in which she slipped a Glock 9mm and a smaller 357 Magnum. Like many women who rarely leave their house without earrings or other pieces of jewelry, she never went anywhere without her guns. In less than an hour, she would be boarding a small jet bound for Saudi Arabia. She would blend in flawlessly with the other businessmen and women, logging their frequent flier miles and trying to make a decent living.

Once changed she pulled out her phone and her fingers punched out a quick text.

DD DEAD

She paused a moment before hitting SEND. DD

stood for Dr. Death, which was how Rashid Jafari was referred to in her world. She almost smiled. Every now and then, she let herself realize how strange her world truly had become. A world of secrets, violent deaths, constant paranoia and covert operations. A world where a seemingly harmless Turkish waitress slips a lethal dose of drugs into a glass of water. A world where a seemingly noble, brilliant, life-saving research scientist dies of a freak heart attack.

The woman blinked hard and hit SEND. She started her car and shifted into gear. Nothing in this world is what it seems.

Chapter Four

Langley, Virginia

James quickly walked across the private tarmac located discretely on the south end of the Ronald Reagan Washington National airport. Awaiting him was a sleek private jet idling on the runway. A barrage of unmarked, dark SUVs were scattered throughout the area. Security was in full force. He had a feeling someone who was more important than himself was already aboard that plane.

James gave a quick salute to the young Air Force private standing at attention at the entrance of the stairs. James bounded up the stairs, taking them two at a time. Sure enough, Gabrielle O'Connor was there drinking coffee and working on her laptop, fully engaged in their current problem.

"Are you hard-up for entertainment? I didn't expect that you'd come along," James stated as he tossed his leather duffel bag into the overhead compartment.

"Disappointed?"

"No. Maybe slightly alarmed. Certainly surprised. But not disappointed," James replied. "Have you been waiting long?"

"Not long. Traffic?"

"It was a bitch. I hate cities," James replied. "Any new developments?"

"Not with Chance."

"What else is going wrong?" James asked, knowing that at any given moment, Gabrielle was likely juggling several missions in various parts of the world. Just the fact that she was flying to Spain was a strong indication that something wasn't right.

"I'm sending another agent to finish up a job that Chance was in charge of. I don't think he will be available as soon as we need him," Gabrielle stated, as she pulled off her reading glasses and looked over at James.

"I don't like your lack of confidence." James replied.

"It's not lack of confidence. No matter what situation Chance is or is not in, he's obviously been sidetracked. This job in Kuwait is time sensitive."

"Is this job an OGO matter or a CIA matter?"

Gabrielle paused before carefully choosing her words. "There are no clear lines of distinction in this work, James."

"Who is this agent you're sending? Must be CIA since I'm not aware of any other OGO agents."

Gabrielle only slipped her glasses back on and went back to reading whatever was on the screen of her laptop.

"Oookay," James answered slowly. "Chance won't be happy. He hates it when someone treads on his territory."

"He's a professional, James. The success of this mission trumps any irritations he has about teamwork. He'll do whatever it takes to get the target. Even if it means he has to put up with someone else finishing one of his tasks."

James shrugged his shoulders, not convinced Gabrielle truly understood how difficult Chance could be. She may have known his little brother for six years, but James had known him for all of his thirty-two years. Tough didn't even begin to describe his little brother.

The military jet's turbo prop engines whirred to life as the jet made its way down the runway. The pilot pointed the nose south and pushed the lever forward. The powerful thrust set James and Gabrielle back into their seats. They watched out their windows as the tires let go of the earth and the plane's wings grabbed the sky.

Once they had reached 4,000 feet, James unbuckled and flipped open his own laptop. "I can't believe he hasn't activated his phone," he mumbled, pulling up the GPS screen. "Usually he has the decency of at least doing that."

"When was the last time his phone was activated?" Gabrielle asked.

"Right before he entered the church. He texted me that he was going to confession and that he would be out of contact for awhile."

"Nothing at all after that?"

"Nope. I kept an eye on the church with the drone, but I lost all visual after the explosion. There was just too much smoke to see anything."

James pulled up images from the charred church on his laptop and he studied them closely, trying to find anything he may have missed the first time. Nothing. When his cell phone chirped beside him, he jumped. When he saw the caller ID, his heart stopped.

"It's Chance's phone," James stated with controlled excitement.

Gabrielle sat up straight and took off her glasses. "Stick to protocol," she reminded him.

James nodded as he pressed a button. "B and E Pizzeria. What would you like to order today?"

Typically, Chance would respond, "sardines and bacon, please" along with a variety of smart-ass additions to his "order." This response usually garnered a laugh and a sigh of relief as James knew everything was safe. As per protocol, if Chance responded with a "Sorry, wrong number," James understood that his brother was in trouble and in need of assistance. Ever since the brothers disappeared into this world of espionage, Chance had never responded "Sorry, wrong number."

Call it luck or skill, or the combination of the two, Chance had built a remarkable reputation as the man who got the job done- regardless of how high the odds were stacked against him.

James began to wonder if the caller had hung up, as he heard nothing but silence on the other end. He was about to repeat his whole Pizzeria spiel when a voice interrupted him.

"To whom am I speaking?" the voice asked.

A wash of disappointment draped over James. Instead of hearing his brothers confidently calm voice on the other end of the line, he listened to a soft, wary voice heavily tinged with a Spanish accent.

"Who are you?" James countered.

"Carlos Sanchez. I'm trying to contact someone who can help me."

James quickly placed the phone on speaker so Gabrielle could listen on the conversation.

"Is there anyone else with you?" James asked, feeling his throat tighten.

"Yes. This is his phone."

"Then why isn't he calling?"

"He's, uh, he's been injured."

"Is he alive?" James asked, trying to keep any emotion from his voice.

"Yes. He fell asleep and I took his phone. I

know he is a very dangerous man, and I fear for my own safety. But, he has suffered a head injury and he doesn't seem to remember anything. He refuses to turn on this phone or make a call. He's convinced someone will track him down and kill him. I pray that you'll help us and not hurt us. This is the first number on his contacts list so I took the risk that you could help."

"Yes, yes, you did the right thing, Carlos. I'll help you. I'll be in Spain in only a few hours. The man who is with you, do you know his name?"

"No. And neither does he."

James was taken aback. Had he heard the man correctly? "What?"

"This man, he's American I'm sure, but he doesn't remember his name."

James felt his stomach knot up. He looked over at Gabrielle but she was intently working on her computer to track Chance's phone.

"Carlos, I need you to activate the camera icon. Look at the screen and find the camera."

"Yes, I see it. Okay, it's on."

"Good. Now, I can see everything you point the phone at. Point it at the American so I can see him," James instructed.

The camera panned over the woods and dim surroundings. Then its viewfinder settled on a man lying prone on a bed of pine needles. The tall, thin blond man was clearly Chance Hughes.

"I see him. Now get closer. I need to see him breathing. Show me that he is alive."

Father Sanchez cautiously tread closer to the unconscious man, holding the camera at an angle to capture the subtle rise and fall of the man's chest.

"I assure you, he is alive."

"I see that. Now turn the camera around. I need to see your face to verify your identity," James instructed.

James clicked a photo of the man's face and forwarded the image to Gabrielle's computer. She began the facial recognition program and within a few seconds, she turned toward James and nodded. The caller was indeed who he said he was.

"Thank you, Father Sanchez. Now shut the camera off, please," James stated. "You were correct in your assumption that the man with you is dangerous. You need to handle yourself carefully around him. I'll be there as soon as I can. When he wakes up, tell him the truth. Tell him you used his phone and called me. Tell him you talked to James, okay?"

"He doesn't even remember his own name, Mr. James. I doubt he will remember yours."

James rubbed his brow, feeling a nasty headache coming on. If only this jet could speed up a few thousand miles per hour.

"Hearing that name might trigger his memory. Just do what I say."

"Is that your name?"

"Just tell him you spoke with James.

"What about his name?" Father Sanchez asked.

"What is your location?" James asked, ignoring the priest's question.

"I'm not sure. This man, maybe he will respond favorably if I can tell him his name?"

"No. Now where are you?"

"Somewhere near the coastal hills. I don't know a specific location."

"Alright, then I'll find you. Look at the screen of the phone, Carlos. Can you find the icon that looks like an eye?"

James waited in silence as Carlos studied the screen.

"Yes, I found it."

"Okay, press that icon. It will ask for a code. Punch in the numbers seven, two, one, five, zero. You got that?"

"Seven, two, one, five, zero. Yes, I got it. What will that do?"

"That activates a GPS tracking beacon. I'll be able to see your location. Once I see where you are, I will figure out how long before I can get to you."

"How long will this take? I'm afraid if this man wakes up and sees me with his phone, he will kill me."

"I'm working as fast as I can. Okay, I've pulled up your current location. Shit, how'd you guys get that far up the coast?"

"We haven't rested until now."

"By my calculation, I can get to you in about seven and a half hours. You need to stay put until I get there."

"How do I keep him here? Once he wakes up, I'm sure he'll want to move to a different location. He's very paranoid about someone finding us."

James sighed and tried to think of a plan. "You need to be strong, Carlos. Don't agitate him, but do your best to convince him to stay close to your current location. I really don't believe he'll try to kill you unless you attack him. Don't, for the love of God, try to physically control him in any way. You will not win that battle."

"I am fully aware of that, señor."

"The phone is activated now. I'll be able to keep track of you as long as he doesn't turn off the GPS."

"I need to go, señor. I need to get this phone back in his pocket before he wakes up, which I have a feeling is soon."

"Okay Carlos. Do your best and I'll be seeing you soon."

The line went dead. James sat back and looked over at Gabrielle.

"That's one scenario I never expected," James stated.

Gabrielle studied the map of Spain and the coordinates of Chance's current location.

"Let's hope that Chance doesn't panic and end up killing Father Sanchez. We desperately need him alive."

"Chance doesn't panic, O'Connor."

Gabrielle looked at James and replied grimly, "Chance doesn't even know he's Chance. I think attempting to predict what he will or won't do at this point is impossible."

* * *

Alvira, Spain

He knew instantly that the priest was guilty of something. As soon as he woke up, or regained consciousness, he wasn't sure which; he sensed the tension in the other man. It was as if he could smell the man's nerves. He didn't comprehend that his own senses were so sharp, and his ability to interpret subtle body language was far superior to that of the average human being.

"What did you do?" Chance asked as he pulled himself up to a sitting position. Damn, if his head didn't feel like it was splitting open.

The priest cocked his head, his heart thumping hard in his chest. The man on the phone told him to tell this guy the truth about the phone call, but Sanchez didn't share his confidence that this injured man with no name wouldn't lose his temper and kill him on the spot.

"Are you going to be okay?" the priest asked, watching as the man winced and squeezed his eyes shut. When he opened them, his pupils were dilated and his skin color had paled to an ashen gray. His gash had been covered in gauze and a bandage that the man had swiped from a small convenience store.

"I'm fine," he grumbled. "How long have I been out and what did you do?"

"About three hours. Why do you think I did anything?"

The man stared hard at the priest for a long moment. He really had no idea why he knew. He just did.

"I took your phone," Sanchez answered quietly, completely expecting the gun to be pointed at his head at any moment. Surprisingly, the American didn't flinch. He just stared.

"And I made a call," Sanchez added, stepping back a few feet. The man continued to watch him quietly. The priest wasn't positive that the man was completely aware of what was being said. He sat so utterly still, his eyes, unblinking cold stones watching him. The result was unnerving.

"I talked to a man named James. He's coming to help us. He'll be here soon," Sanchez spoke quickly, hoping any shred of this information might trigger a positive reaction in the injured brain of the man staring at him.

That name struck a deep chord in his psyche. James. The name had a physical effect on him, like a soothing blanket on a cold night. He pressed the palms of his hands to his eyes, desperately trying to conjure up an image to match the name. He almost had it. He felt as though all the answers were dancing mere inches from his grasp. If only he could snag one, the rest might fall in place.

"I tried to get the man on the phone to tell me your name, but he refused. Whoever, or whatever you are, it's a secret."

The man's eyes shot open and he once again stared at the priest. However, this time those unblinking blue-gray eyes looked right past him, into some unseen world of jumbled memories. He slowly stood up, his gaze still fixated on some unknown point in the distance.

Then, like a cloud passing in front of the sun, irritation flashed across the man's face.

"I must be one hell of rare commodity if they don't even trust a priest with my name."

"Maybe you're military?" the priest asked softly.

The man's eyes instantly focused, a jostled memory righted itself.

"You remember?" the priest asked.

"I'm a soldier," Chance said, sounding unsure, as if he was asking a question, rather than answering one.

Sanchez was far from stupid. Despite being kept in the dark regarding the American's identity and job description, Sanchez figured his guess would hit close to the mark. With his top-tier skills, physical conditioning, and the fact he was packing a high-dollar, custom made pistol not even seen in the Special Forces, this man's name wasn't required in order for Sanchez to know who he was. This man was some sort of mercenary, gun-for-hire, assassin, whatever title you chose, but basically, this man's job was to seek out and kill high-profile targets. In this case, the target was his brother Domino. Who hired this assassin? From the way things were shaping up, the employer was another American who had the money and resources to hop in a jet and fly to his location within minutes of receiving his phone call. He certainly didn't have all the pieces of the puzzle, but Sanchez had enough of them to figure out he would soon be dealing with some facet of the United States military.

Chance ran his hands through his hair, feeling a combination of relief and frustration. He felt closer to remembering who he was. Flashes of scenes that he recognized as war, pounded through his head. He clearly remembered the smell of the desert, the acrid smell of gunpowder and the overpowering sense of death and destruction. He had been a soldier; he had no doubt.

Obviously, he wasn't a soldier any longer. His

hair was shaggy; his weapon was a custom-made, state-of-the-art piece that would never be found in the hands of an infantryman. And then, there was what the priest had told him. Or more what he couldn't tell him. He was a secret. Somewhere in the depths of his memory, he knew what he was. He just wasn't ready to face that truth quite yet.

"Did he tell you anything else?" Chance asked.

"No."

"When is he coming?"

Sanchez checked his watch. "In a few hours. We're supposed to stay here so he can find us."

Chance suddenly grabbed for his phone and activated the screen.

"You turned on the GPS. How did you know how to do that? You need a code."

"James gave me the code. Please leave it on. That's the only way he can find us."

Chance sat back down and sighed, torn between what his instincts were telling him and what the priest was saying.

"If I leave this on, other people can find us too."

"Who? Who is after you?"

"Anyone and everyone," he answered softly. "Trust no one. Everyone lies and everyone is guilty until proven innocent."

Sanchez saw an unexpected glimpse of vulnerable sadness drift across the American's face. It passed as quickly as a shadow.

"Is that what you believe?" the priest asked, sitting down a few feet away from the man.

"It's what I live," Chance said with a sigh. Then he looked up at the priest and asked, "Are you really a priest?"

"Yes. For the past twenty years."

Chance studied the man a moment before saying, "You're around fifty, right? Give or take a few years, I suppose. What did you do before you became a priest?"

Sanchez was surprised at the man's accurate assessment of his age. Most people assumed he was much older than his forty-eight years. Life had not been an easy journey for Carlos Sanchez. Every line on his worn face had been well earned.

"I was in the Spanish Army."

Chance's eyes sharpened. "You're a soldier too."

"No longer. I am only a priest now."

"Once a soldier, always a soldier," Chance replied, his voice barely audible. A fluttering thought tickled his aching brain. He couldn't quite grab it but it did lead to another question that seemed to burn to the forefront of his thoughts.

"What *specifically* were you in the Army?"

"Nothing special, señor. I wasn't cut out to be anything more than a low-ranking foot soldier."

Chance turned and stared hard at the priest. Something wasn't adding up, but for the life of him, he couldn't untangle the mess in his mind. Then he pulled out Sanchez's gun, analyzing the unique weapon closely.

"Where did you get this gun?" Chance asked.

"Am I being interrogated for something?" Sanchez shot back.

"Are you hiding something?" Chance countered, feeling an odd rush of temper. He took a deep breath and snuffed out the extra emotion. "You shouldn't hide things from me, Father. I may be a little screwed up right now, but you and I both know I'm not from the Red Cross."

"But, you're also not evil," Sanchez countered, hoping to keep the American calm and conversational. "I can see it in your face. You saved me from those men who blew up my church."

"I saved you because that's what I was supposed to do, I think," Chance replied, holding his head and wincing in pain as the throbbing nearly became unbearable. He rocked back and forth, squeezing his eyes shut, forcing himself to breath evenly until the pain subsided.

"Is it getting worse?" Sanchez asked.

"Holy fucking shit," Chance muttered, then squinted his eyes open, looked at the priest and added, "Sorry, Father."

Sanchez studied him as he struggled to control the pain. He found it profoundly odd that this man, a likely assassin, trained to hunt and kill, was apologizing for uttering a few swear words. "That's okay," Sanchez replied softly. "I think under the circumstances, God will forgive a little swearing."

Chance nearly smiled as he replied, "I think God has to forgive me for a lot more than just swearing."

Father Sanchez, sensing an odd shift in the conversation, scooted closer and watched as the American inhaled deeply, appearing as though his pain had lessened for the time being.

"There is no sin He won't forgive, you know," Sanchez stated softly. "All you have to do is ask."

In a distant, almost robotic voice Chance said, "If we confess our sins, He is faithful and just and will forgive us our sins and purify us from all unrighteousness."

Sanchez's eyes widened in disbelief. "First John 1:9. You're familiar with the Bible?"

Chance looked away and shook his head. "I think I was an altar boy once," he suddenly stated after a long moment of silence.

"Your memories are coming back?" Sanchez asked.

"No, not really. Everything is blurry."

"Your eyesight? Is it worse? That could mean hemor—"

"No, no, my eye sight isn't getting worse. It's just blurry in my mind," Chance corrected.

Sanchez checked his watch. If he could only

force the hands of time to slip by faster. He wasn't sure how much longer this unexpected, somewhat peaceful lull in the action would last.

"I'm sure it will all come back," Sanchez said. "Permanent amnesia is extremely rare."

Chance looked at the priest curiously. "So, are you a doctor, too? First a soldier, then a priest and doctor. Your resume is impressive."

"I'm not a doctor. I read a lot."

"Of course." Chance idly fingered the safety switch on his pistol. "What if I don't want to remember?" Chance blurted out before he even realized what he had said.

"We all have memories we'd rather forget," Sanchez answered truthfully. Unfortunately, he spoke from experience. His head was full of violent, painful memories of his own.

"What if I don't want to remember every goddamn horrible thing that has happened to me, around me...or because of me? What if I don't want to be whatever the hell it is that I'm supposed to be?"

"Take it easy, señor. Raising your blood pressure will only increase the headaches," Sanchez said soothingly, hoping to divert what looked to be some sort of emotional breakdown.

"Oh, hell no, that doesn't happen to me," Chance replied with a wild-eyed grin. "Not me. The crazier and more dangerous the situation, the slower my heart beats. Weird, huh? Oh, there's more. My resting heart rate settles in at around forty-five and it rarely exceeds ninety beats per minute. I'm not sure why or how I know that, but I know it's true. Did you know that for some reason, my muscles don't produce as much lactic acid as the average person, so I can exert myself at one hundred percent for much longer and not get tired? I know that when most people would run out of a burning building, I'd choose to run into the fire. Why the hell do I know this, and I can't tell you my fucking name!"

Chance was speaking loudly, gun in hand, waving it around wildly as he spewed words he had no control over. Sanchez stood quickly and began retreating; seeking some place to hide in case Chance's grip on sanity slipped and he began pulling the trigger.

Chance stood up and began laughing hysterically. "Look, you're scared as hell of me. I must be one freaked-out son of a bitch, right? I have no idea who or what I am, but I do seem to recall some interesting little snippets of information, right? For instance, I know I'm supposed to kill someone, right?"

"Please, now calm down," Sanchez tried to speak calmly. "Put the gun down and let's talk this out, señor."

"Who am I supposed to send a bullet through this time? That's what I do for a living, right?

Who's the lucky bastard I get to terminate? Is it you? Is that why I was at your church, Father Sanchez?"

"No! Now please, calm down! You are not well. You've been hurt; you're not thinking straight."

"I can't think at all! My fucking brain is messed up," Chance said with a grimace as a fresh wave of pain pulsated through his skull. He held his gun hand softly against his head and mumbled incoherently. He dropped to his knees as the darkness of unconsciousness once again claimed him.

Carlos Sanchez rushed toward the tall man and helped ease him onto the ground. He felt for a pulse and even though his heart wasn't racing, the beats felt weak. Given the pallid color of the man's skin, Carlos could bet with good odds that his blood pressure had dropped. This guy needed medical attention-the sooner the better. The priest gingerly opened each of the American's eyelids and found that his pupillary reactions were equal. Hopefully, the man's condition wouldn't worsen considerably before James arrived.

Sanchez sat near the American for over an hour, watching him breathe, twitch and occasionally groan. When the man finally squinted his eyes open, the sun was beginning to set.

"How long was I out this time?"

"Almost an hour and a half," Sanchez answered.

"Feel any better?"

Chance slowly sat up and rubbed his eyes. "Just great. Any better and I'd be twins."

"How's your vision? Blurry?"

After blinking a few times, Chance shook his head. He ensured his gun was still in his possession and held it gently, once again rubbing a finger over the etching on the slide.

"What does that image mean?" Carlos asked carefully.

"The blue star is Rigel and the red one is Betelgeuse," the American replied softly, seemingly surprised at his own answer.

"The brightest stars in the constellation of Orion," Carlos stated. Looking through the lens of a high-powered telescope and studying the stars had become a recent hobby of his. It was far more enjoyable than peering through the scope of a rifle. "What's with the dice?" he asked curiously.

"It's all me; the stars, the dice, it's me."

"You remember?"

"No, but I know that's me," he replied, tapping the image on his gun.

Suddenly, Chance's attention was diverted in a new direction. He scrambled to his feet as he aimed his gun at the shadows in the trees. Carlos Sanchez stared into the darkness where he was focused, but he couldn't spot any movement or hear any sound. He began to think that the young man was imagining things when a voice spoke out from the shadows.

"Drop the gun. It's me, James. If you shoot me, I'm gonna be beyond pissed."

Sanchez checked his watch. James had made his arrival nearly forty minutes ahead of schedule. He breathed a sigh of relief. Then he noticed that the American hadn't budged in his stance, his gun firmly cocked and locked onto the voice calling himself, James.

The voice soon materialized into a long-legged, dark-haired man dressed in black fatigues toting a heavy utility bag and armed to the teeth. He didn't smile but he didn't appear overly rattled that the injured man didn't drop his weapon to run over and shake his hand.

"Drop it, Stones. That's enough. It's over," James spoke calmly.

Chance blinked hard. Something clinked into place in his brain. Stones. His childhood nickname. His gun hand lowered slightly.

"That's right; it's just me so lower the gun and cool it. I'm not qualified to get in a shoot-out with you, you little shit."

That voice seemed to melt the violent temper brewing beneath Chance's fragile control. This tall, dark-haired man standing in front of him did look familiar. James. Then another dislodged piece of his memory fell into place. James. James Allan Hughes.

James was his older brother. He remembered!

Chance lowered his weapon and felt his hands begin to shake. Exhaustion seemed to flood his overwhelmed system and his vision tunneled. He struggled to fight against the numbing darkness draping over him, but he lost the battle and consciousness as he slowly dropped to his knees before falling flat.

James quickly holstered his gun and ran up to his younger brother. He glanced over at Father Carlos Sanchez and asked, "How many times has he passed out?"

"Several."

James carefully turned Chance so he was lying on his back. He felt for his pulse, counted and then nodded. "Fast and shallow. His blood pressure sucks."

The priest approached the pair and knelt down next to them. "I've noticed that his pupils have been dilated but they seem equal."

"That's good," James replied as he pulled out a pen light. He pulled open the lids of Chance's eyes, checking the pupillary reaction.

"If he's got any intracranial hemorrhaging, it's a slow leak. It's been, what…about thirty- six hours? He would've been dead by now if he had a significant leak."

James paused and looked closer at Sanchez. "Are you a doctor or a priest?"

Sanchez shook his head. "Priest, I read a lot."

"Sure you do," James replied as he pulled out his satellite phone. He pressed a button and spoke. "I've got him and the priest. Orion is out cold. Definite head injury, so we need a medical team on standby. Let's get outta here."

James slipped the phone into his backpack and then gently shook his brother. "Come on, Stones. Wake up. I ain't carrying your ass outta here."

Chance's eyelids fluttered a moment before they popped open, dazed and dangerous. Before James had the opportunity to get himself out of the way, Chance attacked. He used his body perfectly to flip James off kilter. With the agility of a jungle cat, Chance pounced. Within seconds he had his brother pinned with one hand in a vice grip at his throat.

"I swear, if I could, I'd beat the shit outta you right now," James' voice was strained as his throat constricted beneath Chance's tightening hold.

Chance blinked hard, staring down at the person he assumed was the enemy. His eyes slowly cleared and the adrenalin left his system leaving him shaken and confused. He let go of his brother's throat and groaned as he rolled to the side.

The chopping sounds of an approaching helicopter suddenly filled the air. Chance scrambled to his feet, reaching for his gun.

James held his brother's gun. "I've got it, Stones. You're dangerous enough without it. That

chopper is gonna get us out of here and get you
fixed up. We're gonna fast-rope it out of here.
You've done this a thousand times. You know what
to do. Just hang on tight."

Chance tried to concentrate on the chopper, but
intense memories flooded his brain, making focus
on anything impossible. He was seeing a different
chopper, descending upon him at a different place, a
long time ago. He clearly saw the faces of soldiers
that he helped secure onto the ropes and watched as
they were raised into the security of the chopper. He
heard the constant gunfire and felt the snap of the
air as bullets whizzed past him. Finally, finally, it
was his turn. He grabbed the rope and watched the
ground fade away beneath the swirling dust and
sand. He looked up at the chopper and the guys
waiting for him as they gave him a 'thumbs up'.
Then, oh God, something ripped through his arm.
The force was so great it knocked him off the rope.
He tried to grab it again, but it was too late. He was
falling, falling back into the hell he had tried to
escape.

"Stones! Snap out of it, bro! We gotta go!"
James yelled shoving the rope into Chance's hands.

Still foggy from the vivid memory, Chance
robotically secured himself to the rope and stared at
nothing as he was raised into the belly of the Black
Hawk hovering overhead.

James turned toward the priest. "Okay. There's

nothing to this. You ready?"

"I'm fine."

James watched in surprise as Father Carlos Sanchez deftly secured the ropes and gave the pilot a 'thumbs up' before ascending into the sky. Obviously, and strangely, this particular priest had experience in fast roping into a helicopter.

Lastly, James grabbed the rope and lifted rapidly into the chopper. The doors closed and the pilot turned the bird south toward the American hospital in Rota.

* * *

U.S. Naval Hospital
Rota, Spain

"I believe it's quite remarkable that he was able to remain conscious and function as long as he did," Dr. Thomas Redding stated, as he paged through the results of Chance's CAT scan. "He has a significant subdural hematoma. He must've suffered a severe blow to the head."

"It would take a hell of a blow to get through his thick skull," James mumbled, immediately receiving a strong look from Gabrielle who sat next to him in the small confines of Dr. Redding's modest office.

"What's his prognosis, Doctor?" Gabrielle

asked patiently.

"He should recover completely from this injury." Redding was no stranger to treating an occasional covert agent here and there. He had been informed immediately upon this patient's arrival that he was to be treated under the strictest of confidentiality. As a matter of fact, the medical staff was not even privy to his name. He was only known as Patient X. Throughout his inspection of Patient X's condition, Redding could only wonder what had caused the countless odd, jagged scars that he noticed on the man's body. Some appeared thin, smooth and surgical. Others appeared rough, jagged and deep. Then there were the four perfectly round scars: remnants of bullet wounds.

And there were the noticeable mental scars. Even though Patient X had been sedated in the helicopter en route to the hospital, he required more sedation upon arrival, as his reaction to anyone approaching him was violent. He spoke of a cave, Afghan rebels and begged anyone to "please don't let them torture me again."

Doctor Redding lay down the reports and folded his hands under his chin, thinking.

"Miss O'Connor. Your agent is obviously not well; I'm not just talking about his head injury. Physically, he will be fine in a couple of weeks. Other than being a bit thin, his overall conditioning is top notch. What concerns me is his mental state.

He has obviously been through some sort of trauma. Couple that with the amnesia, and he may need more professional help to deal with whatever he has gone through. I realize I am not privy to this patient's history so forgive me for bringing this up, but his repeated statements regarding torture and imprisonment have certainly troubled me and the staff."

O'Connor's only response was, "How long will he have amnesia?"

James smiled slightly. He had grown to respect Gabrielle's cool demeanor in dealing with anything ranging from terrorists, political turmoil, incompetent coworkers, and in this instance, a nosy doctor asking about an agent with amnesia.

Chance's time spent as a prisoner, held captive in the Hindu Kish Mountains by torturous Afghan terrorists, was not a topic to be discussed with this medical staff-or anyone. As far as the rest of the world was concerned, the young soldier who was shot down and disappeared after a bloody battle deep in the harsh desert mountains of Afghanistan, was dead. He was never found. Chance Hughes, the gifted Marine Sniper died in a desolate cave. Special Agent Chance Hughes, American assassin, was alive and, up until the last few days, well.

The doctor sighed. He hadn't expected a straight answer from the likes of Miss O'Connor; however, he did expect to see a little bit of concern or compassion toward her agent who had narrowly escaped a major trauma with his life.

"Not long, but everyone heals differently," Doctor Redding replied. "I'm sure he will be remembering more by the end of the week. However, there may be pieces of memories, especially those moments right before and after his head injury that he will never regain. It's very important that you don't push him to remember."

"Of course, Dr. Redding. I will plan to fly him back to the States by the end of this week, then. Oh yes, we'll be flying in a psychologist to meet with our agent. Please, put a Dr. Anthony Reinholt on the admissions list. Starting now, he is the only psychologist allowed access to my agent. Reinholt will be arriving later tonight. He is to have free access to the patient, day or night."

The doctor looked surprised at Gabrielle's request. "We do have excellent psychologists on staff here who specialize in handling a variety of issues."

"As you may have noticed, Dr. Redding, our agent is a bit unusual. I think its best that we stick to what has worked in the past."

"Okay. I'll put Dr. Reinholt on the list. I get the sense that you believe your agent will be able to go back to work in the near future. I just want you to understand that even though the physical injury will heal within a couple of weeks, it's my strong opinion that your agent needs more time off."

"You've been very clear, sir. I've heard your opinion and I will keep it under consideration," Gabrielle replied coolly. "Thanks for your time Dr. Redding. If anything changes regarding my agent, let me know immediately." Gabrielle stood up. "James, let's go."

Once in the hallway, James turned toward Gabrielle. "I see now why you've never won a Miss Congeniality contest."

A hint of a smile graced her face. "And what makes you think I haven't?"

James looked at her in surprise and then huffed, "If you won, I'd hate to see the other contestants." As they made their way over to the elevator, he asked, "You're putting him back to work, aren't you?"

Gabrielle nodded and stepped inside the elevator. James pushed the first level button and the doors closed.

"Chance has been working on this particular operation for the past year. We can't afford to lose all that information and connections he's put together. You and I both know that he's our best shot at stopping Domino."

"What if he can't remember?"

"I think he will," Gabrielle answered. Then she smiled as she added, "he hardly ever lets us down."

James shrugged his shoulders. He couldn't

argue with her about his brother's successful track record. He also understood the need to utilize Chance as much as possible. Despite all of that, James would make certain that Chance was both physically and mentally capable of going back into the field before allowing that decision to be made.

"Where's the priest?" James asked.

"He's being held in a secure room in the psyche ward," Gabrielle answered.

"He's here? In this hospital?"

"It's the building across the parking lot. I need you to talk to him. Find out exactly what happened in the church, and most importantly, what Chance told him."

James nodded. It had been awhile since he was put in the position of interrogator, but the job didn't bother him.

"When should I pay him a cordial visit?"

"Whenever you're ready," Gabrielle answered.

"No time like the present. I'll talk to you later."

* * *

James quickly made his way across the Emergency Entrance and spacious parking lot separating the main hospital complex from the building that housed the mental health treatment facilities. He flashed his credentials to the woman at the front desk before bounding up the one flight of stairs that led to the high-security floor. He found Sanchez's holding cell, which was guarded by an armed sentry.

The guard had been given a heads-up about a man matching James description that was to be granted access into the priest's room. When James approached him, the guard checked his ID and opened the door.

Father Sanchez sat in the corner of the room on a vinyl chair paging through a newspaper. He carefully folded the paper and eyed the tall man as he entered his room.

"Father Sanchez," James said with a warm smile. "I apologize for keeping you in here like this, but there simply is no other choice."

Carlos watched as James pulled up a chair and sat across from him. He couldn't miss the resemblance between this man and the injured man he had spent nearly two nerve-wracking days with. Their imposing heights, lean strength, strong jaws and facial features were similar. Yet, the man sitting across from him today didn't give him the same sense of danger as the injured man had. Instead of cold hardness, this man's dark blue eyes were warm and friendly.

"What do you need from me? Señor James, right?" Sanchez asked.

"That's right. Just a little information, that's all. I'm not great with speaking Spanish, so I'm gonna have to ask you to talk to me in English."

"That's fine, señor."

"Your English is pretty good, Father. Other than Spanish, do you speak any other languages?"

"No. Why?"

James shrugged and smiled. "Just curious."

"How's the injured man?" Sanchez asked. "He's your brother, is he not?"

"He's fine," James replied softly.

Even though the man didn't answer the second question, the look of surprise that flashed across his eyes was as good as a "yes."

"Who is he? What was he looking for at my church?" Sanchez questioned, wondering if his own brother would be entering this conversation or if the American's plan to hunt and kill Domino was a secret only he knew.

"When he came to see you at the church, what did you two talk about?" James asked, still sounding perfectly casual.

"We didn't have much time to talk. Soon after he entered the confessional, he noticed two men who he claimed were coming after me. He and I escaped through a vent in the ceiling and managed to jump from the outdoor shaft before the church exploded."

James watched the priest carefully. He had no doubts that his brother was a much better, much more intimidating interrogator than he was. Chance could see through a lie faster than most. Yet, James had picked up a few skills along the way. There was something in the way Sanchez glanced up and to his left a few times while telling his story that indicated to James he wasn't telling the truth.

"So, nothing was discussed between you and…let's call him John, regarding your brother, Dominique Rodriquez?"

Sanchez's heart fell. He looked down and clasped his hands.

"Tell me," James demanded quietly.

"He wanted to know where he could find Dominique. That's all."

"And did you give him that information?"

Sanchez looked up and directly into James' eyes. "I do not *know* where my brother is. That is the truth. I try to stay away from him."

"Do you speak Arabic?"

Sanchez's eyes widened and he shook his head, worried about this line of questioning. "No, señor. I don't. I understand a few words, but that is it."

"Your brother has spent the majority of the past twenty years in the Middle East. He speaks predominantly Arabic. How do you communicate with him?"

Sanchez recognized the interrogation technique. James was using questions aimed at tripping up a suspect's story. He was looking for lies.

"It's been a long time since I've spoken with

Dominique. Our native language is Spanish. This is the only language we have ever used to communicate with each other."

"When was the last time you had contact with Domino?"

"A long time. I'm not sure when exactly."

"Not after John came to the church? Not in the woods while waiting for me to arrive?"

"No! I said a long time. Years!"

James studied Sanchez a moment before shifting gears.

"When did you realize that John was injured?"

"As soon as I woke up and found him unconscious lying on top of me."

"How long was he out? Seconds? Minutes? Hours?"

Sanchez thought a moment, remembering the confusion that followed the explosion.

"A few minutes maybe, but not longer. I wanted to take him to a clinic, but he refused."

"Did anyone see you and John after the church exploded?"

"No, no one. Your brother broke into a small shop and took medicinal supplies, but there was nobody there. He had dismantled the two security cameras he found near the doors before he went inside."

"Let's keep calling him John, please."

"But he's your brother."

75

"So, the two of you didn't meet up with a single soul until I arrived."

"Right, señor."

"What happened to your cell phone, Father? I know you own one."

"I leave it in my apartment while I conduct confessions. I don't want any interruptions."

"So, it blew up with the church?"

"That's my assumption."

"So, if we find your phone, we won't find any recent calls made to your brother?"

"You won't find *any* calls made to my brother."

"Fine. Did John talk to you much? Did he mention who he worked for, who he was, what he was doing?"

"He didn't remember anything, señor. You already know that."

"Never mind what I do or do not know. What did he talk about?"

Sanchez rubbed his eyes quickly, bringing up as many memories as possible. "He talked about how he could push himself harder than most, and how his heart rate is slow, strange things like that. He was very frustrated at his memory loss. Oh, he did mention that he thought he was an altar boy once."

"Really?" James replied, trying to remember their childhood. Chance was right. He had been an altar boy as a child.

"He also quoted the Bible. A passage about

forgiveness. Why would someone like your brother do that?"

James sighed and sat back in his chair. Being whacked on the head had certainly brought about some strange behavior in Chance. Now he was quoting the Bible? James wondered what other unusual residual effects his head injury might have.

"Along with the Bible," James began, "John can cite quotes from the Koran, the Constitution of the United States, most Grisham books and nearly every line from Jerry McGuire. Don't waste your time trying to label John by the quotes he makes."

"Why does he have stars and dice on his gun?"

"To make people curious," James shot back.

"Rigel and Betelgeuse are the two brightest stars in Orion. Why is this important to your brother?"

James studied the priest closely. He was surprised that Chance had told him the names of the stars on his gun.

"What did he say about the dice?"

"Nothing. He couldn't remember."

James stared hard at the priest, unable to discern if he was withholding information.

"Can I please ask just one question señor?" Carlos asked, feeling uneasy under James' scrutinizing look.

"You can ask anything you want. I may or may not give you an answer."

"You're obviously American and I calculated

the time between my call to you and your flight time. That put your location on the east coast. CIA is in Virginia. Is that who you're working for?"

"Okay, Father, I think that's all I need from you at this time. I'll try to get someone to send in some more reading material to keep you occupied."

"Please, señor James. Who are you? Who is your brother?"

James stood and started for the door. Then he hesitated and softly replied, "We're the good guys, Father. You need to trust us."

* * *

Dr. Anthony Reinholt softly knocked on the door of Chance's room. He couldn't ignore the similarities between this moment and the first time he had ever laid eyes on Chance Hughes. The first time, however, was in a hospital in Landstuhl, Germany and no one was sure if the young, tortured soldier would survive, much less be capable of carrying out the dangerous, nearly impossible missions they would plan for him.

Hopefully, this meeting would find Chance in much better condition.

Reinholt turned the knob and walked in to find Chance wearing a blue baseball cap, a ratty gray Yankees sweatshirt and faded denim jeans. He was sitting on a bright blue vinyl chair in the corner, plunking away on a laptop. He glanced up over the screen, met Reinholt's eyes and grinned.

"You have *got* to be shitting me," Chance said with a laugh. He pushed the flimsy rolling table that his computer was sitting on to the side and stood up. "They flew your sorry ass all the way over here to see me? They must truly believe I've taken a serious dive off the sanity train."

Reinholt grabbed Chance's hand in a firm shake and felt relieved to see that notorious mischievous spark hiding in those odd colored eyes of his. The two of them hadn't always smiled when in the same room. For the first few years, their relationship consisted of Reinholt doing his damnedest to analyze Chance, describe him in some sort of professional psychiatric terms, and contain him and his issues in a nice neat report. Meanwhile, Chance did his best to frustrate the therapist. Reinholt learned early on that Chance was not going to reveal any deep thoughts or troubling emotions. He guarded his privacy as staunchly as he did his country. Still, it was Reinholt's job to ensure that Chance was mentally stable enough to carry out the jobs asked of him. Following each mission Reinholt would sit in a room with Chance trying to determine if the latest round of killing, trauma or disaster had weakened the agent. Each time, Reinholt left the meeting feeling as though he was beating his head against a brick wall. A brick wall named Chance

Hughes.

Finally, they called a truce. They went through the motions that were required of each of them. Chance would sit through the post-operations analysis and Reinholt would quit trying to find a chink that wasn't there. Chance promised that if he ever felt himself slipping, Reinholt would be the first to know.

Chance never actually admitted to "slipping," per se, but he did slowly start to trust Reinholt enough to vent a little after each job. As the years passed by, the time spent with Reinholt became less confrontational and more conversational.

Now, Chance considered Dr. Anthony Reinholt a friend. For Chance, that was a rarity. Including James, the number of people Chance considered a friend could be counted on one hand, with a finger to spare.

"I'm afraid you finally revealed your true personality. Scared the shit out of everyone so they called me up," Reinholt replied as he motioned for Chance to sit back down. Reinholt pulled up a folding chair from the corner. "So, what the hell happened to you this time?"

Chance ran his hand carefully through his long hair. "I got knocked on the noggin. Rattled everything around up there for a while."

"Still hurt?"

"Yep. Headaches from hell. What do my charts

say?"

"Subdural hematoma, amnesia, schizophrenia, herpes, irritable bowel syndrome, athlete's foot, etcetera, etcetera. You know-all the normal stuff you have."

"Anything I should worry about?"

Reinholt grimaced as he said, "I wouldn't take the Gonorrhea too lightly."

"Funny."

"Amnesia getting better? You remembered me right?"

"You're so ugly I can't forget you. I've tried many times. Just can't do it."

Reinholt smiled and nodded. Chance sure seemed like his old self. The reports, however, painted a different picture. Violent reactions and outbursts are fairly common side effects from a significant head trauma. The average person might yell, throw something, or say things that hurt people's feelings. Chance Hughes was nowhere near average, though. When a person like Chance lost control for even a moment, someone could die.

"How come you're so pissed off, buddy?" Reinholt asked. "Something happen out there that we don't know about?"

Chance lost his smile as he shook his head. "I don't remember anything about going into that church. Or leaving it, for that matter. I guess we got blown up a little."

"Just a little."

"I actually don't remember that much about getting here either. I hear I caused a little ruckus when I got here. But, you know I checked out the strength of drugs they were pumping into me and no wonder I was acting crazy. Man, I'm lucky they didn't kill me with all that shit."

"From my understanding, your behavior caused the staff to feel in danger and they increased the dosage."

"Maybe they shoulda tried talking nice to me, instead."

"I'm sure that would have worked," Reinholt answered sarcastically.

Chance laughed and gently rubbed the stitches on his forehead. "I guess I'm naturally kind of pissed off and when you mix that with some drugs, it all gets amplified."

"You're just naturally difficult to work with, Chance."

"Seriously, why are you here? Is O'Connor scared my brain is permanently scrambled?"

"We just need to know what the extent of your injuries are. Any flashes of light, numbness, irrational thoughts lately?"

"Nope. Look, I'm fine."

"You need to take better care of yourself. You put your body through the wringer day-in and day-out. You're gonna be a pile by the time you reach middle age."

Chance laughed. "That's not likely, Doc. I traded in my longevity when I signed up for this gig."

"Nonsense. With your luck, you'll live to be a crotchety old man."

"Nah, I'm a realist, my friend. My shelf life is limited in this profession, and it's not because my skills are perishable. There are only so many bullets a guy can dodge."

"Don't be so pessimistic."

"I'm not! That's being optimistic. There's far worse things than death. Believe me!"

Reinholt leaned forward. "You have a death wish."

"No. I have a death *acceptance*."

"Interesting," Reinholt stated quietly.

"Say what you're really thinking, 'That Chance Hughes is one brilliant son-of-a-bitch'."

"That's not even remotely close to my thinking. I was actually thinking you're a little weird."

"Weird. Is that a professional term?"

"I gave up being professional around you a long time ago," Reinholt replied with a smirk.

Chance shrugged and said, "Yeah, well, I always say if you're gonna be weird, be confident."

"You have succeeded in that, my friend."

"I'm not gonna succeed in much more than that if I don't get out of this place soon. I want to get back to work. Once these headaches are gone, I'm good to go."

"What operation were you working on?"

"What?"

"What operation were you working on, Chance? Why were you in Spain?" Reinholt asked.

"I told you, I don't remember going into that church," Chance answered, irritation creeping into his voice.

"That's not what I asked. Why were you going to that church in the first place? What was the end goal of this mission?"

"I needed something from that priest," Chance answered, rubbing his eyes hard.

"Remember what you needed from him?"

Reinholt could see Chance deflate a tiny bit as he answered softly, "No."

"How about that priest's name? Remember that?"

Chance concentrated until his head throbbed. He shook his head and looked at Reinholt sadly. "When will I remember?"

Reinholt smiled reassuringly. "It'll all come back soon, don't worry. I didn't want to stress you out."

"Well, you did, asshole."

"My point was to show you that you need to take it easy and follow orders. You're not 'good to go' as you said earlier. Trust me, we need you to come back as soon as possible to finish this operation but we can't afford to have you going off half-cocked, screwing up all the work you've done this past year. Clear?"

"Crystal. You always know how to brighten someone's day."

"Then I believe my work here is done," Reinholt stated with a chuckle. "I'll be back tomorrow to brighten your day once again."

"Bless your sympathetic heart."

"Seriously, Chance, take care of yourself."

"Yeah, yeah, yeah. Got it, Doc. Go flirt with the nurses or something. Leave me alone," Chance grumbled angrily, yet he couldn't quite hold back the grin on his face. It sure felt good to jab at his favorite therapist.

As Reinholt walked out the door, he nearly bumped into Chance's brother.

"James, good to see you," he stated, shaking James's hand.

"You too, Doc. Did the knock on his melon make him any smarter?" James asked, pointing in at Chance.

Despite James teasing manner, Reinholt could see the deep worry in the man's serious blue eyes. James's personal mission in life was not to work covert operations for the United States. It wasn't even to protect the United States, even though he felt a duty to do so. James' primary goal was to protect his little brother. It was an impossible job, really. The wear and stress of trying to keep Chance alive were carefully hidden behind the sarcasm, jokes and his completely disarming charm. However, Reinholt had known James long enough to see past all that. He admired James, but didn't envy him in the least.

"I don't know about that, but it sure as hell didn't make him any less stubborn," Reinholt replied. "He needs to take it easy."

"He's never taken it easy, Doc."

"I know."

"Well, good to see you again. I'm sure you'll be hanging around the rest of the week?" James asked.

"I'll stay until he is discharged."

James nodded at Reinholt before turning and walking into Chance's room.

"You know, if you wanted to have a vacation, you could've just said so," James stated seriously, as he sat down in the same chair Reinholt had occupied only moments earlier. "This whole memory loss-slash-head injury thing is a touch dramatic, don't you think?"

Chance only looked at his brother with a blank stare. "I'm sorry, do I know you?"

"And I should warn you, you're on the tippy-top of my shit list for pulling a gun on me, and," James continued, holding up his hand to silence Chance's response, "your name gets a check mark next to it for physically attacking me."

Chance could no longer keep a straight face; he grinned and shook his head. "Sorry, bro."

"Sorry? That's it? That's all an attempt on one's life gets? A half-assed 'sorry'? That's pathetic."

Chance laughed. "Okay, okay. I'll buy you some new underwear, since I'm sure the whole episode scared the shit right outta you."

James smiled back and looked around the hospital room. "I'm surprised we haven't spent more time in places like this. Other than a few little patch-up jobs, we've been pretty lucky."

"Lucky, my ass. We're good. Well, at least I'm good enough to keep us both alive and mostly unharmed."

"I'll let that slide since you're obviously still suffering from a scrambled brain." James turned to study his little brother closer. "How's the melon?"

Chance shrugged. "Headaches, but they're getting better. Give me a day or two and I'll be ready to get back to work."

"Memories back?"

"I'm working on it. Little bits and pieces are floating around, just waiting for something to trigger everything to fall into place. If I could get outta here, I could think better."

"I had a conversation with the priest, Father Sanchez," James said casually, but carefully watched his brother for signs of recognition.

Chance snapped his fingers. "That's his name. Carlos Sanchez. I've been working on that name all morning. So, what did he tell you?"

"Not much, other than the few odd facts and information you told him."

"What dumb-ass things did I say?"

"Nothing too revealing. You just quoted the bible, talked about stars and a few other odds and ends."

Chance lifted a brow and asked, "Does he know who I am?"

"He's pretty dang smart and I wouldn't be too surprised if he guesses your identity has something to do with Orion. He recognized the names of the stars on your gun. Other than that, I think your name is safe."

"I need to get outta here. I have this nagging feeling that things are happening fast."

James leaned forward on his elbows. "I think Gabrielle is cracking you out of here by the end of the week. We really need your brain to straighten out, Stones. You've got more stored in that jumbled up head of yours than the rest of us have put together. We need your information to finish this job."

Chance rubbed his eyes in frustration. "I know this, James. I just need…I don't know, I need something. I feel like it's all right there," he held his hand right in front of his face. "I just can't grab onto it yet."

"It'll come back, don't worry," James replied. "I'm getting a tad bit concerned that Gabrielle is entertaining thoughts of me taking your place out in the field, and that doesn't amuse me in the slightest."

Chance's eyes sharpened as he sat up straighter. "That is a terrible idea."

"I couldn't agree more."

"Just give me a couple more days and I'm sure everything will come back. Don't, for the love of God, do anything as stupid as trying to take my place."

"It's not *that* stupid. Geez, you make it sound like they'd be sending out Elmer Fudd to replace Superman."

Chance smiled and shrugged.

James got up and walked toward the door. "You're a little shit, that's for sure."

Chance stood and quickly strode across the room reaching the door at the same time as his brother.

"I need a change of scenery," he stated seriously. "Let's go see what trouble we can find. I heard they have great muffins down in the cafeteria."

* * *

"I'm sending you home for a week, and then we will re-evaluate," Gabrielle stated sternly.

Chance bounced his knee underneath the small table in the corner of the coffee house. He hadn't worked up the nerve to try the steaming mug of triple mocha loca latte, or whatever the hell Gabrielle called it.

"Would it kill you to just get me a plain old black coffee?"

"You're in a foul mood. Still have headaches?"

"I wouldn't if I had a reliable source of caffeine on the table." Chance took a microscopic sip of the steaming beverage and shook his head. "This is terrible."

"Go home, and by that I mean Montana. Drink black coffee. Ride your horse. Do whatever you need to do to clear your head and then we'll talk."

"I know if I can just get back out there and work, everything will come back to me," he replied, his frustration obvious.

"You aren't an accountant, Chance," Gabrielle replied, softening her tone. "You operate in life and death situations. You can't afford to make a mistake. *We* can't afford you making a mistake."

"What makes you think I'll make mistakes?"

"I know you'll deny it, but I can see the pain in your eyes. You're not yourself and you know it. It's essential that you take the time to recover.

Chance stopped bouncing his leg and rested his elbows upon the table closing the distance between him and his boss. He stared at her a long moment before saying, "Fine. I go home. I rest. I catch up on my favorite soaps, maybe do some baking. Then what?"

Gabrielle ignored Chance's sarcasm and slowly sipped on her latte. Chance was typically intense, usually difficult, and he always enjoyed bucking the rules. Despite that, Gabrielle rarely saw him actually angry. Frustrated, impatient, ornery? Yes. But, hardly ever angry.

Now, as frustration mounted over his jumbled memories and his impatience to get back to work, Gabrielle saw Chance's anger rumbling near the surface.

"Look, I need some time to put together a plan. You haven't been home in over a year. This is a good time to take a few days to put everything together. Come back next week and we'll all have more focus, okay?"

Chance realized it was no use arguing. Despite his desire to push forward, Gabrielle's words made sense. And, he hadn't been back to his home in Montana in a while. He didn't want to admit it, but he wouldn't mind spending a few days in the mountains to clear his head and breathe in that crisp, fresh air.

"You're the boss," he mumbled.

"Yes, I am," Gabrielle answered with a smile. "But you're the only one who can finish this operation. Go rest up and come back ready to work."

"Yes, ma'am."

Chapter Five

Kuwait

She had to admit, the intelligence gathered by Orion was exceptional. His profile of the target was spot on, as were his predictions of the target's movements and actions. Given different circumstances, he would easily have completed this little snatch-and-grab operation, but due to an incident, that her boss refused to elaborate on, she had been reassigned to take Orion's place and complete the mission.

She hunched down behind the thicket next to the cold brick wall of the water treatment plant. Sitting there, she felt a tingle of adrenaline skip through her system. Just knowing that Orion was supposed to be the one sitting in this very same spot was a thrill. This was as close to the legendary spy she had ever been. Even though they were employed by the same organization and operating within the same shadowy lifestyle, Orion was not the sort of guy you just happened to run into. People didn't find Orion.

He found you. This was a fact that she was learning the hard way. Still, she was getting closer. Heck, she was actually doing *his* job. Something must have severely incapacitated him to render him unable to do this job. Orion didn't take vacation days.

She blinked to clear her mind of distracting thoughts and focused on the task at hand. She had arrived here three days ago and had had no trouble at all locating the target and tracking his day-to-day activities. Now, her only decision was when and where she would grab him. Her orders were strict. He was to be captured alive and maintain the ability to communicate. This target would be a fountain of valuable information once he was in the hands of the interrogation team.

She held the pair of binoculars up to her eyes and watched as her target strolled leisurely along the tree-lined avenue. This particular neighborhood of Kuwait City was home to the very affluent, wealthy citizens of Kuwait. The streets were smooth, the landscape groomed and meticulously maintained. Traffic was quiet this time of day, as was the pedestrian traffic. She smiled, thinking how this man had no clue what was about to become of his life. At that moment he was completely at ease and confident that his secrets were safe. He had no idea how wrong he was.

She placed her binoculars in her backpack,

prepared a dose of a strong sedative and slipped the hypodermic needle and syringe up her sleeve. She slipped on a pair of thin leather gloves, adjusted her ponytail and stepped out from behind the bushes. She quickly, yet casually, cut across a parking lot and grassy park and within minutes was mere paces behind her target. She kept her hands in her pockets and one eye on the benign looking dirty white delivery van parked along the street ahead of her. Her boss had arranged for one of her many mysterious assets to come up with viable transportation. The folded-in passenger side mirror on the van was the only clue she needed.

Malcolm Juarez had no idea he was a target. At that moment, his mind was filled with thoughts of travel plans. He was flying to Morocco tonight for a business trip. Never one to miss an opportunity, Malcolm would most certainly mix in plenty of pleasure to offset the business. He smiled as his mind wandered to Morocco and the beautiful women waiting for him. His personal wealth was increasing rapidly, and with that, the gorgeous women that had once been light-years out of his league, were suddenly easily accessible. Only a few years ago, flying in a plane to go anywhere, was nothing but a lofty dream for someone as poor and insignificant as Malcolm. Now, he was being flown everywhere in the world in private jets and staying in five-star motels. Life was good.

The only requirement he needed to fulfill in order to have this lifestyle was to do whatever was asked of him. Never, under any circumstances, question the orders. Malcolm gladly worked to meet the expectations of the man who had changed his life.

When he had met Domino, Malcolm was a nobody. With Domino's guidance and trust, Malcolm was now poised to help change the entire world. All he had to do was deliver messages between Domino and his followers. With the understanding that digital messaging could potentially be hacked, most of the correspondence within Domino's network was simply the spoken word.

Malcolm lit up a cigarette and heard soft footsteps behind him. He glanced over his shoulder and saw a long-legged blond woman who appeared to be a tourist strolling around to see the sites in this beautiful city. She had a camera slung over one shoulder and a bright purple backpack hanging from the other. She wore sunglasses and her long ponytail swayed in rhythm of her stride. He smiled and she offered a shy smile back at him. Malcolm felt his ego swell. Once, his life was full of nothing but poverty, ugliness and hopelessness. Now, there seemed to beauty everywhere. Even following him.

He paused at the intersection and smiled again at the pretty tourist as she also paused, just a few feet away from him. He stepped out into the street cautiously. He couldn't see any oncoming traffic due to an annoying delivery van parked in his line of sight. He was about to step out further to see around the van, but he never made it. Simultaneously, he felt a sharp jab in his neck and a pair of arms drag him toward the van. Darkness quickly numbed his senses, but before he completely lost consciousness, he swore he smelled a hint of jasmine. Did his eyes really see that pretty tourist's face as he was shoved into that delivery van?

The woman quickly tightened zip ties around Malcolm's wrists and ankles and pulled a black hood over his head. Even though she had pumped enough sedative into his bloodstream to keep him snoring for hours, she was never one to take a risk. The last thing she wanted was for him to wake up and get a good look at her.

She slipped into the driver's seat, twisted her long hair into a makeshift bun and shoved a baseball cap on her head. The logo on the hat matched the logo on the side of the van. She double-checked her surroundings once again to make sure there were no witnesses. She saw no one. She turned the key, but before shifting into drive, she pulled out her phone and texted, SUPERMARIO SECURE. Due to Juarez's striking similarities to the video game figure, right down to his groomed black mustache and odd short black eyebrows, his code name was a perfect fit. She quickly received a text saying simply, GET WINGS.

She carefully shifted the rickety van into gear and began a drive that would eventually take her to the private airstrip owned by a wealthy Saudi businessman who happened to owe Gabrielle O'Connor a few favors. Of course, O'Connor remained tight-lipped about the reason behind his cooperation, but the businessman granted her free use of his runway with no questions asked.

The timing perfectly coordinated, a small private jet was idling at the end of the runway when the woman and her "guest" arrived. The pilot, heavily armed and wearing black combat fatigues, assisted in getting the unconscious man into the plane.

"I might have to charge you an extra baggage fee for this," the pilot joked good-naturedly.

"Bill me," the woman shot back. She was in no mood for jokes. Especially coming from a cocky pilot who was looking to flirt with her. She despised flirting. She hated games and she especially hated men who immediately assumed she was someone they could play with.

The pilot visibly cringed and whispered "bitch" as he climbed into the cockpit. He slid down the partition separating himself from the passengers. He wanted nothing to do with the cranky woman and her hostage.

Good, the woman thought as she reclined in her chair and closed her eyes. She was tired. She hadn't had a good sleep in a few days and she was relieved that this was a long flight. She was heading back to America, land of the free and home of the brave. She sighed. The United States was a truly wonderful country and she did believe in her ideals and in the power of democracy. However, the good ole US of A would never feel like home to her. Her roots ran too deep in the frozen soils of Russia. Some ties just couldn't be severed.

She pulled the rubber band out of her hair to let her blond tresses fall loosely around her shoulders. She slipped out of her shoes and stretched out her long legs. She took one glance at the bound, unconscious man lying in the back of the plane and determined that he wouldn't need another injection for a couple of hours. She leaned back her head, closed her eyes and let herself drift off into a restless sleep.

Chapter Six

Bear Creek Ranch
White Sulphur Springs
Montana

The private helicopter hovered a moment over the open field, before slowly lowering to the ground. Once the wheels touched down, the pilot cut the power and the rotors slowed to a stop. James and Chance stepped out of the bird, leather duffels in hand, squinting in the bright, mid-day sun.

"There's our ride," James stated pointing at a jeep bouncing across the large field.

The old, weathered face of the Native American behind the wheel split into a wide toothy smile the moment he laid eyes on the two men watching him.

He skidded to a stop causing a cloud of dust to envelop them.

"Crazy old man," Chance said with a smile.

"Where's your cast?" James demanded pointing at the Indian's left leg.

"Cut it off."

James and Chance tossed their bags into the back of the jeep. James hopped into the passenger seat, leaving Chance to crawl into the cramped quarters of the nearly non-existent back seat.

"It's only been a month," James stated grabbing onto the roll bar as the jeep jerked to a start.

"I heal fast," George Big Eagle replied with a grin. "Glad to see you brought home a stray," he added, pointing at Chance.

"Yeah, he kept following me around in the parking lot looking all pitiful and hungry. I felt sorry for him so I brought him home."

Chance slapped James on the back of the head.

"What happened to you this time?" George asked loudly, glancing over his shoulder.

"Fell off the merry-go-round."

"How come you only come home when you're all banged up?" George hollered in reply.

"I'm always banged up," Chance muttered, holding tight to the roll bar as the jeep's worn shocks failed to absorb the drastic bumps in the non-existent road. "We're all gonna meet an untimely demise if you don't quit driving like a lunatic!" Chance yelled over the loud motor and wind whipping in their ears.

"Don't be such a pansy!" George yelled back.

George maintained the bone-jarring pace until dramatically slamming on the brakes bringing them to a gravel-spitting stop near the front of the massive log home the Hughes brothers had called home their entire lives.

Their father, the late United States senator William Hughes had over-seen every aspect of this house's construction. He wanted the Hughes' home to represent strength and power, while also encompassing the wild beauty of Montana. He had succeeded.

Sandra, William's wife and the boys' mother, had painstakingly decorated and furnished the log home in a manner that bespoke of both beauty and simplicity. Dark leather furniture, hardwood floors, earth-toned rugs, rough-hewn coffee tables with black iron accents could be found throughout the various rooms of the house. The exposed pine rafters accentuated the impressive stone fireplace that was the centerpiece of the layout.

Even though the brothers had lost their mother, along with their father, in a terrorist bombing at the U.S. Embassy in London nearly twenty years ago, the house still closely resembled how it was kept when Sandra was alive and the Hughes family was whole.

However, looks can be deceiving. Despite the friendly appearance of the house and the entire ranch, the place had undergone a few changes. During the nine months that Chance was struggling to stay alive in a miserable Afghan cave, James had spent every last dime searching for his brother. As a result, the once flourishing Bear Creek Ranch was nearly lost to the bank. Fast forward nearly seven years, with renewed health and top secret job descriptions for Chance and James, the ranch was not only in the black, but it had also under gone some very costly upgrades.

James's affinity for technology, security and surveillance systems led him to install the latest gadgets throughout the ranch. Chance's general mistrust of basically everyone, encouraged James to fortify the house with bulletproof windows and doors, motion detectors, silent alarms, pressure sensors, countless cameras, and a bunker in the basement stocked with all types of weapons and ammunition. The Hughes' ranch had become a nearly impenetrable fortress.

Like most homes, the Hughes ranch perfectly reflected its owners: Handsome, strong, and full of secrets.

* * *

Chance knelt down to rub the ears of the young Red Heeler, aptly named Red. The dog wriggled in close, appreciating the attention.

"Is this little guy learning how to be a ranch dog yet?" Chance asked George who was walking up behind him.

"Dumb as a post," George replied. "All he

wants to do is chase rabbits. He don't want nothin' to do with cattle."

Chance laughed as Red put his paw up in his lap. "Don't listen to the crazy old Indian." Chance stood up, yet the dog continued to stare at him. "He doesn't look dumb. I think he's so smart that he finds cattle boring. Rabbits are more challenging."

George huffed and walked past mumbling, "He's sure not as smart as Toad was."

Chance caught up with George. "I remember you thinking Toad was dumb, too," Chance stated, referring to the old Blue Heeler that had been a member of the Hughes' family for nearly fourteen years before he passed away three years ago.

George paused a moment before replying, "I never thought any such thing."

Chance laughed out loud. "Bullshit!"

"Watch your language around me, sonny boy."

"Ha, ha. You're the one who taught me how to swear," Chance shot back.

"How come you seem to only remember the bad shit and none of the good things I taught you?"

"Settle down old man," Chance said as he patted his friend on the back. "I recall a few good things you may have passed on."

George entered the barn, approached a stack of small square hay bales and sat down on one. "Like how to fight?" he asked with a mischievous grin.

"Yeah, like how to fight," Chance answered

with a smile.

George didn't miss the flash of coldness in the young man's eyes. He may be old, but his instincts were as sharp as ever. Even though neither one of the boys revealed any details of their occupations, George had a pretty good idea of what they were being asked to do. He loved James and Chance as if they were his own sons. Despite the immense pride he felt knowing that they had the skills and talent to succeed in their dangerous lifestyle, George would've given just about anything if they could come home and run this ranch.

"At least your memories are comin' back."

"Don't sound so disappointed," Chance laughed. "How's the leg feeling?" he asked as he grabbed a horse halter from a hook on the wall.

George rubbed his left leg, just below the knee. "Still aches a bit, but it'll be fine."

"Probably should've left the cast on awhile longer."

"Nah. It was time to let it breathe. You gonna ride?"

"Yep. James wants to check the longhorns pastured out on the west eighty."

George looked around and asked, "Where'd he go, anyhow?"

Chance looked around and then shrugged. "Beats me. He's probably satisfying his obsessive-compulsive need to check the ranch's security system."

"It's all good. I checked all the systems this mornin'."

"Oh, you know how he is. My brother has a lot of people fooled into believing he's normal."

George snorted a laugh. "Neither one of you has lot of 'normal' in you."

"Normal is no fun."

"How would you know that? You've never given normal a try. I have plenty of fun."

"Oh shit, old man, you aren't even in the same dictionary as normal," Chance shot back.

"You haven't ridden in over a year. Better take it slow so you don't fall off."

Chance paused as he stood in front of his horse's stall. "If you weren't such a fragile old coot I'd come over there and pound you."

George laughed. He hadn't laughed like this in years. He held his ribs and laughed some more. He looked up to see Chance eyeing him suspiciously. For a fleeting moment, the tall, broad-shouldered man who was capable of carrying out the sort of God-only-knows type of unspeakable missions all over the world looked like the gangly, smart-ass, tow-headed little boy he once was. George blinked hard and the boy was gone. In his place stood the man Chance had become. George's good humor dissipated.

George's odd laughter and weird expressions

gave Chance an uneasy feeling. He had always believed that George possessed the ability to see right through people's lies, masks and facades. George could see the truth, and Chance desperately wanted to keep his truths carefully hidden.

Turning away from George's piercing stare, Chance shook his head and mumbled, "He's lost his mind."

George gathered his wits and slowly raised his bony frame up and off the hay bale. He limped over to the stall and Chance handed him Mac's lead rope. George led the tall bay gelding out of the stall and tied him next to the tack room. He grabbed a brush and began brushing the horse's glossy coat.

"He sure looks good," Chance commented as he came out of the tack room carrying a heavy western saddle.

"He should. Damn horse thinks he's some sort of royalty. I've never seen a horse so particular."

Chance carefully placed the saddle up on his horse's back, slowly pulled the cinch tight and patted Mac on the neck. "Particular? How?"

George tossed the brush back into the box and rolled his eyes. "Oh hell, where do I begin? First, there's the food. He only likes a certain kind of feed, of course. And then the hay. If it has even the tiniest bit of dust in it, he won't have nothing to do with it. Of course, the weather's always an issue. Too warm? He has to be inside in front of a fan.

Bugs? Needs constant fly spray. Too cold outside? Gotta have his goddamn blanket on."

"Sounds like he's got you trained," Chance stated as he slipped the bridle on Mac's head.

"Hmmpf. He's prissy, that's what he is. He's a big old prissy fool."

"What are you two girls gossiping about in here?" James asked loudly as he strode down the hall.

"George was just telling me how brilliant a cattle dog Red is and how Mac is the toughest horse he's ever met," Chance answered.

James laughed as he said, "I bet. Let me get Jig ready and let's ride."

James quickly saddled his gray gelding and the two brothers set off at an easy lope across the rolling hills.

* * *

As the brothers approached their home place, they remained quiet, absorbing the beauty of a perfect Montana sunset. They had ridden over fifteen miles through rough terrain and were now perfectly content to let their tired geldings walk the last mile. As the ranch buildings came into view, they spotted a late-model white Ford pick-up meandering slowly up the drive and watched it pull to a stop in front of the barn.

The guys reined their horses to a standstill and Chance pulled his rifle out from the carrier on his saddle. He lifted the weapon and looked through the scope. The strong magnification erased the mile distance between himself and the visitor, giving him as clear of an image as if he would've been standing a foot away.

"Who is it?" James asked.

Chance looked a moment longer before he lowered the rifle. "A woman. And a pretty one at that."

"Ah, shit," James grumbled.

Chance smiled as he carefully placed his rifle back into the nylon carrier. "How come I have a feeling this is gonna be entertaining?"

James sighed and shifted in his saddle to look directly at his grinning brother. "It's Dr. Ramsey. She must be out here checking up on those sick calves."

"Did you tell her to come?" Chance asked.

"No."

"Wow. What an attentive vet. Coming all the way out here, after hours, just to check on a couple of calves that aren't that sick."

James shook his head, wishing he could slap a piece of duct tape over his brother's mouth.

Chance kicked his horse into a trot. "Well, let's not keep the nice lady waiting."

James quickly spurred his horse and caught up

to Chance. "Remember, you don't exist," James reminded. "Don't do or say anything stupid. Matter of fact, don't say anything."

Chance laughed and replied, "A little touchy with Miss Ramsey, are we?"

"Dr. Ramsey. I'm just trying to keep you out of trouble, as usual. So, don't be a smart ass; just follow my lead."

"Relax, geez. You're only making me more curious."

James glared at him as they trotted up to the barn. Chance winked back.

"Casey, what brings you out this fine evening," James asked with a smile as he dismounted and handed Jig's reins to George who led the horse inside the barn.

Dr. Casey Ramsey couldn't help but return the smile. She realized it was a little late in the day to make a farm call, but she did want to make sure the two sick calves were responding well to the antibiotics she had given them a few days ago. Even more so, she wanted to see James. Since being hired on at the vet clinic at White Sulphur Springs six months ago, she found herself more and more drawn to the dark rangy man who owned this impressive ranch. Despite the rumors and mystery surrounding James Hughes' wealth and lengthy disappearances, Casey found him warm and engaging. When he had asked her to join him for supper last month, she gladly accepted.

Even though she learned nothing more about James' life during their date, their time together felt comfortable and easy. She found herself sharing far more about herself than she typically did with anyone. Something about James made her trust him. Without prying, he got her to open up. When he kissed her good night, she felt both exhilarated and exhausted. She wasn't sure what to think about James Hughes, except that she wanted to see him again. Then, when she had stopped out at the ranch the next day, George informed her that once again, James was on a business trip and had no idea when he would return.

Casey took a chance he'd be home this evening and she felt her heart thump as she watched him ride his big gray horse up to her. She was surprised to see he had a companion, who hung back, yet watched intently.

"I wanted to see how those babies were feeling. Didn't know if I'd catch you at home or not."

"Well, you caught me sweetheart. I knew it was my lucky day," James said as he winked at her. "A little late in the day for you to be working, isn't it?"

"A vet's work is never done."

"Remember what I said about all work and no play?" James asked with a grin. "Calves are doing fine, by the way."

Casey laughed and felt her cheeks flush. Yes, he

certainly got to her. She suddenly noticed that the man sitting quietly on the bay was watching her closely.

"So, who's your friend?" she asked and gave a little wave in his direction. The man tipped his hat and smiled.

James glanced back at his brother before replying, "Oh, he's just visiting. He's the son of a business partner of mine who happens to live in Norway. I promised he could come visit a real working American ranch, and so, here he is. He won't be here long. He has some sort of crazy fantasy of starting up his own ranch in Norway."

James stepped closer to Casey and spoke softly, "If you ask me, he's not quite right in the head, but his father is an important business partner, so I have to play along."

Casey nodded and looked over at Chance sitting on Mac. "Oh, okay. That's nice of you to let him ride Mac. I'm sure he's never been on such a nice horse before."

James huffed, "I'm nothing if not a nice guy." Then he turned toward his brother and yelled, "Sven, come on over here," he waved dramatically. "He doesn't speak or understand English that great so he's a little tough to communicate with."

James had spoken the last comment loudly enough for Chance to clearly hear him. Chance arched an eyebrow at his brother as he walked Mac up closer. Since he apparently had been renamed Sven, he quickly discerned that he must be of Norwegian heritage, or Swedish or Danish, or somewhere in that vicinity. He didn't really know any of those languages but was certain they would be fairly closely related to German, and he had a pretty firm grip on the German language. In a matter of fifteen feet, or ten of Mac's strides, Chance transformed into Sven, a German-speaking rancher-wanna-be.

"Sven, this is Doctor Ramsey. She's a veterinarian," James introduced.

Chance figured his height and mannerisms were easier concealed if he stayed on his horse, so he smiled what he hoped appeared to be a shy smile and reached his hand down to shake the pretty young vet's hand.

"Vet-r-ane-um?" Chance repeated awkwardly.

"Animal doctor," James clarified. He pointed at Mac and repeated, "Doctor, animal doctor."

Chance pretended to be in confused thought for a moment before saying, "Ah, doktor. Tier arzt."

"Yeah, tier arzt…whatever," James stated. "So, wanna take a look at those calves?" James wanted to get Casey away from Chance before his brother began getting creative.

"Sure," Casey replied. She looked back at Sven and said, "Nice to meet you Sven."

Chance smiled broadly. "Verstehen Sie, was ich

sage?" *Do you understand what I'm saying?*

Casey tilted her head. She wanted to be polite, but didn't have a clue how to respond. "I'm sorry, I uh, I don't understand."

Satisfied that Miss Casey didn't comprehend an ounce of German, Chance kicked Mac up a few steps closer. His smile brightened as he said, "Sie sind einfach wunderschön. Wenn Sie sich langweilen mit meinen Bruder, komm wieder, und ich zeige euch eine gute Zeit." *You are gorgeous. When you get bored with my brother, come back and I'll show you a good time.*

Sven's bright smile and fluid words were charming, even if she had no idea what he said. She stepped closer and said, "I'm sorry, what?"

James grabbed her arm and pulled her away from Chance. He glared at his brother over his shoulder. He couldn't speak German but he understood enough of the language to get the gist of what Chance had said.

Chance shrugged and gracefully dismounted his horse. He waited until James and his pretty vet were out of sight before he led Mac into the barn and began unsaddling him. He sensed George approaching and asked, "What's the story with the hot vet?"

"I know that she sure is extra attentive to anything that might possibly be sick around this place. Never knew a vet that made so many farm calls for no reason," George answered as he stiffly sat down on a hay bale.

"I bet she's got great bedside manners," Chance stated sincerely, getting a loud snort of laughter out of George.

"Speaking of stories, what's yours?" George asked.

"I'm a numbskull named Sven who wants to tag along with the all-knowing, talented and handsome James Hughes."

George nodded as he pulled out a piece of hay and began chewing on it. "Sounds about right."

Chance led Mac into his stall and threw an armful of sweet smelling hay into the corner of his stall. His felt his phone buzz in his pocket and quickly pulled it out. He recognized the number and all thoughts of Norway and pretty vets vanished.

"Yep," Chance answered softly. He listened only for a brief moment before saying, "Will do." He shoved the phone back into his pocket.

George felt sadness drape over him like a wet blanket. "You're leaving."

Chance didn't look at the old man as he replied, "Before dawn tomorrow morning. Back to work."

"James, too?"

"Yep."

George slowly stood up and walked over to Chance. He placed his gnarled hand upon his shoulder. He wanted to say something but couldn't find the words. Chance seemed to understand as he smiled and said, "I'm good at what I do. Don't worry. James will be home before you know it."

"And you?"

"I'll be fine. I always am."

Chapter Seven

CIA Headquarters
Langley, Virginia

Chance Hughes had never been known as a team player. Truthfully, Chance wasn't known at all. However, his call sign, Orion, was racking up quite a reputation for being a top-notch bad ass. Other agents and operators within the covert world of espionage and national security were privy to bits and pieces of information regarding a man only known as Orion, who had yet to fail a mission. He was a hunter who never failed to find his prey. His abilities to efficiently gather human intelligence and produce results were impressive, even to the jaded minds of his peers.

Despite his accomplishments, Orion wasn't in a position for accolades. Matter of fact, his only reward for a job well done was coming home alive, and possibly a week or two of rest. He wasn't in the running for honorary medals or even government protection. Orion willingly put his life on the line for his country, yet his country had no idea he even existed. His job title fell outside the confines of the rules placed upon anyone being paid by the government. Gabrielle O'Connor hired and utilized her most lethal spy on her own. Paid exceedingly well with money left behind by an anonymous billionaire who's dying wish was to see the American people remain safe and unharmed by the world's radical thugs, Orion was quickly amassing a small fortune himself. However, with his lifestyle and introverted personality, splurging on luxury items simply seemed silly. Therefore, most of his money was divided amongst several bank accounts under aliases throughout the world. Orion was constantly prepared to quickly disappear and had the funds to support an escape if needed.

Chance's meetings with his boss typically occurred at safe houses, or ambiguous locations such as malls or coffee houses. He had never stepped foot inside the impressive brick monstrosity of the CIA headquarters. When O'Connor requested his presence at a meeting held in the conference room down the hall from her office, he was more than a little surprised. But not nearly as surprised as the others in attendance at the meeting.

When Gabrielle O'Connor stood in front of a group of three of men who themselves were highly respected deep cover operators, and introduced the man standing next to her as Orion, a shocked silence dropped over the room. Curious glances aimed at the tall man yielded few answers to the questions in the minds of those in that room.

He stood with his arms crossed, leaning casually against the wall. Yet, nothing about him felt casual. An intensity radiated off the man like gamma rays. He wore a ratty Devil Rays baseball cap pulled low to shade his face. His eyes were concealed behind mirrored Oakley's and a dark, three-day stubble covered the lower part of his face. The effect was perfect. Despite standing right in front of a group of people, he was nothing but a shadow.

The only facts anyone could gain as they eyed the infamous Orion standing in front of them was that he was taller than average, thin but broad shouldered. His black leather jacket concealed his body, but did nothing to hide his strength. A few strands of dark blond hair stuck out from underneath his baseball cap. There was one nagging question in everyone's mind as they laid eyes on America's top assassin: Why was he here in the same room as them?

Quickly, so as not to allow imaginations to run wild, Gabrielle O'Connor re-directed everyone's attention to their current operation: Find and kill one of the world's most dangerous terrorists, Dominique Rodriquez, aka Domino.

"First of all, I hand-picked each of you for this

operation because of your talent. We have new intelligence indicating with high probability the current location of Domino. We need to move quickly and efficiently as a team to extract him. It's imperative we capture him alive. He may be the only one with information we can use to stop an impending attack."

All eyes sparked with the idea of embarking on this highly sensitive mission, encountering unforeseen dangers, and confronting intense pressure. This is what was continually sought after by these highly trained, unique individuals sitting in this room. Gabrielle recognized this trait and could see their eyes light up at the prospect of being deployed once again. Even though she couldn't see his eyes, she knew that the man standing beside her was the most driven to head back to work. He didn't feel alive unless he was toe-to-toe with death.

"This operation will be in the hands of Orion. He will be calling the shots. You answer to him. I'm confident that you're all fully aware of his abilities. He has been deeply involved in the Domino Operation longer than any of you."

With that, Gabrielle took her seat at the head of the long table and Chance grabbed the chair next to hers. The three other men followed suit and pulled up chairs.

"Now, as I had mentioned, we have reliable information as to the whereabouts of our target.

Orion, take it from here," Gabrielle stated as she turned toward Chance.

Chance paused a moment as an unexpected stab of pain shot through his concussed brain. Despite the return of his memory, the headaches, occasional dizziness and nausea still crept up on him. He insisted to anyone who asked, that all his symptoms were gone. Lying was another well-honed skill in his repertoire of capabilities.

Once the pain subsided, Chance pulled off his shades and rested them on the bill of his cap. Immediately, he sensed the increased curiosity of the three men sitting at the table. Typically, Chance did his best to conceal his most memorable trait, his eyes. At times, they could appear sky blue, other times, stormy gray. At all times, however, Chance's eyes were intense and usually delivered an unforgettable feeling of cold intimidation and unease. Still, he wasn't worried about hiding his face from these guys. They were seasoned operators, used to secrets and shadows. Introduced to him as Tim, Jet and Roger, Chance understood that their real identities were also classified. If he had wanted to, he could've dug into their personal files and learned their actual names, but Chance preferred keeping his acquaintances, good or bad, at a distance.

One man, the one known as Roger, studied Chance closely. Chance remembered Gabrielle informing him that Roger was an ex-Navy SEAL and veteran dark ops agent. As Chance met his gaze, he sensed something off. Curiosity was expected, but this guy seemed completely entranced. Chance shook it off and redirected his focus on Domino. He stood, picked up a small remote control and pointed it toward a large flat screen monitor mounted on the wall behind him. Immediately a detailed city map of Fallujah appeared.

"Our latest intel is that Domino is residing in this neighborhood." Chance tapped on the screen and the image zoomed in to show a residential area on the south side of the city. "According to our sources, he has been seen off and on, in and around this area for the past year. This information was corroborated by one of his advisors that we now have in custody."

Chance walked back to the table and leaned over, placing his hands flat on the table. His eyes almost twinkled as he added, "We're going over there and we're gonna get him."

When Gabrielle informed Chance that their target's location had been pinned down to Iraq, Chance felt the familiar surge of adrenaline. Iraq and Afghanistan had been the stage for many life-changing experiences when he was a young Marine. His skills as a sniper, a fighter and soldier had been honed in this part of the world. It was here that he learned who he was and what he was capable of. It was also the part of the world that had nearly broken him. The desert was his favorite place to seek revenge.

"We've had a drone on this area for a few days. It appears that he may be residing in several houses making him tougher to track. This whole area is residential. In all likelihood, our target is hiding behind women and kids," Chance stated. He looked back toward the burly guy and noticed him staring again at him.

"Roger," Chance singled the man out. "Is there a problem?"

The man gave a small smile before shaking his head. "No, sir."

Chance felt that weird "off" feeling as their eyes met. Chance was second-guessing his decision. He wished he had dug into Roger's files further. The guy was giving him the creeps.

Chance eyed Roger a bit longer before returning his attention to the map on the wall. "We've acquired an asset that will help us pin-point the target's locations."

"And who would that asset would be?" the ex-Army Ranger, Jet, asked.

Gabrielle flipped open a file in front of her and said, "Carlos Rodriquez Sanchez. Domino's brother. He's agreed to help us secure our target."

For the first time Roger pulled his eyes away

from Chance. "How do we know he's not leading us into a trap? Blood's thicker than water, you know."

Chance began pacing in front of the map. "We don't know. Not for sure. That's why we'll use him as bait. If he's lying to us, I'll take care of him."

The three hardened sets of eyes watched as the man they knew as Orion paced the floor in front of the room. None of them had any doubt whatsoever that the man would do whatever it took to complete this mission.

"Wheels up tomorrow morning," Chance finished.

Gabrielle stood, prompting the three men to stand, as well. They shook hands with each other, and then glanced at Orion who had pulled his shades back down over his eyes and retreated to the other side of the room, clearly not wanting to interact any further. Jet and Tim let themselves out of the room, but Roger hesitated only a moment before approaching Orion. He reached out to touch the man's arm to get his attention, but before he made contact, the tall man spun around to face him. Nothing about his demeanor was friendly.

"Roger," Chance said, sounding a tick irritated.

"I never thought I'd ever see you again, Gunny," Roger replied.

Chance pulled off his shades. It was his turn to study Roger closely.

Roger glanced over at Gabrielle who appeared

to be organizing her briefcase.

"The last time I saw you, you were nothing but a beat up, broken kid. We never expected to find you alive."

Chance's irritation melted away as flashes of painful memories tried to break through the carefully guarded walls of his psyche. He would occasionally have odd dreams about the blackened, mysterious faces that pulled his nearly lifeless body from the cave, but those faces were always nameless. Once, he had been asked if he wanted to know the names of the men who had saved his life, but he had declined. He didn't want to remember any part of that experience. What he did know was that the men who found him were members of SEAL Team 6. Now, looking at Roger, he realized he was looking at one of those faces that he had laid eyes on a lifetime ago.

Chance wanted to say something but the words escaped him. He just stared.

Roger smiled and held out his hand. "I've seen a lot of shit, but I've never seen anyone as tough as you. I'd like to introduce myself. I'm Aaron Cash. I was the commanding officer of the team that found you. I'd be honored to finally shake your hand, Sergeant Hughes."

Chance blinked, feeling more shaken than he would've expected in this situation. He met the man's hand in a firm shake.

"Likewise," Chance replied, knowing his response was massively inadequate. What he wanted to say was, "You're the real hero," or "you're a pretty tough bad-ass, too," or "thanks for spending nine months of your life looking for me," or most importantly, "thanks for saving my life." But, ornate verbiage and wordy responses were not Chance's forte.

Roger seemed to understand. He nodded and smiled. "Don't worry. I won't tell anyone who you are."

"I'd appreciate that. I'll do the same for you."

"See you in the morning," Roger said as he turned and walked out the door.

Chance eyed Gabrielle over by the table.

"You can quit pretending that you're not listening, O'Connor."

Gabrielle smiled. "I honestly never thought he'd recognize you. You don't look anything like you did when he saw you last."

Chance strolled over to her, forcing himself to ignore the throbbing headache beating a pulse once again. He fingered the small bottle of pain pills in his coat pocket but would have to wait until he was alone to down a few.

"You were wrong."

"Yes, I was. I picked him for this team because he is good. You can trust him."

"I know. Now drop it." Chance slipped his

shades back on, hoping to hide the pain Gabrielle might spot in his eyes. "A couple of questions for you."

"Okay. Go."

"Who grabbed Super Mario?"

Chance had spent a fair amount of time pinning down that little slime ball and he had every intention of grabbing Domino's advisor himself. Obviously, the little blow up in Spain had redirected his plans. He was surprised the capture had happened so quickly. Apparently, the operative who had taken his place was capable of following the trail of breadcrumbs he had left.

"Take your sunglasses off. I can't talk to you with those on," Gabrielle snapped. "What is it with you and those things, anyhow?"

Chance slipped his shades off angrily. "You sure snatched up Super Mario fast. I must've left easy directions."

"Your intel certainly helped. I had an asset in the area, and yes, his capture went smoothly. Now he's talking and everything is pointing to Fallujah." Gabrielle paused before asking, "Are you okay, Chance?"

"Never better. I'll be on my way, unless there's anything else I should know?"

"I'm adding someone to your team."

Chance stared hard at his boss. "Now, wait just a second, O'Connor. I agreed to those three guys because you convinced me we could get the job done faster with them. If there's someone else involved with this, then why weren't they here in this meeting?"

"This particular operative was in-flight and couldn't be here. Besides, I wanted you to meet this agent privately." Gabrielle checked her watch and said, "Matter-of-fact, the agent should be here now."

"Please, tell me you're joking," Chance stated darkly.

"You've known me quite a while, Hughes. Have I ever joked around with you?"

Chance noticed the extra little gleam in her dark brown eyes. Gabrielle was full of fire and had the guts to make the decisions that would make most people crumble. She was capable of doing almost anything, but as far as Chance was concerned, she wasn't capable of telling a joke.

"Are you doubting my ability to do this? If you are, trust me, I'm fine. There's nothing wrong with me. I don't need any additional baby-sitters along. It's bad enough I've got a *priest* along."

"This has nothing to do with your ability. I wouldn't be sending you back out if I didn't believe you were capable. Now, just listen for once and maybe you will see my point of view, okay?"

Chance tossed up his hands. "I agreed to the priest because somewhere in the back of my screwed up head, I think I can trust you. But, you need to know I have some serious reservations about having him along, O'Connor. I can see about a thousand different scenarios where this is just not a good idea," Chance began pacing the floor. "He'll never be able to handle what's going to happen out there."

Now it was Gabrielle's turn to smile. "Oh, my dear Chance, you are so good at what you do, but there are times when you completely fail to read people correctly."

Chance stopped and looked at Gabrielle in surprise. The word "fail" used to describe anything regarding himself burned uncomfortably. "Explain, please," he demanded.

"You spent nearly thirty-six hours with Father Carlos, right?"

"Technically, but my brain was swollen and bleeding, so forgive me for not being as observant as normal," Chance replied sarcastically.

Gabrielle shrugged and grabbed a folder out of her briefcase. "Father Carlos hasn't always been a priest."

"Wait," Chance interrupted. He paused a moment as he gathered the recollection. "I remember him telling me he had been in the Spanish Army."

"Actually, he spent nine years as a GEO."

"Grupo Especial de Operaciones," Chance

replied quietly. "His gun. A USP Compact. Of course, that makes sense now.

"Yes, the Spanish Special Forces. I believe you'll find that he can hold his own if necessary. However, I fully expect you to keep him out of harm's way."

"I don't trust him. Domino is his brother. I happen to know a little something about brothers, and brothers don't just turn on each other. My money is on Carlos leading us into a trap."

"Maybe, but I believe if we handle this right, he'll help us. But, of course, you shouldn't trust him completely. If you sense that he's misleading you, then you have my blessing to use your charm to extract any information from him he may be withholding. Trust your instincts and use good judgment."

"According to you, I fail to read people properly," Chance grumbled.

"Don't take it personally. Not everyone is perfect," Gabrielle responded as she stuffed the folder back into her briefcase.

"Hey, I would've picked up on Sanchez's past if my brain hadn't been scrambled. Hell, I was hardly conscious most of the time."

Gabrielle smiled up at Chance. "Let it go. I trust your judgment. Don't get hit on the head again, and everything should turn out fine."

"Okay, enough about the priest. Who's this

other spook who gets to join in the festivities?" Chance asked.

"Yes, there is another agent who has been deeply involved in this operation and it's time to collaborate. This operative is also used to working solo, but I trust you both will exhibit professionalism and learn how to work together."

Chance looked hard at his boss. "You do realize you're talking to *me,* right O'Connor? I can pretty much guarantee I'm not gonna live up to your ideals of teamwork. There's nothing in my history to suggest otherwise."

"How's your memory? Any missing pieces?" Gabrielle asked prompting Chance to look at her in confusion.

"That's random, but yeah, I've got almost everything back. There's a few scenes missing from the whole church adventure, but other than that, I'm good. Why?"

Gabrielle almost smiled as she pulled out her cell phone. "You'll figure it out," she replied before she spoke into her phone and simply said, "Come in, please."

The conference door swung open and a long-legged woman with azure eyes and long platinum-blond hair stepped confidently inside. Appearing both elegant and tough in her slim fitting black leggings and curve-hugging black turtleneck, she moved with precision and control.

Her eyes momentarily glanced at Gabrielle before locking onto the icy stare of the tall man standing only a few feet away from her. His face remained expressionless as he met her gaze, which she completely expected. Besides, he was Orion, ruthless killer who never let his emotions run the show. He was a master at concealing his thoughts. Still, she swore she saw something flash in his eyes. Anger? Shock? She hoped it was fear. She chastised herself silently as she realized what she saw in his eyes was nothing more than her own hopes and imagination. For all she knew, he had no idea who she was.

Years ago, she had discovered Orion's true identity. Since then, she had focused on completing her missions, becoming a talented operative in her own right. She learned how to live in the same dark, covert world of espionage that Orion had mastered, hoping someday fate would bring her to him. She prayed that someday she would finally get to look into the cold eyes of Orion. Someday had finally arrived.

Those eyes had haunted her for six years. She had been an idealistic young woman when she first looked into his eyes. Back then, she had dreamt of becoming a successful businesswoman and following in her father's footsteps. Now, as she stood in front of the man who had forever changed the course of her life, she felt a surge of emotion.

She squeezed her eyes shut, trying to stop the memories.

Gabrielle quietly watched her two operatives stare at each other. Then she turned her focus completely on Chance. She studied him closely trying to get a read on his reaction as he laid eyes on Anna Petrova for the first time since he had killed her father six years ago.

As usual, Chance gave no outward indication of his thoughts.

Gabrielle sighed, stepped closer and after giving Chance and Anna another long look asked, "Is this arrangement going to be a problem?"

Chapter Eight

Fallujah, Iraq

"What do you mean, you don't know where he is? Your only job was to find him and bring him to me!" Dominique Rodriquez Sanchez screamed into his cell phone before throwing it across the room. The small device broke into several pieces as it slammed against the adobe wall and fell with a pitiful clatter to the floor.

A portly man, short in stature, blotchy olive complexion and buzzed black hair hidden beneath his turban, Domino was not a physically intimidating man. But one look into his snaky black eyes deeply set within the round contours of his round, pudgy face told the real story. Domino was capable of pure evil. His carefully groomed goatee only magnified his malicious expression. Domino angrily paced a few steps and adjusted his tightly wrapped turban before spinning around to face the three men standing at attention against the wall. None of them made eye contact with the seething man staring them down.

The men caught in Domino's burning glare wore dated Russian army-surplus fatigues and ratty combat boots. All the money in their organization went directly toward buying information, technology and traitors, not new uniforms. Typically, they each carried a trusty 9mm Berretta in their belts, but today they had been told to leave their weapons outside during this particular meeting. None of them held any misconceptions about what would happen in this seemingly benign-looking house. They had been assigned an important job, handed to them by the leader of their organization. They had failed. Now, they must face the repercussions.

"Where is Juarez?" Domino demanded, his dark eyes flashing as he studied them, and waited.

The oldest of the three cleared his throat and replied meekly, "The Americans have him."

Domino's eyes flashed. "He's alive?"

The three men nodded.

Domino immediately pulled out his revolver, aimed and fired. The older man fell to the ground, a gaping hole in his forehead. Instant death. He had gotten lucky. The remaining two men watched in horror and began trembling. Their fear was not of dying itself, but of dying a slow, torturous death. They need not look further than the cellar of this very residence to solidify that fear.

Domino stepped closer to the two men and aimed his gun at the tallest, who also happened to be his third cousin. "Do you see why your failure could cause my whole plan to fall apart?" he snarled, his voice raspy with rage.

His cousin nodded as tears filled his eyes.

Domino pulled the trigger. His cousin's body crumpled to the floor as his face was blown off. A few twitches, and his body was still.

Domino then turned and aimed at the last man standing, who had tears streaming down his dirty face. He silently pleaded for his life, shaking his head, his eyes wide with fear.

"Do you see what failure means? It means death. Do you want to die, my friend?"

The man shook his head aggressively.

Domino lowered his gun. "Okay then. You go out there and track down my brother. Do. Not. Fail."

The man nodded and with trembling lips sputtered, "I won't fail," before turning and running out the door.

Domino shoved his gun back into his belt and rubbed the palms of his hands over his eyes. These past few weeks had been less than optimal for Dominique Sanchez. When one of his most trusted and valuable business partners had died unexpectedly from a massive heart attack, Domino was left reeling. Dr. Jafari had been responsible for one third of Domino's entire operation, and the brilliant doctor was nearly finished with the deadly formula that was to be the key component of the dirty bomb destined to wreak havoc at the LAX airport in Los Angeles. His death put a major wrinkle in the plan. Los Angeles, for the time being, was off the hook.

Domino was not stupid. Truthfully, he believed himself to be far above average intelligence. In actuality, his peers and acquaintances were drawn to him more likely because of his passion and charm, rather than his brilliance. His weaknesses of temper and greed constantly threatened his control, however. He made more than a few mistakes early on in his development into a full-fledged leader of Jihadists. But with the passage of time, Dominique Rodriquez had quickly learned how to lead, how to control his emotions and how to implement a plan. He didn't remember exactly when he lost his earthly identity as that of a man with humble beginnings. He just knew that he was now something much bigger. Someone much more important. Someone who had the power to wreak havoc on the heathens in America. He was Domino, and he was above all those who followed him. Allah had bestowed upon him the great honor to eradicate the infidels.

Domino had no delusions that the plans Allah wanted him to follow would be easy. The Americans would fight, of course. He believed them to be the sneakiest of foes. So, when he received the news that Dr. Jafari had died from a heart attack, Domino knew the truth. Yes, Dr. Jafari's heart stopped, but it was no act of nature. He was convinced that Jafari's death had somehow been caused by those devils from Satan's playground. Domino hated nothing more than the United States of America with all its liberal thinking, hypocritical meddling, its wealth, and most of all, its power.

Dr. Jafari's death had been a victory for his enemies, forcing Domino to scramble to seek out a scientist who could decipher Jafari's complicated recipe. However, Domino would not let this setback stop him from implementing his grand scheme to knock America to her knees. His enemies could have Jafari. He planned to make America give up much more in return.

As he walked down the hall and past the door leading to the basement, Domino couldn't keep himself from grinning. Even if Juarez sang like a bird to his enemies, Domino felt invincible. He was strategically miles ahead of his opponents. Of course, he would have preferred that his top advisor was dead, unable to talk and spill secrets. Still, nothing would impede the progression of the plan at this point. The wheels were in motion, the key players in perfect position.

What bothered Domino far more than Juarez's capture was the disappearance of his brother. He had sent a team of his top guns to retrieve Carlos, yet somehow they failed. His men were operating under strict orders to bring Carlos back alive, and to leave no witnesses. He had handpicked the best team for the job, and still they had returned empty-handed. Not only did they fail to bring Carlos back, they couldn't even seem to find him.

Domino was well-aware of his older brother's skills and capabilities to evade potential threats. It was this awareness that brought about a small amount of hope and comfort to Domino's thinking. Perhaps his brother's innate instincts kicked in and he escaped from the church, believing he was in danger when Domino's men arrived. Maybe Carlos was in hiding, remaining invisible to avoid capture as he had done several times as a younger man. If he was, Domino had little doubt that his older brother would find his way to him. In times of trouble, that's what the brothers did, stuck together and often times, would fight together toward a common enemy.

A significant flaw marring Domino's hopes was his knowledge that Carlos did not believe their enemies were one and the same. Even a darker thought fluttering through Domino's reluctant line of thinking, was that Carlos' ideas regarding the truth had become twisted these past twenty years. As much as Domino didn't want to believe it, his older brother could actually look upon the enemy as a friend. Domino understood the drastically different paths he and Carlos had chosen in life. He believed Carlos to be a good person, just tragically misled. Carlos was following the orders of the wrong God. Somehow, his own brother had fallen into the web of lies known as Christianity and was now powerless to find the truth.

Domino knew the truth. Domino *was* the truth. He knew if he could only make his brother see the error of his ways, Carlos would come to the side of truth and understand the reason why Domino had to do what he was doing. If anything were better than leading the facilitation of the fall of democracy, it would be to do so with his brother at his side.

Carlos was strong, well-trained and a formidable ally. Unfortunately, he also had the potential to be a dangerous enemy. If Domino could not convince his brother to join his ranks, Carlos would have to be killed. Despite the anguish he'd feel over Carlos's death, Domino realized he would be dying for the greater good. The big picture. No one, not even his own brother, could impede the big picture.

As his plan developed further and neared the end goal, Domino knew that the Americans would soon seek out his brother. He had to find Carlos first and bring him under his protection. Domino was confident that his far-reaching contacts, deeply imbedded informants and talented hunters would find his brother and bring him home. He wouldn't quit until Carlos was safe from the Americans, even if that meant killing him. Unlike Jafari and Juarez, Domino would not concede Carlos to the enemy. Not his own flesh and blood. No, those dirty Americans would never have his own beloved brother.

Chapter Nine

Langley, Virginia

"Why would this be a problem?" Anna asked
sarcastically.

Gabrielle waited for Chance to respond; yet he
remained silent.

The tough thing about Chance was the more
turmoil going on inside his head, the quieter he
became on the outside. Having worked with and
closely studied Chance for the past six years,
Gabrielle may not have known exactly what was
going on in his head, but she knew him well enough
to realize that when he went still and silent, trouble
was brewing.

Chance was completely immobile. He gave no
outward appearance of stress: No twitching jaw
muscles, no fidgeting fingers, no reddening face or
increased breathing. Nothing. He just stood there,
his hand resting loosely on the back of a chair,
quietly studying and thinking.

"Chance? You remember Anna Petrova?"

Gabrielle asked, knowing full well he remembered every last detail about Anna, but she wanted to break his silence and begin the process of figuring out how they would work together.

Finally, he moved; he stood a little straighter, pulled his mirrored shades off from the bill of his cap and slipped them on his face, hiding his eyes.

"She's not coming along. Not on this operation or any operation, for that matter," Chance spoke softly, a deadly edge to his voice.

"Chance, she's alrea-" Gabrielle started but was abruptly cut.

"You arrogant ass," Anna growled as she strode up to stand directly in front of Chance. Despite her fluent English usage, her voice still held a touch of the Russian accent that gave away her heritage. She had hoped that her memories of him had somehow exaggerated his aura of strength and intimidation. His imposing height and impossibly handsome face were fixtures in her imagination. Now, standing mere inches away from him, reality did nothing to diminish his impressive features. If anything, the past six years only magnified his intensity.

"This is my operation, and I'm not going to let you screw it up. I don't need you to finish this," Anna spoke carefully, determined not to let any emotion squeak through.

Chance smiled. "Your operation? You are way out of your league here, Princess. I'm sure your talents would be better utilized somewhere else. I saw that Chik-fil-A was hiring down the road."

Chance barely got the words out before she took a swing at him. It wasn't the typical open-handed slap that most women went for. It was a full-fledged right-handed uppercut that came at him a lot quicker than he anticipated. Still, he managed to stop and hold her small fist easily in his large hand.

"Wanna try that again or do you have something else in mind?" Chance asked casually.

Before Anna could work herself into a full temper, Gabrielle stepped in.

"Would you two stop acting like children?"

"I can't work with him," Anna proclaimed angrily as she stepped away the moment Chance released her hand.

"Well, that solves that," Chance replied. "Don't let the door hit you on the ass."

"Chance!" Gabrielle snapped. "Anna, we need you on this op."

"I know you do," Anna quickly shot back. "So, send that Neanderthal home," she added, motioning toward Chance.

"No one knows more about this op than Chance," Gabrielle argued. "I need you *both* in order to find and capture Domino. I think the two of you have misunderstood the situation here. Your collaboration is not an *option*. It's a *necessity.* So, let me be clear, once and for all: I'm not asking; I'm telling you. Both of you need to figure out a way to work together until this operation is complete."

If Gabrielle wanted some sort of confirmation from her top operative that he understood, she was left disappointed. Chance simply walked past her and out of the room, slamming the door on his way out.

* * *

James gently tossed his duffel bag into the cargo compartment of the large military plane. Sometimes the guys got lucky and were flown first class in private jets to their destinations. This was not one of those times. They had to arrive in Baghdad in complete secrecy and in order to do that, they would fly in on a C-17 Globemaster III military cargo plane under the cover that they were missionaries accompanying a supply of essential medicinal supplies for the suffering refugees of the country.

James was about ready to seek out the pilot in order to get the details of the flight when he was interrupted by the arrival of a short, fine-featured man with a dark complexion, gray-streaked, closely cropped black hair and dark steady eyes that seemed much older than the rest of him.

"We meet again, señor James," the man stated with a cautious smile as he held out his hand.

"Father Sanchez. You ready for this?" James asked, shaking the man's hand and searching his face for signs of weakness, or betrayal.

"I hope so."

"You'll be fine. I'm sure all that military training hasn't been forgotten, right?"

Sanchez stared a moment at James. He tried to discern if these American's had dug up his past as an officer in the Grupo Especial de Operaciones. James' eyes gave away nothing.

"That was a long time ago, señor James."

James held Sanchez's gaze a moment before he smiled knowingly. "A man with your level of training doesn't forget those skills."

In that smile, Sanchez could only assume his past as a GEO was no longer a secret. Still, he wasn't willing to reveal anything more about himself than absolutely necessary.

"I believe I'm accompanying you on this operation as a source of information. Not a source of fire power, correct?"

James' smile widened. "That's right, Father. Hopefully you don't have to resurrect any of those forgotten skills."

"Do you think this could end peacefully?"

"I wish I could make you feel better and say yes, but truthfully, any sort of peace is unlikely." James watched as an old-school, nineteen-sixties something black Chevy Camaro sped across the tarmac and skidded to a stop a few feet from the plane. "When a guy like that is involved," James stated, pointing at Chance as he got out of the car, "peace has already been ruled out."

Carlos stepped over to stand next to James and looked out the door. "He appears to be angry."

"He is," James replied.

"Good to know."

"Oh, look, there's O'Connor's car," James said as he motioned toward a black Denali SUV with smoked-out windows pulling up and parking next to Chance's car. "Did you bring any popcorn, Father? This might be entertaining."

Carlos looked at James in surprise as the tall man sat down in the doorway and swung his legs out over the edge. James looked up and said, "Might as well take a seat." Carlos sat down next to James and watched curiously, as Gabrielle stepped out of her SUV. A tall leggy blond woman stepped out of the passenger side.

Chance and Anna eyed each other warily as she walked to the rear of the vehicle, opened the hatch and pulled out a large black leather duffel bag. Chance meanwhile circled the other way around and found Gabrielle.

"Chance your goi—" Gabrielle began but was quickly interrupted as Chance closed the distance between them.

"I trusted you," he growled. "I trusted that you

would make sure she was okay."

"I wa—" Gabrielle tried to explain but to no avail. Chance was in no mood to listen.

"This is how you protect someone? You turn them into killers and make them work for you?" Chance tried to keep his anger and voice controlled.

"She wan—"

"No. No way, O'Connor. Don't you dare give me any of that shit about her wanting to do this. No one *wants* to do this. No one. She had a chance to be normal, and you took that away from her."

Gabrielle wanted to grab Chance and push him back a few steps out of her personal space. But, she knew it would not be wise to lay a hand on him while he was in this current state of mind. Instead, she stepped back and took a deep breath.

"I gave her a choice," Gabrielle stated firmly, looking directly into Chance's angry glare. "This was her choice. She didn't want safe. She didn't want to be stuffed away someplace safe, forced to live life on the sidelines."

Chance looked away and watched as Anna climbed up the ramp into the belly of the plane. "You knew this whole time. She's been working for you this whole damn time and you never said a word to me," he stated quietly. He turned back and met Gabrielle's gaze.

The anger had diminished some, but in its place was a healthy spark of betrayal. Gabrielle realized when she first hired Anna that she was taking a risk. Chance's trust was fragile and she knew once he discovered that the woman he tangled up with in Russia during his first undercover job was now working under the same auspices he was working under, his trust in her would weaken. Gabrielle hoped that with time, Chance's strong sense of logic and strategy would override his sense of betrayal.

After Chance insisted on getting Anna out of Russia and away from the dangers her father's life had put her in, Gabrielle had promised to personally take charge of Anna's protective custody. She did not intend on doing any more than the customary actions needed to keep the Russian woman safe. However, it wasn't long before Gabrielle recognized Anna's talent and potential. Anna's athleticism, her incredibly high IQ and her instinctual decisiveness were strong traits Gabriel sought in her operatives. But, it was the underlying layer of coldness and emotional distance that she sensed within Anna that drove Gabrielle to offer her a job. Gabrielle was pleased that she had accepted and even more pleased with Anna's job performance. She was a relentless hunter, and as an attractive woman in this business, she had added advantages that Anna's male counterparts couldn't exploit.

Once Anna decided to work for her, Gabrielle knew that telling Chance wasn't an option. He would immediately do whatever he could to get Anna out of the program. He would have made it impossible for Anna to become the operative that the Team needed. There was also another reason for keeping the secret. A reason that Chance brought up now.

"She wants to kill me, O'Connor. You know it and I know it. I killed her father and she wants revenge." The anger had run its course and he was feeling calmer and clear-headed.

"I have weighed that possibility. You may be right."

"I'm right."

"But, the one thing she wants more than your head on a stake is Domino. She's been after this guy since she started with the organization. She hates to lose and Domino has evaded her every time she's gotten close. She'll do whatever it takes to get him."

"Even work with me?"

"Even that."

* * *

As Chance and Gabrielle held their intense discussion, Anna entered the plane only to see two men sitting in the open doorway, swinging their legs.

"Good show?" she asked sarcastically.

"So far," James replied with a grin. "How's it

going, Princess?" he asked, referring to her code name from the operation in Russia. "Long time no see."

Anna shoved past the men and huffed, "Not long enough."

James looked at Carlos and smiled. "See, this is gonna be fun. I mean, seriously, you can't script a better cast for this adventure. A pissed off, dangerous woman who has a torrid past with our trouble-prone superhero, a deceptively meek priest who has the ability to kill a man nineteen different ways with nothing more than a twig, and me, the humble horse wrangler who just hangs out in the eye of the storm with chaos swirling around him."

Carlos stared at James for an uncomfortably long moment before he finally said, "You have a colorful imagination, Mr. James." Then he stood and walked back into the plane.

James laughed as he watched Carlos pick out a seat along the side of the plane's interior. When he turned back to watch as his brother continued to spar with Gabrielle, his smile disappeared. His initial impression of Father Carlos was troubling him. The man held his emotions in check like a pro and his resume certainly indicated he was a dangerous man. Carlos may be wearing the priestly collar, but he still had the skills of a GEO.

Seeing Anna brought back a lot of memories for James. He glanced over and she was already

strapped into her chair, eyes closed and legs kicked
out. He had been shocked when Chance told him
she was working for O'Connor and was going to
accompany them on this operation. When James
first dealt with her, Anna was a bona fide spoiled
daddy's girl who didn't know life without luxury.
Hence the nickname, Princess. Yet, when that
Russian operation turned ugly, she didn't crack.
Even more telling of her true personality, Anna
pulled the trigger of the gun that sent the fatal bullet
into an American traitor. She also happened to send
a bullet into his brother. Luckily, for Chance, Anna
was untrained and emotional at the time or else he
wouldn't have escaped with his life instead of yet
another round-shaped scar on his body.

Anna Petrova was much tougher than her
Cover-girl looks would suggest and to
underestimate her would be a grave mistake.

Within minutes, the rest of the Team, Roger,
Tim and Jet arrived. As they boarded the jet, they
passed questioning glances toward the confrontation
going on between their boss and the legendary
assassin. Then their eyes landed on the beautiful
woman, resting on the seat in the plane.

"Who's she?" Tim asked loudly.

"And what the hell is going on out there?" Jet
asked, pointing out to the parking lot.

"That's Anna and she's with us," James replied.
"And that's nothing to worry about," he added as he

jabbed a finger out the door.

The three men claimed their seats, stowing their bags. Roger was the first to approach James.

"You must be the one Orion calls, Cowboy," Roger stated as he extended his hand. "I'm Roger. Good to be working with you."

"Call me, James. Good to be working with you guys too."

James met his hand, and then shook hands with Tim and Jet as they, too, made their introductions. Their warmth dissipated as they acknowledged Carlos. Their mistrust was palpable.

Carlos couldn't blame the men for their paranoia. He would feel the same way if he were in their situation. In what seemed like a lifetime ago, he had been in similar situations. They were smart to worry.

"Show over?" James asked sincerely when Chance bounded up the ramp and strode past him without so much as a glance. "I guess it is," James mumbled as he swung around and found a seat a safe distance from his still-angry little brother.

Chapter Ten

Fallujah, Iraq

Upon arriving at the safe house located near
the target's presumed location, the team tried to
break the tension that had riddled the long flight
from Virginia. Fifteen hours of fairly close quarters,
yet the only conversations had been between the
three men who had previous experience working
together. Jet, Roger and Tim discussed everything
from the upcoming operation to world events to
NFL football.

James swallowed a stout dose of sleeping pills
and subsequently slipped into a heavy sleep for the
majority of the flight. Anna dozed, checked and
cleaned her small arsenal of handguns and stared
blankly off into nothing. Chance made zero attempt
to bond with his new teammates. Wearing his dark,
mirrored shades, it was impossible to detect where
his eyes were looking or if he was even awake. For
the most part, he remained unnervingly still. Then
there was Father Carlos Sanchez, who probably

would've have been happy to engage in some sort of conversation to help pass the time, but no one wanted to be the first to cross that invisible line. He wasn't quite the enemy, yet not quite a teammate. He was untested, therefore, not trusted.

The comfort level didn't improve once inside the safe house. It was small, designed to house two, maybe three agents at any one time. Five men and one woman were crowded.

"Okay, listen up," Chance stated, nearly causing the rest of his team to jump. He had been silent for so long, no one expected him to be the first to speak.

Chance tossed his duffel bag to the side. "Here's how this thing is going to go down. I'm going to prep Carlos and set him in motion. Once he's in and the target is confirmed, we make our move."

James pulled out a chair by the small table in the kitchen and immediately began pulling out wires and surveillance equipment from his duffel bag. Anna shook her head in obvious frustration at having to take orders from anyone, much less Chance. Tim, Jet and Roger glanced briefly at each other before Jet stated, "I thought the plan was to wait for a go signal from headquarters."

Chance pulled off his shades and stared intently at Jet.

"Did it sound as though I was open to suggestions?" Chance asked, his voice controlled, yet there was no mistaking the violent undertone.

Roger pulled on Jet's arm, knowing Jet had a short fuse and a tangle with Orion would be just plain stupid.

"We got it," Roger replied. "Let's get to work."

"You're being foolish by rushing in," Anna suddenly spoke up. "Wire up the priest, turn him loose for a couple days. Let him build trust with our target. Moving too fast could—"

"What? Catch the target off guard?" Chance snapped. He walked until he was mere inches from Anna. "That's the idea, Princess. We don't need to establish trust with our target. I'm not sure what you're used to doing, but sitting around a campfire singing Kumbaya while the enemy moves closer to carrying out an attack isn't my style. Don't question my authority again."

Chance turned toward the priest and said, "Come with me."

Chance led Father Carlos into the privacy of a bedroom. Once inside, he closed the door behind them.

Carlos carefully eyed the tall man who filled the small room with both his physical presence and his overt intensity. Carlos felt his trigger finger tingle and his senses sharpen. He hadn't seen this man since they were on the rugged shores of Spain together. Then the man was injured, confused and at times, strangely vulnerable. Now, there was nothing but a confident predator pacing the confines of the small room.

"I know you are a GEO," Chance finally stated.

"*Was* a GEO," Carlos corrected. "I'm now a priest."

"Once a GEO, always a GEO," Chance shot back.

Carlos remained silent, sensing correctly that it was useless to try to argue.

Chance paced a small circle before turning to glare once again at Carlos. Speaking in soft fluent Spanish, he stepped closer to the priest and said, "Mira, si por un segundo que intento y doble cruzar este equipo o me voy a hacer tu muerte lenta y miserable." *Look, if for one second you try to double cross me or this team, I will make your death slow and miserable.*

"Esa no es mi intencion, señor Stones." *That's not my intention, señor Stones.*

Chance's penetrating glare quickly changed to surprise. "Why did you call me that?"

"I overheard señor James call you that."

Chance turned away and cursed softly under his breath. When he faced the priest again he said, "Do yourself a favor and don't call me that again."

Sanchez nodded.

Chance's jaw muscle twitched. He paused a moment, thinking over his plan. He really had no choice but to place a small amount of trust and faith in this priest.

"James retrieved Domino's cell phone number. You're going to call him and lead us right into his house," Chance instructed.

Carlos shook his head and replied, "My brother is a very suspicious man. This whole situation will raise many red flags with him."

"You will convince him to trust you. And he will because you are his brother."

"Get him to trust me and then betray him by giving him up to you," Carlos said softly.

Chance stared hard at the priest. Moment of truth. Would Carlos go through with this operation? Would he turn on the only family he had left in this world?

"I know that señor James is your brother. Would you do this to him?"

What the hell has James been telling this guy? First my nickname, now this? Chance tried to push his frustration aside one more time.

"I will easily kill anyone who is a traitor to my country and it's my duty to ensure that anyone posing a threat to freedom is terminated. If I had a brother that was responsible for such atrocities against innocent people as your brother, I'd kill him without a second thought."

Carlos witnessed an almost imperceptible flash in the man's steely eyes. However, in a blink, whatever he had seen vanished underneath the glacial shield.

Chance took a step closer to Sanchez. "I was under the impression that you were a willing participant in this operation. If you've had a change of heart and continue along these double-crossing lines of thinking, your brother is going to find you with a little less blood flowing through your veins.

"What do you want me to do?" Carlos asked, giving up on trying to break through Chance's barriers.

"You will wear a wire and call Domino. He knows you've been missing since the church explosion but he doesn't know that we have you. You are going to tell him that we did have you but you escaped. He knows you have the skills to do such a thing, right?" Chance asked, studying the priest closely.

Carlos wanted to say, "No, I couldn't do what you think I'm capable of," but the lie was impossible, and he realized that Chance already knew the truth. Carlos nodded.

Chance studied the priest a moment longer, making Carlos wonder what he was looking for, or already seeing.

"You went into hiding and you're now reaching out to him for help," Chance finally concluded.

"He's going to wonder how I knew he was in Fallujah and got his cell number."

"Tell him you used some of your old contacts to

track him down. I'm sure you still have some buddies from the good old days that owe you a favor, right? Tell him whatever you want. Just make sure he takes you back to his house, or shack, or cave, or wherever the hell he's staying. Once you're in and we can confirm that Domino is there, as well, we'll come knockin'.

Carlos inhaled deeply, the reality of the task at hand sinking in. "You will take him alive?"

"That's the goal but if he threatens the lives of my team, he's dead."

A soft knock on the door interrupted their conversation.

James stuck his head inside, "Ready to go?"

Chance nodded. "Get him wired and let's do this."

James entered with a handful of the latest technological advances in nearly invisible human surveillance and tracking equipment.

"You need to have a chat with the team regarding cameras," James added as he passed by his brother.

"Cameras?"

"Yep. Apparently it's standard for them to record every shot and step they take. Suits back stateside get to recline in comfy chairs, sipping sodas while they entertain themselves with a reality show starring us. I tried to tell them about our no-cameras policy but it fell on deaf ears. They're mounting all sorts of camera shit on themselves out there."

Chance stared a moment at James as if to say, "Are you kidding me?" Then he began to pace the perimeter of the small room.

"This is rapidly approaching a Charlie Foxtrot," Chance said in disgust. "I've got a team that doesn't want to follow me, a woman who wants to kill me, bait having second thoughts, my own brother blabbing secrets, and cameras being installed to record the whole damn circus!"

"Bait?" Sanchez asked angrily.

Chance spun around and faced the priest. "Yes, bait! That's what you are. Deal with it."

A searing pain slashed through Chance's head, causing him to bend over at the waist, hands gripping his knees. James stopped what he was doing and quickly approached him.

"What the hell, Stones? You okay?" he asked quietly.

Chance slowly straightened trying not to aggravate his throbbing brain any further. "I am not made to work in a fuckin' team environment," he whispered. "And what have you been telling him?" He added, motioning towards Sanchez.

"Nothing. Look, unless one of has some plastic surgery to rearrange our handsome mugs, it's obvious that we probably dropped off the same family tree."

"I don't look anything like you," Chance grumbled.

"Keep telling yourself that, Sunshine."

Chance's only response was to flip him the bird before softly massaging his aching temples.

"Let's get this done. Someday you'll look back on this and laugh. Hey, I already think it's sort of funny," James replied as he patted his brother on the back. "Oh, and while I'm thinking about it, regarding your whole Kumbaya theory, I believe this team is more of a 'Ninety-Nine Bottles of Beer On the Wall' sort of crowd."

Chance didn't comprehend a word James was saying. The majority of his focus was on getting to the bottle of Vicodin stuffed in the side pocket of his duffel bag. If he didn't swallow a few pills soon, he'd be unable to think clearly. The last thing he needed was a foggy brain during a raid that demanded sharp thinking. He walked out of the bedroom past the rest of his team who were attaching all sorts of tiny, state-of-the-art technological wizardry on their helmets and vests. He dug into a side pocket of his bag until he found the bottle of pills. As inconspicuously as possible, he popped off the lid, poured out a few pills, popped them into his mouth and swallowed. After gulping down some water, he turned to face the team.

"No cameras."

The men stopped what they were doing and

looked up at Chance as though he were speaking a foreign language.

"We have to. It's policy," Roger replied.

"How much do you guys know about me?" Chance asked.

Tim and Jet looked at each other. Roger only shook his head and said, "Not much."

"Exactly! That's because I don't allow cameras. Period. Take them off."

"What about the OPORD?" Tim asked.

"OPORD?" Chance repeated in surprise.

"You know, the Operations Order, that little memo about how the shit's all gonna proceed. Weren't you in the military?" Tim asked.

"I know what OPORD is," Chance replied, realizing the last time he laid eyes on any official orders was back when he was Marine soldier known as Gunnery Sergeant Chance Hughes. Nowadays, the only rules he cared about were his own. The execution of this mission rested on his shoulders, which was the way he operated best. "Look guys, I don't give a shit about the OPORD. I'm calling the shots. That's it. That's the only thing you need to worry about."

"Maybe in your world, Orion, but in our world we have to answer for our actions. Our asses will be in a sling and our careers over if we pull any insubordinate stunts," Jet spoke up.

Chance looked past Jet and Tim and locked eyes

with Roger.

Roger nodded in understanding and stated, "Technology suffers glitches from time to time. We'll tell them our equipment had a malfunction of some sort."

"If anyone gives you trouble, I've got your back," Chance stated sincerely. Then he walked up to Roger and softly said, "Thanks, man."

Roger replied with a wink and then turned his focus to helping Tim and Jet dismantle the cameras and recording devices. Even though they didn't know much about Orion, they did know he held a position of high-esteem on Gabrielle O'Connor's roster. If anyone had the power to sway people's thinking, Orion did.

One issue resolved; Chance focused on the next. His eyes settled on Anna who was clad in black combat pants, boots and a tight black tank top. Her long blond hair was pulled back into a ponytail. She looked like a deadly angel. Her eyes met his with a bolt of intensity that nearly felt physical.

"You'll be staying with James in the surveillance van during the raid," Chance stated before turning away to get his own gear ready.

With the grace of a panther, Anna jumped out of her chair and grabbed Chance's arm before he could reach his duffel bag. She spun him around to face her.

"I will do no such thing," she hissed at him,

prompting Tim, Jet and Roger to stop what they were doing and stare at them and what appeared to be some sort of domestic dispute.

Chance glanced curiously down at her hand on his arm, causing her to immediately release her grasp.

"You seem awfully eager to get your hands on me," Chance whispered. "Remember, work before play," he gave a quick wink. He readied himself for another potential right-hook, but she never took a swing. Instead, her small fists were clenched tight by her side, her anger obvious, but unlike their first encounter, this time she maintained control.

She breathed a deep cleansing breath, stifling the red-hot anger that coursed through her veins and focused on whatever it would take to get this stubborn man to see things her way.

"I have been tracking Domino for years," she stated intently. "I deserve to go in there and help hunt him down."

"My operation, Princess. My rules," Chance answered as he began organizing his gear.

"You have no idea who I am now," Anna spoke between clenched teeth. "I'm perfectly capable of handling myself with the rest of the team. I'm just as good as you," she spit out before she could stop herself.

Chance looked back at her and smiled, but it did nothing to defrost his eyes.

"Honey, 'good' is not a word many people would use to describe me. Don't try to aspire to my level. I'm not someone you ever want to be. You're going to accompany James in surveillance and that's it."

Chance stared at her in uncomfortable silence, waiting for Anna to back down.

Finally, she stepped closer and stuck her finger in his face as she whispered, "You don't scare me, Chance."

Chance met her challenge. In a blink, he had reached and grabbed her finger that was intruding into his personal space. His grip tightening, he inched even closer to her. He loomed over her by a solid four inches, outweighed her by at least a hundred pounds, yet there wasn't a speck of fear in Anna's liquid blue eyes. Only unfiltered hatred.

"Pozdravlyayu," *Congratulations,* Chance replied ever so softly in Russian. Then he leaned down closer so that his lips were nearly touching her ear before he added, "ne govorite, moye imya snova." *Don't say my name again.*

The moment he released her finger from his uncomfortably tight grip, Anna spun around, walked over to the table, picked up her gun and turned back to face Chance. She noticed that he instinctually placed a hand on his own weapon. No doubt, the safety was off and within the blink of an eye, his sleekly designed gun would send a bullet into her brain before she could raise her own weapon and pull the trigger. She was a well-trained marksman and she prided herself in precision. Yet, she knew she was out of her league when it came to competing with Chance. His weaponry and sniper skills were unrivaled.

The two assassins stared at each other for a long moment, both with their hands on their loaded weapons. Both wondering who would make the first move. Finally, Anna relented and angrily jammed her gun in its holster.

Chance noticed Jet, Tim and Roger staring at him. He could only imagine what they were thinking. He briefly pondered an explanation, but quickly decided against it. Anna was a long, complicated story.

So far, this whole "team" thing was turning out to be a giant pain in the ass. Chance felt himself longing for the simple partnership of only himself and James. They had worked together for so long that they barely had to vocalize their plans. James handled the surveillance and had Chance's back. Chance focused on the dirty part of the job. Nice and simple.

Carlos and James entered the kitchen, breaking the tension. James eyed Anna who appeared to be in the mood to tear someone apart as she stood with her arms crossed near the rear door.

"Sorry to break up what appears to be a special

bonding session," James stated, "but Carlos is ready to rock and roll."

Chance pulled out the rest of his gear. He pulled off his shirt, revealing his ultra-fit body that would have been the envy of any fitness magazine if it weren't for the countless scars crisscrossing his tanned skin. Four round scars, the results of bullets, were easily visible, along with jagged rough scars left from knife wounds, straight, randomly-scattered scars left from vicious whippings he had suffered under the hands of the Taliban terrorists, and a few clean, surgical scars left by the skilled surgeons who had put him back together again.

The scars quickly disappeared beneath a black t-shirt, Kevlar vest and tactical jacket. He walked up to Carlos, studied him closely before opening the priest's jacket and patting him down, searching for any visible sign of the listening devices. Seeing nothing, he flashed his brother a thumb's up. Once again, James had made his work virtually invisible.

"The only way they'll discover your wire is if they scan you," James stated as he handed Carlos a cell phone. "Don't let that happen. Another possibility is that they have a scrambler. In that case, we won't hear you but we can still follow your movements with the GPS chip you swallowed. Of course we can track your phone, but I'm sure they'll dispose of that before they take you anywhere."

"Does he get a gun?" Roger asked.

All eyes turned toward their leader. Would Orion trust the priest enough to allow him to arm himself?

"Nope," Chance answered without hesitation. "If everything goes to hell, he's on his own."

James grabbed his favorite 9mm Glock and stuffed it into his shoulder holster. "A cowboy's best friend," he stated with a grin and wink. "Let's get to work, boys." James glanced over at Anna, still fuming in the corner and added, "And girl."

"Speaking of the girl," Chance began. "She's doing surveillance with you."

Now, it was James' turn to glare at Chance. No wonder Anna was hopping mad. He wasn't so thrilled himself. He had zero desire to spend any alone-time with the Russian who had unclear motives.

Chance perfectly understood the look in his brother's glare. But, his mind was set. He wasn't about to put Anna in the line of fire nor did he trust her enough to put his life in her hands. Actually, he was convinced that given the opportunity, she wouldn't hesitate to take kill him.

"Alright. I'll take Carlos to the drop zone. Let the games begin," Chance said as he grabbed Carlos by the arm and escorted him out the back door.

* * *

Luck appeared to be on their side. Within an hour of making contact, Father Carlos was picked up in a rusty Toyota pickup and driven to a residential section of Fallujah. The driver was not Domino, but a trusted aid, and Carlos was rapidly on his way to meeting up with his younger brother, face to face, for the first time in years.

Even to an outsider, Fallujah had a different feel and rhythm than the rest of Iraq. Combining rigid religious conservatism, strong tribal traditions and a fierce loyalty to the ideals scripted by leaders like Saddam Hussein, Fallujah was constantly primed for battle. Many times, what might appear to be simply residential sections of the city were actually combat zones masquerading as neighborhoods. Young boys were often seen standing on street corners, selling bananas and Kleenex boxes. The boys served as an early-warning system for the city, notifying the fighters if they spotted foreigners. Women were equally, if not more, radical than the men, as they willingly sacrificed their sons to fight the infidels.

As was typical in Fallujah, many of the houses looked like mini-palaces on the outside. The insides, however, would be a total mess. Upon entering, one could find most anything, and strange combinations of things, such as goats and flat screen TV's. High-tech satellite equipment was everywhere. AK 47's could be found hidden underneath babies' cribs. Most of the properties were walled off from their neighbors by thick brick and stucco walls. The neighborhood that Father Carlos was nearing fit this description perfectly.

James huddled over his laptop and other equipment, controlling the small drone as it followed the route taken by the Toyota. The bumps in the road rattling his sensitive computer equipment brought about more than a few mumbled swear words as James did his best to keep everything steady. Most of his attention was on a green blip moving across a small screen. With every change in direction the green blip made, James relayed instructions to Roger as he maneuvered the vehicle. As expected, Domino's driver confiscated Carlos' cell phone almost immediately and removed the SIM card and battery. The small chip in Carlos's stomach, however, worked flawlessly as the Team watched the GPS track the vehicle.

The Team was crowded into a large van; its outward appearance was that of an electrician's van, the inside however, told a different story. It was packed with surveillance equipment, tracking devices, flat screen computers; weapons ranging from handguns to missiles lined the walls, and five heavily-armed humans in tactical gear were ready to pounce at a moment's notice. The van was no longer a van. It was now the TOC, or Tactical Operations Center, for "Operation Domino."

171

The heat inside the van produced by the computers and surveillance equipment, along with the five humans, quickly created a stuffy, uncomfortable environment. Chance channeled his attention outward, looking through the windshield, wishing he were driving. He had learned long ago how to control his claustrophobic tendencies, but the ability to stifle his panic didn't lessen the fact that small confined spaces made him absolutely miserable.

"Good thing we're all friends, or else this would feel a little awkward," James mentioned off-handedly, as they slowly followed their target.

No one laughed. Everyone was trying to prepare for whatever this upcoming raid had in store for them.

Very little conversation took place in the vehicle that Father Sanchez was riding in, and what was said, was in Spanish. Of course, Chance understood Spanish perfectly, as did as Anna. Roger understood a few words, but Jet, Tim and James were left behind as the rapid words were spoken.

"I trust that if anything of importance is said, one of you muchachos will let the rest of us know?" James asked in frustration.

"He just asked if his brother would be at the location they are driving to," Anna suddenly spoke out, translating the words heard over the wire.

They all listened for the driver's reply but none

came.

"Are you sure this is a safe location?" Carlos asked the driver.

"It is safe," the driver finally responded. "Your brother would not be there if it were not safe."

"So, he is there?" Carlos asked again.

"He is waiting for you."

With Chance and Anna's translations, the team heard what they had been waiting for. They were being led directly to one of the world's most wanted terrorists. Roger slowly drove the van through the city streets, following the drone and GPS directions without actually keeping a visual on the Toyota. They could not risk blowing their cover.

"They're pulling into a gated drive. They're stopping. I think we've got our spot, boys. And girl," James stated, wincing from Anna's dirty look.

Roger sped up and quickly found the location. They drove by the residence once, then circled the block. Parking on a side street, the Team zipped up vests, flipped off their guns' safeties and felt the excitement mount. Still, they had to wait for the perfect time.

"I'm point man," Chance stated, covering last minute tactics. "Roger, you take up the rear. You two are the breachers," he added pointing at Tim and Jet. "Get in, get out. Fast and clean. Nothing to it"

Issuing orders was something Chance had not

done in a long time. As a young Marine, he had excelled in the leadership role, easily getting his fellow soldiers to follow him into danger. Since his transformation into a lone assassin, he didn't feel nearly as comfortable moving into a violent situation with a team. A team felt cumbersome, clumsy and loud. To Chance, it felt more like a herd, than a stealthy squad of skilled tacticians. Yet, he understood that his teammates were no slouches when it came to these situations. He was doing his best to adjust and dust off his old management skills.

"He's going in," James stated, watching real time images produced from the drone. "I'm trying to get thermal imaging," he added as he typed a multitude of commands into his computer. He shook his head in frustration, "That might look like an ordinary house but it's not. I can't get thermals. That place is built like a bunker."

The team listened closely for conversation but after a few words of welcome, static filled the air.

"Scrambler," Chance mumbled.

"I recognized that voice," Anna spoke up with certainty. "That voice that welcomed Carlos was Domino. I'm sure of it."

James pulled up the GPS tracking information generated from the chip in Carlos' stomach.

"We can track every step he takes. The best I can do is create a map of the house from the moves he makes," James talked rapidly, lost in his own world of technology.

"That's all fine and good but we can't get definitive confirmation that Domino is in that house," Tim spoke angrily. "We can't break in there with guns a'blazin' if he's not in there. Our asses will be in a sling if we shoot up the place and our target is sunning himself in Brazil. The suits will make sure we never carry a gun again."

First the cameras, now concern over shooting up a place without proper documentation. Chance was quickly realizing why Gabrielle kept him off the grid. Tim, Jet and Roger were all legitimate spies, with actual files and records and a salary from the United States Government. Their actions were strictly controlled, their results scrutinized. Up until now, Chance and James had operated under no rules. They were not expected to remain confined within all the governmental red tape. The United States government couldn't criticize their techniques when they didn't even know they existed. Gabrielle O'Connor straddled a very dangerous line between doing her job as Director of the CIA while managing a covert team of operatives that abided by only one rule: Get the bad guy.

Chance was not about to change his ways.

"Remember that part about me being in charge?" Chance asked loudly. "We're doing this my way. I'll take the heat if things go south.

Fuckin' terrorists don't give a shit about the Geneva Convention and that's the playing field I operate on." Then he turned toward Anna and asked, "You sure you heard Domino?"

Anna nodded.

"Then he's there." Chance responded with confidence, showing that despite their strained relationship, he did have a certain level of trust in her.

"He's going up a couple of flights of stairs. He's on the third floor," James interjected.

"That's the best place to tag him," Chance said as he slipped in an earpiece. "Vamanos, muchachos."

"Let's go," repeated Roger.

The team of four men moved silently and quickly over the brick wall, through the small dirt yard and up to the grated front door.

"You copy, Cowboy?" Chance asked quietly into the wireless bone mic.

"Loud and clear, Stones," James responded. "Target's location remains steady."

"Copy that," Chance stated before getting into position next to the door. He held up three fingers for a silent countdown to break-in. With one finger remaining, Roger's eyes widened as a man appeared at the front door. He only opened the door a crack and peered through the grate.

Chance, speaking in Arabic, told the man to

open the door. The man shook his head and replied that only his wife and children lived there, and to leave them alone. Chance demanded once again that he open the door. This time, instead of arguing, the man disappeared inside the house. His footsteps could be heard running up the stairs.

Knowing the man was running to warn others in the house, Chance immediately yelled, "Go! Break the grate in!"

The Team rushed in. Their pace was quick and automatic, each of them experienced in this exact situation. Not long after their entrance, they were under attack. Bullets whizzed by their heads and slugs ricocheted off the brick walls. Still, the guys remained controlled and professional. They wouldn't return fire unless they had a clear target, because, along with the blasting of gunfire, they could hear children's terrified screams. The Team dodged bullets as they continued to push the enemy further into the house.

In one of the bedrooms, Roger found three women huddled into a corner. Behind them hid a small child, a boy who looked to be around five years old.

Chance quickly approached the women and asked in Arabic, "More children?"

One woman nodded slowly and pointed to the wall next to her.

"In the next room?" Chance asked and she

nodded.

"You need to keep moving, Stones," James voice spoke into Chance's ear bud.

"We've got kids in here. I'm gonna get them all in one room," Chance replied and then turned to Jet and said, "You stay here with them and we'll go clear the next room. If there's more kids we'll bring them all in here."

Jet nodded and stayed behind as the rest of the Team left the room to check what they would find next door.

There were three more children. There were also five armed men waiting to put an end to the American's unannounced visit.

In a frenzy of bullets, Chance, Tim and Roger prevailed. The terrorists were well-armed but undisciplined and unprepared for the high-level lethal talent of the Americans. As the team searched for, and secured, the dead men's weapons, one of the young boys that had cowered in the closet during the gunfight walked out of the shadows. In his small hands, he held some sort of old Russian-made sniper rifle. He couldn't have been more than ten years old, yet he knew exactly how to hold that rifle, and he aimed it at the closest American intruder.

Immediately Tim and Roger aimed their weapons at the boy and were about to fire when Chance yelled, "No!"

Without lowering their guns, their fingers putting slight pressure on their triggers, they were ready to fire the instant they believed that boy would make good on his threat.

"Just hold on," Chance said firmly. His weapon remained lowered as he held it in his left hand. He took a small step closer to the boy and spoke softly in Arabic.

Tim and Roger continued to watch steadily, prepared to intervene, certain that Chance was about to commit suicide. In Fallujah, as in pretty much anywhere in Iraq and Afghanistan, children were not necessarily innocent. Jihadist-crazed terrorists were known to warp the minds of children at a painfully young age and turn them into brainwashed little killers.

The boy's skinny arms trembled as they tried to support the weight of the heavy rifle, yet his dark brown eyes looked determined. Just as he shifted the weapon to better fit into the crook of his bony shoulder, Chance made his move. The boy had intended to pull the trigger but by the time the message got to his finger, the tall intruder had kicked the rifle out of his hands. In another blink of an eye, he was being held tightly in the grasp of the American, lifted off his feet and carried across the room.

"Some sort of tough guy, huh?" Chance grumbled as he strode toward the room. "Get the rest of the brats and let's go," Chance ordered to his teammates.

After confirming the women were unarmed and the room was empty of hidden terrorists and weapons, Chance ordered Jet to stay with the women and children to ensure their safety until the raid was over.

"Watch that punk in particular," Chance added, pointing to the boy who had aimed the gun at Chance. "Okay, boys, let's finish this."

"Where's our target?" Chance asked into his bone mic.

James voice replied, "On the roof. The drone has a visual on him, along with three gunmen awaiting your arrival. You better go in hot."

"Copy that. We're on our way."

Chance raced up the stairs to the third floor and moved to a doorway that led out to the roof, leaning against the wall, as the rest of the guys stacked to follow. He nodded once before breaking through the locked door. As expected, they faced gunfire from three different gunmen. Like the five that were currently assuming room temperature in the bedroom below, these three were not nearly as skilled as their adversaries. Two were quickly dropped, while the third cowered behind the small shack that sheltered the house's water supply.

Using concise hand signals, the elite Americans maneuvered themselves into the best possible positions for success. Tim moved to stand guard by the door to prevent any sort of last ditch escape attempt by Domino. Roger and Chance worked together to silence the last gunman without a dramatic hail of bullets, which could potentially kill Domino and Carlos. Roger fired his weapon into the sky as he ran for cover behind a pile of bricks and lumber. His actions drew the attention of the lone remaining Taliban fighter, giving Chance his split second opportunity to silently slither along the shadowed wall of the well-house. He heard Roger's voice in his earpiece telling him that the tango was positioned only a few feet from him. All he had to do was look around the corner. Without hesitation, Chance peeked around the corner, clearly saw the tango and fired. The Iraqi fighter never knew what hit him. The 9mm bullet hit him square in the back of his neck, severing his spinal cord and delivering instant death.

The silence after a firefight is deafening. The human ears are comfortable detecting 60-65 dB, which is about the volume of conversational speech. OSHA requires hearing protection in factories experiencing at least 85dB. Pain threshold is 120dB. The chest wall begins to vibrate at 150dB. The average 9mm handgun firing at close range is 160dB. Even with earpieces, soldiers engaged in a firefight, indoors, sustained for even a few minutes, can experience ear pain and ringing lasting hours after the last shot was fired.

Chance pulled out his earpiece and popped his jaw several times, trying to reduce the ringing so he could use his hearing to help detect where Domino and Carlos were hiding. He remained in the shadow, his back pressed against the wall, his senses trying to cut through the deafening aftermath of the firefight. The subtle sound of a shuffle, a whisper, or even a flicker of light could help pinpoint his target's location.

Then he heard a voice; it sounded almost as if it was coming from his own head. Quickly, he shoved his earpiece back in his ear when he realized the voice was Roger, saying that he spotted movement behind some storage barrels.

Before Chance could get any more useful information, his attention was diverted by the unmistakable clinking sound of a bullet falling into a chamber directly behind him. His brain instantly recognized the fact that the men on his team would never make that sound when chambering a bullet. Only an amateur would be that flamboyant.

Chance slowly turned to face his threat. Standing straight and proud, smiling brightly as he held his Russian Makarov arrogantly in his hand, Domino stared at Chance.

"I will enjoy killing you, American," Domino spoke in strained English.

Chance spotted Roger standing directly behind

Domino but gave no indication of that welcome sight. Roger flashed the exact same hand signal that a major league pitcher would give his catcher telling him that a curve ball was coming his way. Chance understood perfectly.

"I'm sure you would, asshole. Especially since you've tried and failed so many times before." Chance replied with a cocky grin. "This is as close as you'll ever get, so you better hurry up and pull that trigger before you lose your chance, again."

Before Domino could utter his clever response, finish off this particularly meddling American operative and celebrate an impressive victory, the Americans, once again, twisted up his perfect ending.

Chance dropped to the floor as Roger aimed and fired.

Domino crumpled to the floor, losing his grip on the Makarov. He desperately reached for the AK-47 strapped to his shoulder. But, before he could get his fingers wrapped around the weapon, Chance bounced to his feet and pulled the rifle away from the him.

"No you don't, bucko," Chance muttered as he emptied the rounds of ammo from the weapon and tossed it aside. "You snooze, you lose. You shoulda pulled that trigger faster."

Domino clutched his shoulder where the bullet ripped through flesh and bone, his face twisted in pain. Chance noticed Domino's eyes glance upward. He spun around with his weapon drawn.

Roger already had his gun cocked and locked onto Carlos who was holding Domino's Makarov.

"Gimme," Chance ordered, his hand out waiting for Carlos to hand over the gun.

"Kill him!" Domino screamed at his brother.

Carlos tightly held his brother's gun. A momentary, fleeting thought laced with sentimental foolishness caused him to actually consider taking aim at the American. If only he could turn back time. Back to a time and place when he and his brother were innocent and unbroken. Long before evil and greed had taken over his brother's life. Carlos glanced sideways at the tall American standing next to him. Chance was still holding out a hand, waiting. His other hand firmly gripped the handle of his own weapon that he aimed directly at the priest's forehead, the detailed etchings of the stars and dice glinted in the sun.

"If you can't kill him, kill yourself!" Domino demanded. "Don't let them take you alive!"

Carlos studied his brother curiously, alarmed to see the crazed, rabid look of insanity radiating from his dark eyes. The man Carlos once knew as his beloved little brother was lost somewhere behind that insanity.

Chance watched Carlos closely, hoping he wouldn't be forced to pull the trigger. The priest's internal struggle was obvious. When the cold steel of Domino's gun was laid gently into his outreached hand, Chance caught himself wondering what he would do in the same situation. It only took him a second to realize that he'd never betray James. He would have kept that rifle and shot the hell out of anyone standing in his way. Then again, James wasn't a terrorist.

"You betrayed me," Domino gasped breathlessly as he clutched his bleeding shoulder. "How could you do that, Carlos? Betray me? Your own brother?" His eyes pleaded as he stared up at the man he truly believed would always protect him.

Carlos felt tears welling up in his eyes. Hating the show of weakness, he turned away and stood a careful distance from his brother.

Chance emptied the bullets from the Makarov and tossed it over the wall of the roof. Stepping closer to Carlos, he studied him a moment before saying, "You made the right choice." Turning his focus on his team, he smiled at Roger. "Thanks. Again."

Roger patted him on the back and replied, "I knew this was gonna be fun."

Tim joined them and said, "Let's cuff him and get outta here."

"Hold on. Let's make sure this is over," Chance stated before asking into his bone mic, "all clear

Cowboy? We're ready to blow this pop stand."

"What's the status of our Target?" James asked.

"Injured but stable."

"Don't move yet. I'm following a group of maybes. I'll know in ten seconds."

"Copy that."

Roger walked over to the edge of the roof and carefully peered over to see if he could spot what James was referring to. He looked back at Chance and Tim and shrugged.

"Trouble, Stones," James' voice stated into Chance's earpiece. "Eight tangos just entered the front door."

"Hold up, everyone," Chance quickly informed his team. "Not clear. I repeat, not clear. We've got eight tangos on their way up. Reload and regroup, boys."

James typed in one last command and folded up his laptop. He pulled out his 9mm, nodded at Anna and spoke into his mic, "We're coming." He followed Anna as she slipped out the side of the van.

"Well, shit," Chance mumbled as he realized they were in for another fire fight before they were finished with this job. "Jet, you copy?"

"Go, Orion," Jet's voice replied.

"You're getting company soon. At least eight."

"Copy that."

Suddenly Anna's voice entered the

conversation. "I'm coming, Jet. Cowboy is circling around by you, Orion."

"Ten-four, Princess," Jet answered.

"Copy that, Princess," Chance replied, trying not to dwell on the fact that he was now relying on a woman he didn't trust to help him and his team make it out of this shit-hole alive.

Suddenly Carlos knelt down next to his brother, and yelled, "You hit his brachial artery! He's bleeding out!"

"Cover my six," Chance stated matter-of-factly, prompting Tim and Roger to move into protective positions near their leader. Chance holstered his pistol and slung his rifle on his shoulder before kneeling down in front of Domino. He was rapidly losing blood and with it, consciousness.

Tim and Roger stood at the ready, their weapons aimed at the only entrance onto the roof. Chance wiped at the sweat steadily dripping down his face before reaching over and grabbing the hem of Domino's tunic. Quickly tearing off a long strips of the fabric, Chance wadded it into a ball and stuffed it into the bleeding wound.

"Make this quick, Orion. I hear 'em comin'," Roger stated, his voice calm despite the situation.

"He'll bleed out in minutes. We need to get him to a hospital," Carlos demanded loudly.

Extensively trained in survival and the first aid treatments of the countless possible horrible injuries and situations he could face in his occupation, Chance was intimately aware of the dire nature of Domino's wound. He tore off more strips of Domino's clothing and used them as a pressure wraps to slow the blood flow.

Once satisfied that nothing more could be done to help Domino, Chance looked up at Carlos and said, "We aren't taking him anywhere near a hospital."

Carlos' face reddened as his once deadly temper rose to the surface. "You said you wanted him alive," he grabbed Chance by the front of his tactical vest. He pulled the tall man as close as possible and spoke between gritted teeth. "You asked me to betray my own brother for you. Now don't you dare expect me to watch him die."

"Let. Go." Chance spoke softly, but the lack in volume did nothing to hide the menacing tone. Father Carlos released his desperate grip.

"Please. He's my brother," Carlos stated weakly, hating that he was reduced to begging.

Chance's unblinking cold eyes measured the priest for a brief second before turning his attention to the chaos about to erupt onto the roof.

"I've slowed the bleeding. We'll be out of here in a few minutes and then we'll get him patched up just fine. My brother is a medic," Chance stated as he stood and took a stance facing the entrance, ready to shoot his way out of trouble once again.

"Please, give me a gun so I can help you fight," Carlos pleaded. "You'll be outnumbered. I can help."

"No. Just stay down and outta my way."

"Your best out is over the wall," James voice spoke softly into Chance's ear bud.

Chance glanced over his shoulder. They were three stories up. The jump would certainly sting a little. Then he eyed Domino lying semi-conscious next to the water barrels. He was in no condition to successfully complete any roof jumping.

"Target is unable to jump," Chance replied. "Where are you?"

"Getting ready to cover your ass while you climb down off the roof."

Chance sighed and walked over to the edge of the roof and spotted James rounding the corner.

"Tie him on and lower him down," James ordered.

Chance looked over at Roger who immediately holstered his weapon, saying, "I'll buy you some time. Come on, Timmy, let's blockade that door."

As Roger and Tim worked feverishly on creating an obstacle that would slow the fighters' entrance, Chance pulled out the military-grade mountain rope from the small pack strapped on his back. He fashioned a crude harness from what was left of the injured man's tunic, used a sailor's knot to firmly secure him to the rope and then dead-lifted him and carried him to the roof's edge. Carlos followed closely.

"All righty, nice and easy," Chance said as he carefully lowered Domino to the edge. He wrapped the nylon rope around his hands. Then he turned to Carlos and said, "Hang him over the edge. I'll lower him down. Come on, we need to hurry."

Carlos glanced back toward Roger and Tim as he heard the footsteps of more enemy fighters rapidly ascending the stairs. A few muffled sounds of shots being fired on the levels below them rang out. The enemy would be bursting onto the roof at any moment. Carlos picked up his brother and looked over the edge to see James waiting. James nodded at him and he gently released Domino over the edge.

"Two tangos down. Six still heading your way, Orion. Jet is tailing the tangos. I'm getting the innocents out," Anna's voice informed Chance as he grabbed the rope attached to Domino.

"Copy that," he replied, trying not to drop Domino three stories to the hard ground below, while keeping most of his attention on what was about to happen behind him.

Chance's arm muscles bulged and burned as he strained against Domino's significant weight and the pull of gravity as he slowly lowered him to the ground. As soon as the injured man was within James' grasp, the rope went slack. Chance felt a slight tug on the rope, signifying the rope was now available for another escape. At that moment, the door to the roof exploded open and bullets flew. Chance grabbed Carlos and pulled him along as he dove behind the crude plywood wall that served as the well house.

"I'll cover you," Chance said as he popped out the empty clip and shoved a new one into his gun."

"While I do what?" Carlos replied as he ducked from the bullets splintering the wood above his head.

"Climb down."

Carlos looked over his shoulder at the end of the black rope resting on the floor.

"No."

Chance peaked around the wall and fired off three shots before looking at Carlos in surprise. "What do you mean no? That's your only way out, amigo."

"You'll be too exposed. Give me a gun and let me help you fight."

Chance didn't have the luxury of time to ponder the idea of arming a potential enemy. Right now, he could use all the help he could get.

Chance leaned forward, pulled out his spare handgun that also happened to be a one-of-a-kind pistol. This one, however, did not don any artistic etchings on its slide. He handed it to the priest. All his handguns were custom built for his hands only, by a legendary gunsmith in Colorado. To say the least, he was a little possessive of his weapons. Before he let Carlos have it he said, "I expect to get this back."

Carlos shot back, "Unida a sus armas, señor Orion?" *Attached to your weapons, Mr. Orion?*

Chance flashed a quick smile at the priest before turning around. "It's time to switch from defense to offense. Let's play ball."

Carlos felt the weight of the pistol in his hand. He was surprised at how comfortable and familiar the weapon felt. He squeezed his eyes shut, whispered a quick prayer and crossed himself. Then he slid his finger around the trigger turned around and prepared to follow Chance's lead. That was when he realized Orion was watching him.

"Are you sure you can do this?" he asked.

Sanchez nodded and gripped the gun tighter.

"Forget about being a priest for the next few minutes. Shoot to kill and stay close to me."

It wasn't lost on Father Sanchez that as bullets whizzed past, by mere inches from their heads, Orion appeared to be completely calm and at ease, nearly conversational and dare he say…happy? Sanchez concluded that despite all the unknowns about the man, there was one thing that was crystal clear. Orion was wired for battle.

Chance got to his feet, but kept his body low as he scurried from their spot behind the plywood over to the water barrels. Along the way, he fired two shots, killing one enemy and injuring another. Carlos fired and finished off the injured rival. Roger and Tim were pinned behind a pile of bricks, holding their own, not letting the tangos advance any further, but not knocking them back either.

Chance's movements caught the enemies' attention and as they scrambled to respond to him, Roger and Tim both aimed and fired, each taking down one. Two tangos remained. Now they were outnumbered and knew that their seconds on earth were severely limited. Despite that, the terrorists would gladly fight to their death in order to kill a hated American on their way out.

The two Arabs screamed crazily as they gave up on any sort of strategy. They ran straight toward Tim and Roger, firing the remaining rounds from their assault rifles.

Chance stood, took aim and fired twice. One enemy fell, the bullet severing his spinal cord. The other tango was hit and staggered, but remained on his feet. Chance fired a third time. This time the enemy fighter fell, his lifeless body twitching once before becoming still.

Chance ran over to Tim and Roger who cautiously walked away from their protection. Jet burst through the attic door and felt relief to see his team alive and relatively unscathed.

"You're hit," Chance stated as he saw the blood

seeping from Tim's thigh. "Can you walk?"

Tim looked down at his leg in surprise. He hadn't realized he had been injured. Now that the adrenaline was ebbing a bit, he could feel a little burning in his leg.

"Yeah, yeah, I'm fine. Didn't even know anything happened," he quickly responded. "Are we clear? Or are there any others who would like to welcome us to the neighborhood?"

Chance laughed before he clicked on his bone mic and asked, "Is this little party over?"

A few seconds passed before James's voice replied, "You're clear."

Chance looked back at his team and said, "Let's get out of here. We're clear."

Despite the clear signal, the team still proceeded cautiously as they descended the stairs and made their way toward the front door. They remained in their cover positions while maintaining their fields of fire. Booby traps or an unaccounted-for surprise enemy fighter could really wreck a good day. As they passed the bedroom where the women and children had been kept, they double-checked to make sure everyone was out.

"Innocents all out?" Chance asked into his mic.

"Princess is loading them into an armored Humvee as we speak. They'll be questioned at a secure location."

"That was convenient. How'd we manage that

kind of support?" Chance asked.

"I guess that's one of the perks for working for OGA, versus operating solely as Off-Griders," James answered, referring to the Other Government Agency, otherwise known as the CIA.

As the Team stepped into the daylight, they still didn't feel safe. They wouldn't breathe easy until they were out of Iraq. The sooner they were in flight, the better.

"Let's go!" Roger yelled as he jogged to the van and slipped into the driver's seat.

Jet assisted the injured Tim quickly into the back of the van where James was feverishly setting up an IV to pump fluids into Domino's veins. He had already placed a new pressure wrap over his wound to slow the bleeding.

Carlos stood nervously near the open door. His only brother, his only *family*, was about to be placed into the hands of the United States government and treated as a dangerous terrorist. Domino is a terrorist, Carlos knew this, but still, his younger brother's life would now be very similar to that of a dog deemed vicious, locked in a cage, and possibly put to death.

That was *if* he survived.

"Get in, Father," Chance demanded as he jogged up to the van. "We need to pop smoke."

"Sorry?" Carlos asked.

"Get movin'!" Chance demanded.

Carlos crawled inside, trying not to interfere with James' efforts.

Chance had one foot in the door when he realized they were missing someone.

"Where the hell is the Princess?" he asked.

No one knew where Anna had gone.

"Goddamn it, where is that wo—" Chance began.

"Hey, Longshot, we can't leave yet!"

Longshot? Chance stepped back from the van to see Anna running toward him. He was about to start ripping into her for making them wait, but she didn't give him the opportunity.

"I overheard a couple of the women talking about something important in the basement."

"That's where the men keep their girly magazines, Princess. Now, let's move!"

"No. It's more than that. It's something big."

Chance stretched his shoulders and inhaled deeply. "Fine." He grabbed the van door and before he slid it shut, he stuck his head inside and said, "Princess and I need to check something out in the basement. We'll meet up with you guys later."

"Hold on just a half a pickin' second," James replied, stopping Chance from closing the door. "Since when am I a medic?"

"Don't sell yourself short, bro. Looks like you're doing good."

"He needs a doctor. A *real* doctor."

"I can get you a doc," Chance said without hesitation as he pulled out his phone.

"Wait," Tim interjected. "You can't bring a civilian off the street to treat a high-profile terrorist we just captured in a dark op."

Chance ignored the comment as he pushed a series of numbers into his phone. As he waited for the connection, he said, "You should get going. Cropper right?" he asked James, referring to the detention facility near Baghdad International Airport.

Camp Cropper had been an overcrowded prison used to hold detainees for long periods of time and was reported as a potential CIA black site used for enhanced interrogations, aka, torture. Most of its notoriety came while holding Saddam Hussein prior to his execution. Since being turned over to the Iraqi government in 2010, the prison was renamed Karkh Prison and no official United States unit operated there. Unofficial U.S. activity did still occur from time to time in any one of the countless, unmarked steel containers, or concrete bunkers dotting the desert inside the razor-wire fence.

"That's the plan," James replied.

"I'll have Doc meet you there."

"Maybe this basement investigation can wait for another day?" James asked.

Chance shook his head but then turned his attention to the voice who just answered his call.

"My hair looks like shit. It needs a close crop. You available in say, thirty minutes? Great. I haven't seen a scissors in eight months so be prepared for a mess."

Chance clicked off the phone and turned back to his brother.

"I'm assuming the good doctor is not a civilian," James commented.

"Go. We're burnin' daylight," Chance replied.

"Orion," Father Sanchez said suddenly. Then he pulled a gun out of his belt and held it out to Chance. "Here's your friend back," he commented.

Chance smiled and grabbed his gun. "Thanks." Then he leaned into the van and extended his hand toward Roger saying, "It was an honor working with you."

Roger smiled and met his hand firmly. "And with you. If you ever need back-up, give me a holler."

"Since when did you become so social? Quit talking and let's go," demanded Anna as she put fresh ammo into her clip.

Chance rolled his eyes, took in a deep breath and stuffed his gun into his belt. He turned toward the woman and said, "I'm all yours, your Highness."

The van door slid shut and wheels squealed as the van sped away leaving Chance and Anna alone in the dangerous neighborhood. They walked quickly back toward the door they had busted through only thirty minutes before.

"I couldn't make out what they said exactly. I'm not good at whatever language people speak around here," Anna commented as they neared the entrance.

"People here have a weird dialect that doesn't exactly have an official title. I call it Fallujese."

"Brilliant."

"What's with this 'Longshot' business?"

"It's a perfect name for you," Anna snapped.

"And why are you naming me?"

"You took it upon yourself to call me 'Princess'. Now everyone is calling me that horrid name. It's only fair that I come up with a name for you."

"But I already have a name. Two or three, actually. I don't need any more."

Chance briefly wondered if Anna had somehow discovered his past as a record-setting sniper. His secrets seemed to be harder and harder to contain lately.

They walked through the front door and down the hall until they reached the narrow door that led to the basement. Chance waited while Anna grasped and turned the doorknob. His senses on high alert to any noises or movement that would signify danger. He hated basements. Anything remotely resembling a cave triggered a repulsion deep in the core of Chance's psyche. In his experience, nothing good ever happened in a cave, or a basement.

"So, I suppose we better check it out, huh?" he finally asked, not sounding the least bit enthused.

"Lead the way," Anna stated as she stepped aside.

Chapter Eleven

Washington, D.C.

Gabrielle rushed down the hall toward the large conference room in the basement of the West Wing of the White House. The Situation Room. The room where the president, along with his advisors, monitored and dealt with crisis at home and abroad. Gabrielle gave a quick smile to the Secret Service agents standing guard outside the door before she entered.

"Mr. President," she said politely as she pulled out a chair from the long conference table.

President John Dawkins, currently in the final year of his second term as Commander and Chief of the U.S., sat at the head of the table. Vice President Gerald Evans, Secretary of Defense Connor Lindemann, as well as the National Security Advisor and the Deputy for Homeland Security all lined the table.

"Miss O'Connor," President Dawkins stated. "We've been anxiously awaiting your arrival. This operation was set to take place an hour ago, and we've heard nothing."

Lindemann, clearly frustrated, stood and paced behind his chair. "We've had zero audio or visual with our men on the ground. Technicians were here to check our equipment and the glitch is not on our end. Something happened over there."

Gabrielle stood and walked to the front of the room, picking up a small remote control from the counter on her way. She pulled a flash drive out of her suit jacket pocket and placed it into the computer's hard drive. With the push of a button, several of the flat screen monitors on the wall flickered momentarily, and then settled on the image of a neighborhood in Fallujah, Iraq.

"The latest intel I received was moments ago from one of the operatives involved in the operation. The house in which Domino was hiding was this three story brick building in the middle of the block." Gabrielle used the remote to zoom in and enlarge the picture of the house.

"Wait," Vice President Evans interrupted. "Why are you getting information and we aren't getting anything? When will our operatives go after the target?"

Gabrielle hesitated a moment before speaking. "The agent in charge realized that the team was experiencing technical difficulties. Intel showed that the target was currently in this particular building.

The team had no time and they were forced to make a decision. They chose to continue the operation despite the glitches with the audio and visual equipment."

"Are you telling me the agents have already taken action?" the Deputy for Homeland Security asked in disbelief.

Gabrielle nodded and pushed another button on her remote control. This time a picture of Dominique Rodriquez, appearing disheveled, bandaged and beaten.

"This was taken thirty minutes ago. The Team successfully captured our target and is currently giving him medical treatment in a secure facility. I'm very happy to report there were no civilian causalities and our guys only suffered minor injuries. The operation was a success."

The room fell silent as this information sunk in. Obviously, the magnitude of capturing one of the world's most prolific terrorists was huge. There was also the reality that this all happened without any of their eyes or ears involved. With all the billions of dollars spent on the latest in military and surveillance technology, how in the world did this operation proceed in complete darkness?

Finally, President Dawkins cleared his throat and asked, "You said our target was undergoing medical treatment. Was he injured in the raid?"

"Yes. He was shot. It's a serious injury but not

life threatening at this point. You will be notified when he is stable enough to travel."

"Was he shot by one of ours?" Lindemann asked as he sat back down and rubbed his forehead.

"I can't answer that yet, sir."

"Can't? Or won't?"

Gabrielle stepped closer to Lindemann and answered, "You'll get a full report of this operation as soon as I get one, sir. Until then, I suggest we sit back and think about what it means to have Domino in custody." She moved back to the top of the table and continued. "Gentlemen, we have been after this individual for years. He has terrorized and killed hundreds, if not thousands of innocent people. He is a hater of America and a killer of peace. And now, we have him. We owe our thanks to the brave operatives that captured him today." Gabrielle's look matched the seriousness of her words as she met the gaze of each person at the table. "Now, if you'll excuse me, I need to get back to work."

The five men stood as Gabrielle walked back to her seat to pick up her brief case she had left on the table.

"Hold up, for a moment, Miss O'Connor," President Dawkins stated. "I'd like to have a word with you, privately, please."

"Yes, of course Mr. President."

The Vice President and the rest of the advisors quickly realized they were being dismissed and they grabbed their suit jackets and briefcases and left the Situation Room.

Dawkins smiled and rested a hip on the corner of the glossy mahogany table.

"Ok, Gabrielle. Don't bullshit me. What really happened today? I understand technology glitches happen. Hell, half the time I can't get my own computer to do what I want. But if you're trying to sell me the idea that ALL the cameras and ALL the audio equipment had massive malfunctions right before the operation was to take place, I'm not buying it."

Gabrielle smiled back. She and John had a long history of friendship and she respected his no-nonsense approach to politics. He truly did care about the condition of America far more than the condition of his political party. He was an astute, honest man and Gabrielle knew better than to feed him anything other than the truth. She had understood this fact the moment she manipulated this operation. She knew she would eventually have to come clean to the President.

Gabrielle slowly walked around the room, glancing up into the corners. "Are we being recorded, Mr. President?"

"All visual and audio recording devices have been deactivated or removed as you requested this morning. Whatever you have to say is in the strictest confidence. Now, please, what in the world is going on with this operation in Fallujah?"

Gabrielle circled back around so she was standing directly in front of the President.

"You're right, Mr. President. The cameras and audio were never engaged. As far as I know, the equipment is all in perfect working condition. The team was following the orders of their leader and those orders included no cameras."

Dawkins stood up. "But why?"

"The agent in charge of the operation is off the grid. His identity is highly confidential. He has been trained to never be caught on cameras of any sort."

Dawkins ran his hand through his hair in confusion. "The identities of all our operatives are confidential. The audio and visuals of every mission is top secret. Your agent's identity will remain confidential, even with the use of cameras. Why is this operation different than any of the others?"

"This operative is different. When I say he's off the grid, I mean *totally* off the grid. He's not exactly on our payroll."

Dawkins eyes widened. "Are you telling me he's employed by another intelligence agency? Israeli? Syrian?"

"No. He's American. He's been working for me privately, paid for by private funds."

Dawkins appeared stunned. He stood and stared blankly at the wall. Then he turned to face Gabrielle.

"A private contractor? Using the resources of the CIA? Gabrielle, please tell me you know better than this."

Gabrielle felt the tension rise rapidly. She had understood that she would be treading on very dangerous ground when she decided to keep Chance a secret from her own government. Now, was the moment of truth. She could very well lose her job because of her decision. She really hoped it wouldn't come to that.

"I believe once you discover who this particular operative is, you'll agree that I've made the right decision by keeping him off the grid."

"You've certainly piqued my curiosity. I doubt I will change my opinion that the director of the CIA shouldn't be running operatives off the grid, but please, do tell. Who is this mystery agent?"

"Go back seven years, Mr. President. Remember flying to Comanche Point and handing the Medal of Honor to a certain young Marine Sniper who had miraculously survived as a captive of the Taliban for nine months?"

Dawkins eyes narrowed and he took a small step back. "Of course I remember. Sergeant Chance Hughes. I remember that meeting clearly." Dawkins paused while his memories were brought to the surface. Meeting the young soldier had deeply affected him. At that time, Dawkins was a newly elected President, optimistic and motivated to uplift a country teetering on the brink of a depression. Shaking his hand and looking into the eyes of someone who had lived through the worst the world could possibly offer, Dawkins had felt an even deeper urgency to protect America from suffering at the hands of terrorists.

Because of O'Connor's involvement and the top-secret requirements surrounding the young soldier, President Dawkins had been led to believe that if Chance could recover from his injuries, he would be retrained and utilized in some facet of the CIA. Given the extent of his injuries and mental trauma, he had doubted that Chance would ever be considered as a field agent.

"I truly believed that if he could overcome the damage done to him in Afghanistan, he would go on to do great things," Dawkins stated quietly, recalling the determined intensity that had burned in Sergeant Hughes' eyes.

"He did, and he has," Gabrielle replied with a smile. "His talents in the field are unmatched."

"Chance Hughes is your operative?" Dawkins asked quietly, letting the information sink in. "Why not put him on our payroll? The confidentiality of the agents in dark ops is of utmost importance."

Gabrielle looked around the room anxiously. "Are you absolutely positive we are not being recorded?"

"Rest assured, I had everything scrubbed this

morning before our meeting as per your instructions. This room is clean."

Gabrielle inhaled slowly and nodded. "Still, I think it best you don't use his name. You may call him Orion."

"Fine. So, tell me, how did *Orion* end up becoming a top secret weapon?"

"After his capture and the media found out how he saved so many fellow Marines, Orion was made into a national symbol of everything that went wrong and right in the war. I believe even you used his name and story in a campaign speech or two."

President Dawkins nodded his head slowly, remembering how his campaign staff had pushed to use the Chance Hughes story more than he had wanted to. Dawkins had never felt comfortable exploiting such a tragic, and no doubt, traumatic, event for his own political gain. Clearly, Sergeant Hughes had acted heroically in the moments leading up to his capture, but at the time of the presidential campaign, Hughes was still missing, still enduring unthinkable torture at the hands of the Taliban. Using Chance's name like a political bumper sticker seemed disrespectful to a young soldier fighting for his life.

"Yes, yes I remember. His name was all over the place."

"He was a household name and his face was on every magazine for months," Gabrielle continued.

"There is no way, short of plastic surgery to dramatically alter his appearance, we could've have maintained complete secrecy of his rescue and the fact that he is alive and well. This country needed his skills and in order for him to be successful, I had to run him privately."

Dawkins circled the table, his mind reeling with the idea that one of his most trusted advisors had kept this massive secret from him for the majority of his presidency.

"So, why tell me now?" he asked.

"We needed him to run this operation against Domino and in order to do that, he was going to have to come out of the trenches. Plus, it's been almost seven years since the name of that heroic young Marine has been in the media. The public has a short memory."

Dawkins crossed his arms as he mulled over his thoughts. Suddenly, he smiled.

"I think I'm understanding something here, Gabrielle. You believe that Hughes is no longer safe out there without our protection. You said he's good. Has he become too good?"

Gabrielle nodded. "Please, he goes by the name Orion. And, you're correct. I'm afraid he has become somewhat legendary. His identity and his appearance, to a certain extent, remain secret; but yes, Orion's reputation is rapidly spreading. Two months ago, he killed a target with a three thousand meter shot. In case you didn't know, the record for the longest confirmed kill shot is around twenty-eight hundred meters. Would you like to guess who set that record?"

"Cha--Orion?"

"Yes, during his third tour to Iraq. During that time, he also had a kill shot that witnesses claim was longer than that, but it wasn't confirmed."

"Oh."

"No one, since Orion, has even come close to completing a shot at that distance. A long shot like that is almost as identifying as his signature."

Dawkins pulled a pen out from his pocket and fiddled with it as he thought a moment. Then it came to him. His eyes brightened.

"Jose Capinac, the Mexican drug lord who was gunned down two months ago…that was Orion?"

Gabrielle didn't reply.

"I've read the reports. Experts claim an accurate shot taken at that distance would be nearly impossible."

"Nearly."

"Unbelievable," Dawkins replied quietly. "Of course, we adamantly denied any U.S. involvement in his assassination."

"Which was true. There was no official U.S. involvement whatsoever."

"I don't even know what to say about all this," Dawkins stated.

"In the Middle East, our enemies refer to him as Shay tan," Gabrielle continued.

"Devil?"

"Yes. In South America they call him Cacador de Fantasmas."

"I don't know that one."

"It's Portuguese meaning Ghost Hunter."

"We've even picked up chatter in Russian referring to someone as 'Stopar'. It means stalker and we're fairly certain that's Orion."

"You're right. He's going to need protection soon," Dawkins said.

Gabrielle nodded, feeling a sliver of optimism that she might walk out of the meeting with her two goals met: protecting Chance and keeping her job.

"Does that mean you want to bring him inside?" Dawkins asked.

Gabrielle sighed and looked down at her hands. This was the one question she still didn't have an answer for.

"Mr. President, one of the main reasons Orion has been so successful is that he isn't on our payroll."

Dawkins nodded. "Because if we don't pay him, he doesn't have to follow our rules. But, if he isn't officially one of ours, we also can't protect him. This is a dilemma."

Gabrielle quietly waited, watching as the President rolled ideas around in his head.

"Look, this is something we will have to discuss once this Domino operation is completed," Dawkins stated. "I'll think about how we can fully utilize Orion while keeping him under our protection."

"Yes sir," Gabrielle replied, feeling a sense of relief. Finally, her secret was out and her intuition was correct. The President understood, and now she had the world's two most powerful men on her side.

Chapter Twelve

Camp Cropper
Baghdad, Iraq

Doctor Asifa Kahled al-Fulan was accustomed to the chaotic, often dangerous lifestyle thrust upon young doctors trying to work in the hospitals and clinics of Iraq. The main threats came from tribes and families who believed the doctor had committed an error in the care of their family member. Even worse was for a doctor to be accused of causing the death of a patient. With the threat of being accused of causing harm to a patient, many doctors were reluctant to perform surgeries and other procedures. Kidnappings and black mailings were becoming more prevalent. All doctors were expected to provide their own protection. As a result, the severe shortage of doctors in proportion to the population came as no surprise. Being a woman in this environment only heightened the threats.

Despite the dangers of being a woman doctor,

Asifa didn't spend much time worrying about a potential tribal threat. Asifa was accustomed to much bigger threats and dangers. Global terrorism, her country's safety and the world's various wars were on the top of her agenda. Asifa Kahled al-Fulan had been born into a well-respected Iraqi family. She had been educated in the finest medical schools in Germany, was a devout Muslim, and had no aspirations to rebel against or aggravate anyone. Asifa Kahled al-Fulan was also a complete fabrication.

The only truth about the woman called Asifa was that she was a highly trained medical doctor. Instead of Germany, she had attended Harvard University. Her actual parents had both been killed in the brutal terror attacks thrust upon northern Israel by the Palestinian guerilla organizations that eventually prompted the government of Israel to invade south Lebanon, bringing about the Lebanon War. Even though she held a thorough understanding of Islam, she was a Christian. Although schooled in medicine, her current employment involved more killing than saving.

The death of her parents and her experiences of war and destruction at such a young age had forever shaped the course of her life. Deeply threaded through the fiber of her being was an urge to seek revenge, and to rectify all the wrongs done to her family and her country. This obsession, coupled with her natural skills and abilities led her down a mysterious and dangerous path. She was a member of the Kidon, an elite group of expert assassins who operated within Mossad, Israel's intelligence agency. Her birth name had been lost long ago into the darkness of the covert world in which she operated. Now, even to her closest allies, she only went by Lexi.

The moment she received Orion's phone call, Lexi knew she would finally be asked to pay the debt she owed him. Business dealings conducted in the world of espionage were usually based on trading one of three basic things: secrets, lies, or favors. Three years ago, Orion had helped her get out of a rather delicate situation with both her life and her career intact.

They had crossed paths while hunting the same terrorist in Syria. Both felt the other was intruding on their hunting ground and their initial meeting was nearly deadly. However, neither pulled the trigger and they had decided that two assassins working together was better than two working individually and ultimately against each other. Once the operation was complete, Lexi discovered that her handler, a veteran of Mossad, had turned traitor and was about to sell her out to the enemy. That's when their paths crossed again, but this time on purpose. Lexi took a chance, made contact and informed Orion of her predicament. Despite having been assigned to a new mission on a different continent, Orion took a detour to Israel. Coincidently, shortly after Orion's arrival in her country, a particular high-ranking Israeli intelligence officer tragically committed suicide in his apartment. The traitor was dead, Lexi's secret remained safe and she owed Orion a favor.

It had been three years since Lexi had had any contact with Orion, and she was clueless as to how he knew she was in Baghdad, but she had realized long ago that it wasn't wise to throw too many questions at Orion. He wouldn't answer, anyhow. He was a strange and mysterious man, and in her world, trust was a foreign concept. Despite everything she didn't know about Orion, she was certain that it was in her best interest to keep him on her side. Going up against him had ended the careers, and lives, of many.

She walked steadily upon the hard-packed ground toward the grim rows of steel containerized housing units, otherwise known as CHUs. Each unit was basically an aluminum box, slightly larger than a commercial shipping container. With linoleum floors, one window, a roof vent and rudimentary power cabling, they were only a slight improvement over a tent.

She had easily deciphered Orion's conversation, knowing his cropped hair meant Camp Cropper, his reference to having had a haircut eight months ago meant bunker number eight, and when he said his hair was a mess she knew her medical skills were required to fix whatever mess Orion had. She wondered if he was the one suffering from an injury. He did usually work alone, so she didn't expect anyone other than him. His voice hadn't sounded strained on the phone, but then again, she never knew him to sound anything but composed. His voice could sound perfectly calm in the midst of great turmoil and pain.

Lexi was quite aware of the activities that occurred in these bunkers and containers. Most commonly, they were used as isolation cells, or holding chambers for prisoners and detainees awaiting transport to a more permanent facility. These crude buildings were also used for lesser-known, more violent occurrences. Intelligence agencies, including the CIA and her own Mossad used places like this and other black sites around the world to conduct enhanced interrogations. Torture. When crucial information was needed fast, anyone who potentially had answers could be brought here for a special Q and A session and avoid the meddling of lawyers, or congressional rules and cameras. According to some prisoners, Allah rarely even intervened in these activities.

As bunker eight came into view, she slowed her approach, her senses on high alert to anything seeming unusual. Other than swirling sand cyclones and the sound of wind whipping across the desert, the camp was quiet. Lexi stepped up to the door. One hand slipped under her burka and flipped the safety off her 9mm. She knocked softly.

The door squeaked slightly as it opened a crack. Lexi found herself staring into a pair of unfamiliar eyes. For a moment, she believed she had been led into an ambush.

"You the doc?" James asked, cursing himself for not asking Chance for a few more details on the person he was sending over.

"Who are you?" Lexi asked, her hand tightening on her gun.

"You'll never live to pull the trigger if you pull that gun on me," James stated his grip tightening on his own weapon. Then he remembered the odd text he had received from Chance moments ago. He passed it off as a butt text but then realized it may be the key to saving himself from a shoot-out with the angry Arabic woman at the door.

"Pembe," James said cautiously, hoping he wasn't insulting her in some way.

The woman's dark brown eyes immediately widened and then she whispered, "What?"

James had no idea what sort of relationship Chance had with this woman or if she even knew his name. He decided to proceed carefully.

"I was told to tell you 'Pembe'. If you are who I'm hoping you are, that should mean something."

"Who told you that?"

James sighed. "Who do you think?"

"Orion."

James nodded.

"I'm the doctor. Please, let me in."

James opened the door for the woman and shut it quickly once she was in. Without being told, she approached the bleeding man lying on the floor near the wall. He appeared to be sedated and was attached to an IV bag strapped to a makeshift stand. If Lexi recognized the face of one of the world's most notorious terrorists, she didn't show it. She pulled off her shawl and burka, revealing her long raven-black hair and fit body. James still had one hand on his gun, sensing this woman, despite her small stature, was as dangerous as she was beautiful. She had a small leather satchel attached to her belt and she pulled several medical instruments from it. She began gently cutting the makeshift bandages off Domino's wound.

"How long ago did this happen?" she asked.

James checked his watch. "About an hour."

"What have you given him?"

"Saline drip and ten milligrams of morphine. Oh, and a milligram of Demerol for good measure."

She paused a moment to pull her hair into a tight ponytail before resuming her investigation of Domino's injury.

"You a medic?" she asked as she peeled back

Domino's bandage.

"I am today, it appears."

"Who are you?" she asked, glancing over her shoulder at James.

"Orion's partner."

"Orion works alone," she replied.

"I'm the ghost that follows him," James shot back.

"And what about you? Another ghost?" Lexi asked Carlos who was standing in the shadows nearby.

Carlos looked at James who shook his head. Carlos understood and replied, "Yes, señora."

Lexi smiled and nodded. Spooks. They all had weird a sense of humor. When surrounded by constant danger, violence and death, one had to find a way to laugh on occasion, even if it was inappropriate. Sometimes laughing in the face of death helped maintain a semblance of sanity.

"It went through, so it's clean. Must've been close range. What kind of bullet did this?" Lexi asked, tenderly studying the gaping wound. She had seen more than her fair share of gunshot wounds, and most times she could guess fairly accurately at the make and model of the gun responsible for the damage. The wound she was looking at now didn't give her many answers.

"Does it matter? I know it wasn't a poisoned dart," James answered impatiently.

"Am I supposed to patch him up for transport, or something else?" Lexi asked. She wouldn't put a lot of effort into fixing up this man's gaping hole if he was just going be questioned and killed within twenty-four hours. She could put in a few stitches, give him a mild painkiller and be done. Or, she could thoroughly clean the wound, put in several layers of stitches, along with a drain tube, hook him up to an IV with vital antibiotics and continue with the strong painkillers. Her treatment depended on his expected longevity.

Carlos looked at James who directly met his gaze. James then looked down at Lexi and Domino.

"We need him alive. Period. Patch him up the best you can."

Lexi began cleaning the wound. "When will you be transporting him?"

James smiled. "Focus on your job, Doc."

Lexi turned and met James' look once again. She could tell that he knew she was more than a doctor. She also knew he was much more than someone who followed Orion around. First of all, anyone who had any sort of working relationship with someone of Orion's talents was unique. Secondly, the resemblance was obvious. Despite his dark hair and deep blue eyes, the lanky man staring back at her had to be closely related to Orion. She also knew exactly who the man lying on the floor was. She, along with all other operatives in

222

intelligence agencies throughout the world, considered this man to be the top prize in their hunting games. She would gladly give up her current undercover operation to join Orion and his two ghosts in closing the chapter on Domino. At the very least, she'd love to know what these Americans planned to do with him and what kind of information, if any, they had garnered from him. So far, Orion's two ghosts weren't talking.

Chapter Thirteen

Fallujah, Iraq

Chance and Anna stood at the open doorway looking down the dark, narrow stairwell that led to something they were both certain would be nothing short of terrible. Their first clue was the horrid smell wafting up from the dank recesses.

Chance reached around the corner feeling for a light switch. His fingers quickly located the switch. He flipped it up. Nothing.

Of course, Chance thought to himself. Electricity was a fickle luxury in most of Iraq's cities and towns.

"Ladies first," Chance stated as he stepped aside and pulled out his flashlight and night-vision goggles from his backpack.

"How gallant of you," Anna huffed as she double-checked her weapon.

"I'm nothing if not gallant."

"You're chicken, that's what you are."

"Actually, I don't think it's wise for me to turn

my back on you. Therefore, you first."

Anna turned and smiled back at him. "Are you afraid of me?"

Chance stepped close to her and smiled back. "I'm afraid you'll make a rookie mistake and try to kill me, which in turn, will force me to kill you. It's all an inconvenience I'd rather not deal with right now."

Anna stared back at him a long moment before she whispered, "If I really wanted to kill you, you'd be dead by now."

Chance laughed out loud. "That's original. Where'd you get that line? Spending your down time watching old Clint Eastwood movies?"

Anna turned away and mumbled, "I'm not a rookie."

"Then how come you didn't pack your NODs?"

Anna glared at him, knowing she had made a mistake in omitting packing her night-vision goggles. She honestly believed it was a waste of time since this was a day-light operation.

Are we gonna do this or stand around and waste time?" she asked in frustration.

Chance handed her his flashlight. "Don't turn this on unless it's absolutely necessary."

Anna carefully placed one foot in front of the other, slowly descending into the basement. She could hear Chance following as she strained to see into the darkness. The deathly odor was nearly unbearable and something Anna had never experienced before. She paused momentarily to hold her hand over her mouth and stifled her gag reflex.

"Breathe through your mouth," Chance whispered, seemingly unaffected by the smell. He placed his hand on her back and applied gentle pressure urging her forward.

Anna did her best to breathe through her mouth, but it was impossible to ignore the stench. Her eyes were adjusting to the darkness and objects and shapes became visible. She held her gun up, ready to fire at the whisper of a threat. She felt Chance move away from her and a sense of incredible vulnerability enveloped her.

"Orion?" she whispered, hating how weak her voice sounded. Getting no response and unable to hear any footfalls, her heart raced. "Chance?" she asked a little louder and not caring that she sounded scared. She *was* scared. At any moment, she expected one of those dark shapeless objects that her eyes strained to see, to suddenly attack.

She looked back toward the stairs and the dim streak of light filtering down. She backed up until her heels hit the bottom step. Suddenly, she heard something scratching the floor nearby. She turned to face the source of the noise, but then the scratching noise seemed to be behind her- and much closer. As she gripped the flashlight she spun around again, ready to attack whatever was producing that dry raspy noise. In her mind, she envisioned someone's bare feet scuffling along on the floor. Her heart raced. Then a footfall landed nearby. Desperately wanting to turn on the flashlight, she turned around to face the danger. Before she could act, a long arm wrapped around her shoulders, pulling her tight against a long lean body.

"Easy, Princess," Chance whispered.

He let her go and Anna turned around and slugged him in the arm. "Dammit, Chance! You're lucky I didn't shoot you! Why are you sneaking up on me?"

"I wasn't. Try not using my name. You never know who's listening."

"I heard something. Was that you?"

"No. It's the rats. Follow me," Chance replied.

"Rats?" Anna gasped, suppressing an overwhelming urge to sprint up the stairs.

"Come on. They won't hurt you if you keep moving," Chance demanded as he grabbed her arm and yanked her out of her frozen stance.

Anna immediately sensed a change in Chance. His smart-ass tendencies completely disappeared. His voice, although calm, held a tinge of something else. Anger? Urgency? Anna couldn't be sure, but she was certain that she was about to see the reason for his change. She followed Chance down a narrow hall that led to a small room. He asked for his flashlight and then aimed the beam of light toward the corner.

"Oh my, God," Anna whispered.

Shackled to the wall in heavy chains were two bodies, broken, emaciated and abused beyond recognition.

"Are they dead?" she asked softly, feeling suddenly weak and overwhelmed by the inhumanity of what she was looking at.

"Hold this," Chance ordered as he handed Anna his flashlight. He approached the bodies, taking in every possible detail. The smell and condition of the bodies told him they had been dead for quite some time, yet he desperately wanted to know who they were and why they had been kept here.

"Call James," Chance said with a quick glance back at Anna. "Tell him what we've found and that we'll need a QRF to secure the scene. Then have him deploy the CSIers. We've got ourselves a puzzle to figure out. Make sure James informs the team they're gonna need generators. There's no electricity here."

Chance gently touched one of the bodies. Cold and stiff. He was a master at separating emotion from his job, but this scenario was especially traumatic. Being held captive and tortured by ruthless maniacs still haunted his dreams. While standing in front of these two beaten and broken bodies, a lot of buried feelings were brought to the surface. Chance inhaled slowly, stuffing the unwanted memories back into the dark corners of his brain. He refocused and looked closer at the prisoners, keeping his mind focused on the cold, hard facts. He had a job to do.

He heard Anna on her SAT phone explaining to James that the house was now an official crime scene that needed to be secured immediately by the Quick Reaction Force, a team of soldiers waiting on standby ready to react to any situation. She also informed him that they required a team of forensic specialists, the Crime Scene Investigators. No doubt, James would relay that information back to O'Connor, and within minutes, the highly-trained military investigative team would arrive to take over. Until then, Chance wanted to gather as much information as possible.

Both of the bodies were badly mutilated, but he noticed specific things that struck him as odd. Both prisoners were missing their eyes. Both had also had their hands chopped off. Chance crouched closer and peered into their mouths. All their teeth were missing. He spotted a jagged, patch-shaped wound on one prisoner's upper arm, as if the skin had been torn off.

"Ok, Princess, here's a quiz. What are five of the most commonly used methods of identification found on a human body?"

Anna stepped closer and replied, "Fingerprints,

of course. Dental records. Retinal scans. Then I suppose unique markings on the skin, like tattoos or birthmarks. If all that fails, DNA. Did I miss anything?"

"Nope, and all we've got left here is DNA. We need to find out who these two guys were and fast."

"Were they both men?" Anna asked.

"Yes," Chance answered as he stared at what remained of one of the dead men's faces. "This is really bad," he said under his breath. "What happened to you?" he whispered.

Anna watched curiously, momentarily blocking out her own repulsions of the scene and surroundings. *Is Chance talking to the dead men*?

"You think Domino wanted to delay their identification if someone happened to stumble upon his little secret down here?" Anna asked.

"Apparently. But I think there's more to it than that…" he replied softly as he gently picked up one the dead man's shackled arms. Because his hands had been removed, the metal cuff was clasped tightly above the elbow, with a heavy chain attaching it to the wall.

"You think they were important?" Anna asked.

"Everyone's important to someone," Chance answered as he carefully placed the dead man's arm back by his side. He absent-mindedly rubbed his own wrists, remembering the cruel ropes that had once bound him in a foul smelling hole, not much different from this basement.

Anna stepped closer, keeping the beam of light steadily aimed at the bodies. "Orion? Are you okay?" Getting no response, she added, "Domino obviously kept these guys down here for a reason. They must be someone significant, right? I mean he wouldn't just torture and kill people for fun, right?"

Chance shifted so he could look closer at the other mangled body. "He might. That sort of shit happens. Look, this guy had both of his legs broken," he stated as he pointed to the twisted, deformed tibias that were once the man's shins.

"That's sick," Anna replied, finding it difficult to keep emotion from clouding her thinking.

"It's a sick world, Princess. You must get the easy, clean assignments if this surprises you."

Anna stopped herself from snapping back at him. She didn't want to start down the path of comparing careers with Chance. No doubt her experiences paled in comparison to his.

"Can we wait for the reinforcements upstairs?" she asked impatiently.

"These two had to fight a horrible fight down here, by themselves, with no help or mercy for God knows how long," Chance replied seriously. "The least we can do is keep them company until the cavalry arrives."

"They're dead, Orion. They aren't fighting anymore."

Anna immediately regretted her words as Chance glared at her angrily.

"You go ahead. I'm staying," he stated with a dark edge to his voice.

Anna remained, shifting her weight and shining the flashlight at the pitiful sight.

After what seemed like an eternity of silence, Chance finally said, "I think this might be a case of stolen identities."

"For what reason?"

"These two guys had access to someone important and now there are two imposters taking their places," Chance spoke softly, his mind racing over the possibilities.

"That's pretty far-fetched, don't you think? I mean anyone who has access to a high-ranking politician is vetted so extensively I doubt two imposters could break through."

Chance stood up and stretched his legs. "Really? What about that maniac sign language dude who stood right next to the president when he spoke at that Veteran's Day program last month. Turns out, he's a felon with a dangerous past and has no idea how to do sign language. You'd be surprised at who can slip through the cracks."

"Ok. Maybe. When's the QRF team coming? Our job is done. Let someone else figure out the details."

As if on cue, heavy boot steps could be heard

above their heads.

"U.S. Marines! You there?" a voice yelled down the stairs.

"It's clear!" Chance yelled back.

Chance crouched back down and looked closely at the dead prisoners, knowing this would be the last time he'd see them. He tried to memorize every agonizing detail. He understood why he felt the overwhelming desire to seek justice and revenge for the poor souls who endured ungodly treatment in this dark hole. He also understood why looking at this carnage made him physically sick and would most likely amp up the frequency and violence in his own haunted dreams. What he failed to understand, was how any human being could inflict this sort of sadistic torture upon another human being.

Five marines secured the area and prepared to stand guard, while waiting for the forensics team to arrive. Chance understood that he was no longer required to stay, but he couldn't quite make himself leave, either. He felt an odd sort of attachment toward the pitiful bodies chained to the wall. He wondered how long they had been dead. He wondered if he would have somehow found them a month ago, if he could've saved them. He wondered how long they had been shackled to that wall and if they had held out any hope for rescue. His mind was racing from one "what if" to another when he felt a hand on his shoulder.

"Hey, what's going on with you?" Anna asked, impatiently waiting to get away from this death chamber.

Chance blinked hard, bringing his mind back under control. He brushed off Anna's hand. Ever since his little adventure with the Taliban in the Afghan cave, he didn't care to be touched. At one time, even a simple handshake would nearly bring on a panic attack. Despite gaining impeccable control over most of his issues, little things, such as a hand on his shoulder, felt like salt in an open wound. The increased throbbing in his concussed brain wasn't helping his tolerance to little irritations either. Once again, he was craving the relief that few pain pills could deliver. Without them, his headache and mood would quickly turn for the worse.

Anna followed Chance up the stairs and out of the house. Even though the air quality in Fallujah was less than crisp, Anna gulped in the open air, grateful to be rid of the unbearable stench of the basement. She still felt the urge to gag, as the smell remained in her nostrils, so potent that she swore she could taste death. Not wanting to appear weak or dramatic, she forced herself to not react in any way. She pushed back the horrific images of the dead prisoners and focused on the next move. As she looked over at Chance, she realized he wouldn't have noticed a reaction from her, anyway. His attention was somewhere else completely.

"So, we meet up with Cowboy at Cropper, right? How are we getting there? Want me to steal a car?" Anna asked, eyeing several vehicles on the street.

Chance only partially heard her as he fought off a wave of nausea and brain throb. He took a slow breath and rubbed his eyes. The glaring hot sunshine wasn't helping his condition in the slightest.

"Orion! Snap out of it," Anna snapped as she stepped closer to him. "What's wrong with you? How are we getting to Cropper?"

His fingers shook slightly as he fingered through his pack, digging for his Oakley's. Relieved to finally find his shades, he slipped them on and with one more glance back at the house, he walked to the street.

Anna followed, wondering where he was going. She had a feeling he was "off" somehow, but had no idea why. Obviously the grisly scene in the basement would be enough to completely unravel a normal person, but Chance wasn't normal. The ice in his veins was legendary. Still, Anna swore she caught a glimpse of emotion in him as he whispered softly to those nameless, mangled bodies.

Anna's memory swirled around the sight of Chance ingesting pills right before they left for the house invasion. With so many things going on at that time, she didn't spend much time thinking about it. However, she was trained to pick up on the smallest details. One small act may seem random, but several small acts could add up to an answer. She would continue to watch Chance for more possible clues that could explain what she felt was uncharacteristic behavior.

Her eyes flicked back and forth, scanning the surroundings for anything suspicious as she remained close to Chance. He paused a moment before going directly to a rusty Toyota pickup parked a block away. Within a few a minutes he hotwired the vehicle and stepped on the gas. He never spoke a word to Anna, who had the good sense to keep quiet and hop into the passenger seat.

* * *

Domino sat quietly on the floor. His ankles zip-tied together, and despite his injured shoulder, his wrists were also tightly bound with a zip tie. Lexi carefully monitored the slow-dripping IV bag. After closing off the tiny hole in his brachial artery, and placing a few layers of stitches and a drain tube into the wound, Lexi considered Domino stable enough for transport or questioning.

James checked his watch, wondering what was taking his brother so long. After learning of the gruesome discovery in the Fallujah house, James worried a bit about Chance's state of mind. Even though Chance had spent six years proving his incredible toughness of both mind and body, James knew that memories still haunted his little brother. Seeing the bodies of tortured prisoners, would, no doubt, have dusted off a few jagged memories in Chance's mind.

"How are you related to Orion?" Lexi asked, snapping James from his thoughts.

"Third cousin twice removed. What's your relationship with Orion?" James shot back.

Lexi laughed. "I don't even know his real name, so I wouldn't say we're close."

"Does he know your real name?"

Lexi hesitated a moment, revealing the truth.

James laughed and nodded. "So, he knows you a little bit better than you know him, huh? Don't worry, happens all the time with him."

Not wanting to converse with Lexi any further, James walked over to Domino and knelt down in front of him.

"Is your pain going away?" he asked.

Domino looked him in the eye a moment before he nodded.

"Good. I want to keep you comfortable, ok?"

Domino nodded again and whispered, "Thirsty."

James stood, looked at Lexi and demanded, "Grab a bottled water out of my pack."

Lexi brought the water and James unscrewed the cap before handing it to Domino. After watching the man take in a few gulps, James took it back and set it aside.

Kneeling once again, James said, "As long as you cooperate, I'll keep the pain medication and water flowing. I'll even find you some food when you get hungry. The good doctor over there will make sure your wound is taken care of and life won't be so bad for you."

Domino stared at James. This American had soft, gentle blue eyes and a soothing voice. He came across as sincere. But, Domino knew better than to trust any American. Still, he didn't want the pain medication to go away.

"I'm not an interrogator," James continued. "But if you could just answer one question for me, I do have the power to make you a deal."

"Immunity?" Domino asked, his voice sounding stronger.

"I doubt that. But, I could get you a cell in a prison much nicer than Guantanamo. You could have a window, privacy, even a little more outdoor time. If you don't help us, you'll be lucky to end up in a seven-by-seven concrete cell in Guantanamo. You'll be looking at the death chamber, my friend."

Lexi observed quietly, quickly assessing that this wasn't the American's first interrogation. He may claim he's not an interrogator, but his methods revealed otherwise.

"I need to know the identities of the two prisoners we found in the basement."

Domino looked away, silent.

James laughed but there was no humor in it. He stood up; his eyes remained fixed on Domino. "Trust me, if you choose not to talk to me, you'll be forced to talk to someone who has zero tolerance for uncooperative behavior."

Domino looked back at James and sneered. "You Americans like to play good cop bad cop."

James smiled and leaned down closer to Domino, "The man you're about to visit with makes a bad cop look like a flower girl. He *will* get the information from you, with or without your cooperation. You know, you might have actually heard of him. Forgive me for my lack of Arabic skills, but I believe he's known as Shay tan around here." James waited for his words to sink in, then asked, "Ring a bell?"

Domino's already pallid skin lightened another shade. Many people truly believed that the man known as Shay tan wasn't human. Instead, they believed he was some sort of mystical hunter who possessed the skills to track down and kill his prey regardless of where his quarry tried to hide. The stories circulated about his treatment of the men he captured or killed cast a cold shard of fear into the bravest of warriors.

"Why not make it easy on yourself and just tell me the names of those two prisoners?" James asked with an easy smile. "You obviously don't want me to hand you over to Shay tan."

"It's too late," Domino whispered. Beads of sweat forming on his brow. "Names mean nothing anymore. It's too late."

Before James could respond, a loud knock on the door interrupted them. He flicked the safety off his gun and walked to the door. He heard Lexi take up a defensive stance behind him. He unlocked the door and opened it a crack to see his brother looking back at him.

"Took you long enough," James proclaimed as he opened the door for Chance and Anna to enter. "Take the scenic route?"

"Yep. Baghdad is lovely this time of year." Chance strode into the room, quickly assessing his surroundings. "So, I see our guest of honor is still amongst the living. Good job, Doc." Chance remarked, winking at Lexi. "Thanks for helping out."

"I guess now we're even," Lexi responded, lowering her gun and studying the man she only knew as Orion. It had been three years since she had seen him. His hair was much longer now and his lanky body thinner. Still handsome, in a hardened, dangerous sort of way. His rugged, unshaven face portrayed a sort of weariness hidden behind a razor sharp intensity, perfectly complemented by his chilly gray eyes. He was not the type of man a typical civilian would feel comfortable approaching. Good thing she wasn't a typical civilian. He was just the sort of man she was attracted to. She briefly allowed herself to wish she could spend a little time with Orion in non-working conditions.

"Even Steven," Chance stated, his focus now turned to Domino. "Has he talked?"

"Not much except that we're too late, he can't help us, blah, blah blah." James turned to face Domino. "You're gonna wish you talked to me, compadre. Say "hi" to Shay tan," James said as he motioned toward Chance.

Domino fixed his eyes upon the man he had the opportunity to kill on the roof of his own residence. The American spy who had been constantly impeding his plans and wreaking havoc within his organization was the infamous Shay tan? Domino closed his eyes, for the first time feeling a sense of defeat creeping into his system. His mind obsessing over a single thought: *If only I had pulled the trigger faster*.

Chance eyed the interior of the small bunker. "Ahhh, Shay tan, yes, that's who I am here. It's gotten difficult to keep track," he said offhandedly. "The Three Musketeers got out okay?"

James nodded. The moment they arrived at Camp Cropper, Roger, Jet and Tim hopped onto the waiting C-130 Hercules. The four-engine turbo-prop military plane was the tactical go-to airlifter, designed to handle unprepared runways and hurried take-offs and landings. The original plan was for the entire team, plus Domino, to board the Hercules and leave Iraq together. Chance and Anna's impromptu basement investigation had put the kibosh on that idea. Now they would have to find their own way out.

"There's a room not much bigger than a closet back there. Put our guest in there and prep him for an interview," Chance told James.

Domino began to curse and argue, prompting Chance to grab a roll of duct tape out of James's pack. He ripped off a piece and slapped it across the terrorist's mouth. "Save it, Dom. We'll talk in a bit," Chance said with a friendly smile and a slap on Domino's shoulder.

"Gimme about ten minutes, then he'll be ready to sing like a bird," James stated as moved Domino into the back room.

Carlos approached Chance. "What will you do to him?"

"I won't kill him."

"But you will torture him?"

"Not if he talks."

"Please, please have a little mercy," Carlos pleaded.

"Mercy? Like all the mercy your terroristic

242

brother had for those innocent people, mostly women and children, mind you, in that market in Syria? What about all the mercy shown to the United States ambassadors killed in the bombing of the Syrian embassy? I also didn't see any mercy in Israel when I walked around countless dead bodies of young children after their school exploded. Would you like me to go on? Because I could. Your brother has shown no mercy as he spreads his sick terroristic plans all over the world. Now, I'm pretty sure he's trying to carry out his biggest plan yet and I am going to stop it. I am going to stop the killing. I'll do anything to stop it."

Chance almost rubbed his eyes but stopped himself, not wanting to give away the fact that his head was killing him. He had a gut feeling that Anna was studying him closely.

"Maybe he'll talk to me?" Carlos asked. "He trusts me."

"Not anymore, Father," Chance replied. "Don't worry. You'll get your opportunity to help."

"Why do they call you Shay tan?" Carlos asked, not convinced that he actually wanted the answer.

"Because they don't know my real name and they can't pronounce Orion," Chance grumbled. Then Chance looked directly at Father Sanchez and the dread and worry he saw in the man's face unexpectedly bothered him. "I'm not the devil," Chance said quietly. "You can't believe everything you hear, Father."

Chance held Sanchez's gaze for a moment before he walked away. Chance worked at focusing his mind on the part of his job that he couldn't say he liked in the least, but even he couldn't deny that he excelled at it. The role of interrogator exhausted him mentally. He wasn't against torture, whatever that may entail, but he did save those methods as a last ditch effort. He preferred to twist the suspect mentally. His reputation as Shay tan, or whatever else the hell people called him, helped create an intense fear in whoever he was extracting information from, before he even walked into the room. Chance had the upper hand from the get-go in any interrogation, and he prided himself in administrating a king-sized mind fuck to those who chose not to cooperate. Occasionally, the mind games yielded poor results, forcing him to get physical.

"So, who's she?" Anna asked loudly, motioning with her gun toward Lexi, drawing Chance's attention. He had almost forgotten that his favorite doctor was still here.

Cat fight? Here? Really? Chance thought to himself incredulously. He quickly recognized this as the perfect distraction needed for him to swallow a couple of pills and try to quiet the marching band pounding in his head. Putting a little distance between himself and the two women, he stood in the shadows and grabbed the bottle of pills.

Lexi stepped forward, her hand gripping her own weapon. "Why not ask me directly?"

Anna faced the petite, dark-eyed woman. Standing nearly six foot tall, Anna towered over the small, lithe Lexi.

"Okay," Anna spoke softly. "Who. Are. You?"

Lexi smiled before answering, "The one Orion calls when he needs something. Who are you? His bookkeeper?"

Anna flashed a perfectly smug smile when she responded to Lexi's snide comment. "I'm the one who knows him well enough to call him by his real name."

"Knock it off, girls," Chance interrupted angrily as he approached the women. Already the pills were working their magic and the pain was subsiding. Now, he could focus. "Let's retract the claws and focus on the job," Chance stated firmly.

"And what is that job, exactly?" Lexi asked.

Chance snatched Anna's gun from her hand before she could stop him. Stepping between two angry, armed females was just plain stupid. Feeling more comfortable about turning his back on Anna, Chance faced Lexi. "Is he stable?" he pointed to the back room.

"The man I stitched up or the guy who looks like you?"

"In the interest of time, let's focus only on the

stability of the injured man."

"Depends on what you're planning to do with him."

"We're gonna have a fucking tea party," Chance responded, quickly losing his patience. "Is he stable, yes or no?"

Lexi knew better than to push him any further. "Yes."

"Then you're done here. Thanks for your help."

Lexi stepped within inches of Chance and spoke softly so Anna couldn't hear clearly.

"You know I can't just walk out of here," she demanded. "I know who that is," she said, pointing to the back room.

"I know you do."

"I want in on this operation."

"All positions have been filled," Chance answered, knowing this was the price he would have to pay for letting someone like Lexi lay eyes on a target such as Domino. Once again, business would come into play. He just had to decide if they would once again be swapping favors, or if they would dive into the trade of secrets and lies.

"You know me well enough to realize I can't pretend I didn't see any of this," Lexi commented, her eyes blazing with the desire to be privy to whatever Orion was doing with Domino.

Chance reached out and brushed the back of his hand gently against her perfect olive complexion.

He fully comprehended Lexi's attraction to him. He certainly appreciated her athletic beauty, as well. Maybe someday he'd have some downtime and allow himself to explore all the adventures promised in Lexi's dark eyes. Someday. For now, his time was limited and he had a job to do. He smiled and whispered, "Do I know you well enough, Pembe?"

Lexi felt a horrifying feeling of vulnerability when Orion whispered her name. Pembe was the Turkish word for rose. Her father, whom she barely remembered, bestowed her with the name, Rose, thirty-six years ago. It was a name she rarely heard, yet when she did, it touched something deep within her soul. How Orion had discovered her name was a mystery.

"If I let you in on this, you're gonna owe me again," Chance spoke softly. "That's not necessarily a safe position to be in."

Lexi only smiled.

Chance dropped his hand and sighed, thinking momentarily before saying, "You're hard to say 'no' to." He knew the second he asked her to help him that he wouldn't be able to just dismiss her from the operation. Lexi was the epitome of persistence and would never pass up an opportunity of this magnitude.

"Seninle, ben ondan almak Intel paylasacagiz," *I'll share the Intel I get from him, with you*,"

Chance whispered in Turkish. "Ben Israil istihbarat toplulugu bu bilgileri ele verdik nerede hicbir bilgiye sahip olacaktir guveniyorum?" *I trust the Israeli intelligence community will have no knowledge of where you've gotten this information*"

"Elbette degil." *Of course not.*

Chance smiled as he held out his hand. Lexi placed her small hand in his and held tightly for far longer than a customary business handshake. Then she took it one step further and sidled closer to him. Standing on her tip-toes she softly kissed him on the cheek.

"Thanks," she whispered. She looked up and noticed an odd, almost baffled expression on Orion's face. His typically distant, detached demeanor momentarily evaporated as he met her eyes in a penetrating stare. In a blink, whatever door Lexi managed to crack open, slammed back shut.

He took a generous step away from her and said, "Don't thank me yet. You might regret your decision."

"I doubt it. When will we meet again?"

"I'll find you. Get back to being a doctor."

"I'm always a doctor," Lexi replied as she gathered her medical bag, slipped into her shawl and burka, and walked out the door.

Anna waited until the door was locked and latched before she asked, "Israeli intelligence huh? Is she Mossad?"

Chance looked at her in surprise.

"I speak Turkish."

Chance shook his head in disgust. In addition to choosing a little-known language, he and Lexi carried on their conversation in a soft whisper. How the hell did Anna eavesdrop? Then it dawned on him. She was a lip reader.

"She's a doctor," Chance replied, mad at himself for not being more careful.

"Your doctor?"

Chance's headache was ebbing a bit, allowing him to find a trickle of humor in Anna's jealousy.

"I have a complicated medical policy."

"I'll bet. Give me my gun back."

Smiling, Chance laid her gun in her outstretched hand. "Never let someone take your weapon."

"What was I supposed to do? Fight you for it?"

"That's what I would've done."

When James opened the door and walked out of the back room, Chance turned and asked, "He ready to go?"

"I pulled the pain meds and what were in his system should be wearing off soon," James replied. "Sedative is gone. He's wide awake and uncomfortable."

"Took you long enough. Holy hell, it's been a regular soap opera out here. Any longer and there would've been a couple of marriages and divorces take place," Chance said as he pulled off his tactical gear, removed his guns and rolled up his sleeves.

"He's gonna be tough."

"They usually are. I'm thinking we'll need to utilize his Achilles Heel."

James raised his eyebrows and glanced at Carlos. "Should I take care of it?" He asked softly.

Chance nodded and then walked back to the room where Domino was waiting.

James looked at Carlos apologetically and said, "Sorry, Father, but this is gonna get a little ugly."

Carlos backed up a step and shook his head.

"Come on, let's just get this over with," James stated as he knelt down on the floor and began digging through his pack. "Have a seat and take a deep breath."

"Oh for God's sake, I'll make it quick," Anna said as she flipped open her knife and approached Carlos.

For the lack of another alternative, Carlos prepared to fight and stepped into Anna's advance.

"No!" James yelled as he jumped up and grabbed Anna's arm. "What the hell are you doing?"

"What Longshot wants you to do; make the priest bleed a little for the camera so Domino knows we mean business. The face and head bleed the most so a couple of slices in those areas will make a nice dramatic picture."

James let go of Anna's arm. "Back off, Warrior

Princess. Holy shit, you're hard-core. Let's do this my way and save poor Carlos a little bloodshed, shall we? And who in the hell is Longshot?"

Anna rolled her eyes and walked away. James watched her a moment before he shook his head and smiled. "Carlos, sit. We don't have all day."

Anna folded up her knife and stepped aside as James walked past her to begin his work on Carlos. James pulled a small pallet of colored makeup and paints and dialed up his inner artist as he began applying the colors to Carlos' face.

"So, now that you've finally come face to face with him again, you getting any of your questions answered?" James asked with a quick glance over his shoulder at Anna.

"What on earth are you talking about?"

"I think you're calling him Longshot now. You and I both know you don't want to kill him. So, I'm wondering if you're resolving the other issues you have regarding him."

"I have every right to want to kill him," Anna snarled, feeling her blood pressure rise at this line of odd questioning.

"Of course you do. Join the club. But, you won't actually do it. I have a theory. Wanna hear it?"

Anna rolled her eyes again. "Do I have a choice?"

James applied the finishing touches on a freakishly realistic nasty gash across Carlos' forehead.

"You've been so focused on finding Mr. Hot Shot in order to confirm your belief that everything that has gone wrong in your life is somehow his fault."

"It *is* his fault. And he's 'Longshot', not 'Hot Shot'."

"Longshot, Hot Shot, Big Shot, Shot Put, whatever. Why can't we just stick with 'Orion'? It has taken me a long time to get used to calling him that. I'm too damn old to try and learn another new name for the little shit."

"Why are we talking about this? Focus on the priest so you don't make him look like a battered clown."

"I can multitask," James shot back as he winked at Carlos, who was listening to the odd conversation curiously. "Sorry, sweetheart, but you were destined to live an unorthodox life long before my brother entered the picture." James straightened and inspected his work. "If it wasn't Orion, someone else would've gunned down your father. That's how the story ends for people like him. You would've never taken the path of a typical businesswoman. The fact that you're fairly successful in this career is a giant red flag to more than a few personality glitches. Hell, you were about to slice up an innocent priest just to make a good photograph," James said as he shook his head.

He pulled out his camera and turned Carlos to catch better light. He snapped a few pictures before turning to face Anna once again.

"I think you're trying to prove to yourself that you're as good as he is," James stated seriously.

"I am."

James smiled and shook his head. "Not yet, Princess. Not even close. See, there are two major aspects to my brother you have to keep in mind. First of all, obviously, he's got some impressive skills."

"So do I. What's the second aspect?"

"Me."

Anna's eyes couldn't hide her surprise. "You?"

"That's right. Now, you went through all the training and mental toughness shit that Orion went through, but he didn't go through it alone. I was there practically every step of the way, pulling him back from becoming a machine, reminding him he was still human, that there was still life outside of this dangerous dark world he is compelled to work in. I reminded him that hunting down and killing the world's most demented, evil human beings was his job, not his identity. My brother is not programmed to kill. He understands that sometimes the most important shot he handles is the one he doesn't take."

James walked up and stood close to Anna. He studied her a moment before he added softly, "Who do you have pulling you back from the machine, Anna? If you don't find something or someone to hold onto, this job will devour you." James turned away and then looked back and said, "Maybe it already has."

The door of the back room swung open.

Chance emerged, looking much the same as when he began the interrogation. No blood spatter, dripping sweat or any sign of struggle or even exertion.

Looking at Carlos and then at James, Chance said, "Wow, you missed your calling bro. Shoulda been a makeup artist."

"I dream of that every night," James answered as he handed his brother his phone with the pictures of Carlos appearing to be beaten, bloodied and in pain. "You getting anywhere?"

"Nope." Chance heard his own phone ding with incoming text. He quickly checked it. The message was from Pembe and it simply said BOLO. A second text from her contained two letters; IP. Lexi was giving him a Be On The Look Out warning and her second text indicated the trouble could involve the Iraqi Police. Usually cooperative with allied forces, Iraqi law enforcement could cause a significant amount of hassle if they discovered a few American dark ops interrogating one of their citizens in their own backyard.

"What?" James asked, as he began cleaning the

paint and makeup off Carlos.

"Change of plans. We need to move. See what the boss can do to get us some sort of transport out of here, stat. I'm gonna sedate our guest and hood him. Carlos?"

"What, señor?"

"Don't talk to Domino. Not a word, got it?" Carlos nodded.

James tossed a towel to Carlos who finished wiping his face. He picked up his phone and began dialing. He was interrupted when he spotted Chance grab his phone and read another incoming text.

"Never mind," Chance proclaimed with a smile. "Transportation has been arranged."

Lexi offered use of her own vehicle, which she had recently outfitted with a nifty little gizmo called a Blue Force Tracker. The BFT allowed a vehicle to link up with satellites and give the locations of friendly and enemy units, maps and routes. Apparently, Lexi was already paying off her debt.

"I'll get our wheels, you get everyone ready to run," Chance said before he slipped out the door.

He remained close to the containers and in the shadows as he scanned for their escape vehicle. He had no idea what he was looking for, but he understood how Lexi operated. She'd leave some sort of clue. He kept his head low as he slithered through the area reserved for parking that was used mostly by the staff employed at the nearby medical facility. Chance noticed a sleek, black BMW that got his hopes up, but as he approached the car, he didn't see anything indicating it was Lexi's car. Chance had always believed that one's personal car was a direct reflection of its owner. The racy BMW would've been a perfect match for Lexi. Chance continued his search, hoping to find another high-end, fun-to-drive, get-away car. Then something caught his eye. A glint of red flashed from a windshield. Chance cautiously approached what amounted to little more than a bucket of rust, on four bald tires. Sure enough, a small red rose rested inside on the dashboard. Pembe.

Chance circled the Toyota pickup with a dilapidated topper. He quickly hopped inside. The springs in the seats nearly poked through the ragged upholstery directly into his ass. According to this fine piece of machinery, Lexi had a wide streak of redneck hidden beneath her sleek exterior. Chance was feeling a little pessimistic about the odds of them actually making it beyond the razor wire fence in this pitiful junk heap. Then he started the engine. The motor didn't purr. It *roared*.

Chance's pessimism was gone. *That's more like it, baby*. He smiled as he stepped on the gas and drove it as inconspicuously as possible back to CHU number eight. James had Domino hooded, cuffed and ready to transport. With Anna's help, they quickly secured him in the cargo box. He was about to experience one miserably bumpy ride, however, James had generously doped him to the extent that he wouldn't care.

"That's sharp," James commented as he took in the not-so-beautiful appearance of the Toyota.

"It's what's under the hood that counts, bro. Wait till you hear this little sweetheart turn all her ponies loose," Chance replied as he slid back behind the wheel.

Luckily, the humble pick-up had an extended cab, but still, space was limited. Carlos and Anna piled into the cramped confines of the back seat, while James slid into the passenger seat.

"Hang on," Chance said as he glanced in the rearview mirror while slamming his foot down on the gas pedal. He spotted a barrage of Iraqi Police vehicles descending upon the compound. By the way they were driving, they weren't coming in for a social visit. "Nothing like cutting it close."

James first started digging in the glove compartment before moving on to searching under the floor mat. Finally, he found a small device that resembled a watch battery.

"What's that?" Anna asked nervously, knowing detonating devices came in all shapes and sizes.

"The BFT," James answered. He pulled out his phone and typed in a nine-digit code. Immediately, his screen transformed into a map. Their location was indicated by a blue dot. Enemy units were highlighted in red, friendly units in green, various routes and locations favorable for escape quickly snaked across the map.

"Take a left and hammer down," James said.

"That's not a road," Anna stated as she looked around trying to find something to hold on to.

"Off-road time," Chance laughed. "Welcome to my kind of fun."

"This little buggy might have an impressive motor, but the tires and suspension leave a little to be desired," James commented as he held his phone up, trying to study the map despite the rough ride. "Try to keep this thing in one piece, will ya!"

The Toyota kicked up dust as they cut across the expanse of desert.

"We're gonna come to some sort of road in another mile. Once you get there, hang a right," James said.

"What's our destination, señor?" Carlos asked as he gripped tightly to the seat in front of him.

"I think it'll be in another few miles," James answered as he typed more commands into his phone.

"You think?" Chance asked. "Is it going to surprise us?"

"Come on, boss," James said under his breath as he stared at his phone impatiently.

"Should I be concerned?" Chance yelled as he wheeled the pickup in a wild right turn onto a dirt road.

Suddenly James' serious demeanor was busted by a wide grin. "We're about to upgrade our vehicle boys, and girl."

Chance scanned the horizon and saw nothing. Then he felt it before he actually heard it: the rhythmic chop of rotors slicing through the air. He leaned forward and saw the descending chopper.

"Seriously?" Chance asked in surprise.

"Compliments of the OGA," James replied.

"I'm feeling spoiled."

Chance slammed on the brakes only a few feet away from where the Blackhawk touched down. They swiftly unloaded Domino and half dragged him into the bird. After everyone was loaded, Chance ran back to the Toyota. He yanked a few sticks of C4 out of his backpack and wired it to the undercarriage of the pickup. He attached a three-minute detonator, pressed start and ran.

He hopped into the chopper, yelling, "Go! Go!"

The pilot lifted off immediately and banked west to get as much distance between them and the upcoming demise of their humble get-away vehicle. James, Chance, Carlos and Anna stared out the window and watched as the small Toyota blew apart in a violent explosion. A thick black plume of smoke slowly rose into the sky.

"Sorry Lexi," Chance said softly, knowing she'd understand the necessity of ridding any evidence and preventing it from getting into the wrong hands. He checked his mental scorecard. There was no doubt that Lexi had just paid off a big chunk of her debt to him. She was turning out to be a useful ally in this unfriendly world.

Chapter Fourteen

Langley, Virginia

Gabrielle O'Connor's heels clicked smartly on the marble tiling as she strode quickly down the hall. The chief forensics officer from the U.S. Army Criminal Investigation laboratory in Ft. Gillem, Georgia, was awaiting her call. She had been in a briefing with the deputy of Homeland Security regarding the two prisoners that were found in Fallujah last week trying to match them up with any Missing Persons reported in the past three years. When she was notified that the preliminary results regarding DNA tests on the prisoners' bodies were in, she quickly excused herself and made her way back to the privacy of her own office.

These past six days had been a whirlwind within both the CIA and FBI, as Intel slowly came in regarding an impending attack within the borders of the United States. As word spread throughout the terrorism network that the Americans discovered and are now working on finding the identities of the two bodies taken from Domino's residence, the typical frequent chatter picked up by various sources had decreased to almost nothing. Gabrielle and the rest of the intelligence community realized what this meant. The terrorists were buckling down, maintaining radio silence and moving quickly into the final stages of a planned attack.

After the narrow exodus from Camp Cropper, O'Connor directed Chance, James, and Anna, to take Carlos and Domino and relocate to another black site in Poland. Knowing that time was running out, Chance was furiously interrogating Domino, ever so slowly breaking him down and extracting bits and pieces of information from him. So far, they had learned that the prisoners had been kidnapped nearly three years ago; they were young Caucasian men, not from the Middle East.

Back in the States, O'Connor, along with a full task force dedicated solely to finding the identity of the two prisoners, worked feverishly around the clock. The bodies of the prisoners arrived in the U.S. the night after their discovery and were transported directly to the lab in Georgia. Even with DNA testing underway, without narrowing the database, finding a match would take far too long to thwart the attack. The men's identities had been stolen and somewhere two imposters were about to wreak havoc on innocent people. Were they reporters? Law enforcement? Cab drivers? They could be anyone, anywhere.

Gabrielle's cell phone rang and when she checked the number, she quickly answered, "Yes?"

"They were taken from the JJRTC," Chance's voice said a clipped tone.

O'Connor felt her knees go weak. The James J. Rowley Training Center was located just outside of Washington D.C. Its main purpose: to train agents for the Secret Service.

"They were in training to be Secret Service?" she asked in disbelief, trying to keep her voice low so as not to attract unwanted attention.

"That's what I just got out of him, and believe me, it wasn't easy. DNA results yet?"

"I was about to find out."

"Ok. Keep me posted."

Gabrielle slipped her phone into her pocket, feeling stunned. The FBI, CIA and NSA had all had the misfortune of having been thoroughly penetrated by foreign spies. More than 110 years in existence, and not once had the Secret Service dealt with a mole within its organization. A breach of this magnitude would seem impossible. Now, however, the facts were beginning to indicate otherwise.

The phone call with the chief forensics director in Georgia only lasted a few minutes. He gave her the prisoners' genetic profiles, with basic information that was already known: they were Caucasian, young and male. More information would require a narrower search perimeter. Fortunately, Chance had just given that to her. She quickly forwarded the results to one of the CIA's most brilliant analysts, Richard Jacobson. He also happened to be one of the few people that had been involved in Chance's career working with O'Connor from the beginning. He was equally as good at keeping secrets as he was manipulating technology and digging up information. Gabrielle was going to need him to utilize all of those talents. She pulled out her cell and pushed one number.

"Did you get the file I just sent?" she asked as soon as she heard Jacobson's voice on the line.

"Just received them."

"Good. I want you to focus on matching those results with all the recruits enrolled at the JJRTC going back four years."

After a moment of silence, Jacobson said, "Secret Service? Wow. Not good."

"Just find the match and call me immediately. Do not, I repeat, *do not* go to anyone else with this information."

"Of course."

"Thanks. And hurry."

Gabrielle put her phone down on her desk and tried to wrap her mind around the fact that there could be two assassins standing next to President John Dawkins at this very moment. She scooted her chair closer to her computer and began typing in commands. She looked up the names of every agent on Presidential detail and felt a tiny amount of relief when she discovered that all the agents responsible for protecting the President up close and personal had been on the payroll for over five years. Then she began scanning through the files of all the agents on protection detail. There were over three thousand Special Agents. There were those assigned to the President's family members, Vice President and his family, pre-congressmen, past presidents, prominent politicians; the list was long.

When her cell phone rang, she jumped. She glanced at the clock and was amazed that an hour had flown by since she had sent the file to Jacobson. She felt her heart race when she realized that he was possibly calling her with a match.

"Yes?"

"I found the matches. Jared Schmitz and Wyatt Jenners. They both graduated from the program three years ago. I dug up records that appeared to state that they were both accepted into the Uniformed Division and assigned to separate field offices out of the country. But, I can't find a trace of their involvement in the Secret Service after that."

"That's when they made the switch," Gabrielle stated softly.

"Yes. And get this; they were both only children with deceased parents and very little family."

"So, not a lot of people noticed when they

disappeared."

"Except they didn't. They may not exist on the Secret Service payroll, but they both have active bank accounts and credit cards. Addresses in California and New Mexico. Neither one is on social media.

Jacobson continued, "I'd imagine we will find timely tax returns and credible paper trails leading to normal U.S. citizens. This isn't an amateur operation. We're dealing with pros."

"How does this even happen?" Gabrielle asked.

"With all the information they harvested from Schmitz and Jenners, our imposters could've created completely new, entirely believable American men that could withstand even strictest of scrutiny.

"Even that of the Secret Service?"

"Prior to this, I would've said no. With our current information, I'm afraid we both have to admit that it's not only possible, but probable."

Gabrielle sighed, thinking of her next move. Somehow, she would have to weed out two highly trained imposters from this very tight-knit organization that prided itself in loyalty and honor, above all else. Trying to convince a Secret Service Agent that one of their own was a traitor would be next to impossible.

"Okay. Thanks Rick. I've got some planning to do."

"Yes you do. I'll keep digging."

"Thanks."

As Gabrielle thought more about approaching the staunch Secret Service Agency, the more she realized she would never fully gain their support. They simply wouldn't believe her, no matter the facts. She would have to create her own Secret Service Agent. Someone who held no bias toward any agency. Someone who truly believed everyone was guilty until proven innocent. Someone who wouldn't be the slightest bit intimidated about infiltrating one of the world's most tight-knit, loyal organizations. Gabrielle picked up her phone and dialed.

"Orion. I need you to come back home as soon as possible. Bring everyone with you."

* * *

Chance padded barefoot into the spacious kitchen, full of the latest appliances and gadgets. James and Carlos were munching on toast and drinking orange juice. Chance walked past them, poured himself a cup of coffee and gazed out through the window into one of the oldest arboretums in the world. Countless exotic trees and bushes imported from remote corners of the world could be found throughout the hundreds of acres surrounding their current location.

"I gotta say, this is hands-down the best safe-house I've stepped foot in," James stated as he spread raspberry jam on another slice of toasted wheat bread. "Did you check out the Knight's Room down the hall?"

"This is not a house, it's a castle. And we're under strict orders not to go snooping around," Chance replied as he turned away from the window and leaned on the granite counter top."

"I was quiet. Besides, there's no one here. Only a few thousand ancient books locked up in some sort of library upstairs, and few old paintings."

"This is the Kornik Castle. It's the seat of the Polish Academy of Sciences."

"So?"

"That means it contains a shit-load of valuable books. Hey, when you were snooping around in the Knight's room, did you happen to see the painting of 'The White Lady'?" Chance asked as he topped off his coffee.

"No. Who's 'The White Lady'?" James asked, not sure if he really wanted to have this conversation. A topic such as this usually ended up making him feel profoundly uneducated. At times, having a genius little brother had negative side-effects.

"Teofila Dzialyriska Szoldrska-Potulicka," Chance rattled off smoothly.

"Your what hurts?" James shot back in

268

irritation.

Carlos cleared his throat and said, "Every night, after midnight, it is rumored that she leaves the painting and goes for a ride with a knight who comes on a black horse."

Chance's eyes lit up. "Yes!"

"How do you know that?" James asked in shock. "Why would anyone know that? It's completely useless knowledge."

Carlos shook his head and replied, "Knowledge is never useless, my friend. I happened to find immense enjoyment from studying art history."

James studied Carlos closely before saying, "You know, I'm coming to realize that you seem to know a little bit about everything. You remind me of him," he said as he pointed toward Chance. "And that's not a compliment."

Chance arched an eyebrow. "I've never been compared to a priest before."

"I'm nothing like him," Carlos replied softly.

"You are if you know obscure facts about unknown paintings hanging on the walls of private castles," James grumbled.

"It's actually a famous painting, bro," Chance stated with a grin.

James groaned loudly. "Someone please shoot me. Why can't I be surrounded with people who are content discussing the Broncos?"

"Wild horses, señor?" Carlos asked.

"Oh no, not me. I'm forced to take part in discussions about some creepy white woman with a name that sounds like a sneeze." James shook his head in frustration and disappointment.

"It's a struggle to always dumb down for you," Chance commented casually.

Fortunate to be blessed with fast reflexes, Chance ducked in plenty of time to dodge the butter knife James hurled at him.

"What's wrong with you people?" Anna asked as she entered the room. She headed straight for the coffee and poured herself a cup.

"Anything new?" Chance asked, leaving the fun and games behind.

"Nothing. I think we need to discuss advancing our methods," Anna replied.

Once they arrived in Poland and were hidden away within the massive, ancient Kornik Castle, Anna had presented a valid argument for allowing a woman, herself, to join in Domino's interrogation. She reiterated what they already knew, that an Islamic man would react differently to a strong woman who acted aggressively towards him. Much more emotion would be evoked, and when emotion took over, secrets were revealed. Even though Chance hated to admit it, Anna was skilled as an interrogator.

Now, watching her sipping coffee, Chance could see she was exhausted. Between the two of them, they were taking turns working Domino over with sleep deprivation, loud, ear-piercing rock music along with fear-inducing threats. Chance used a few painful techniques of his own to convince Domino that cooperation was his best choice. The photos of Carlos' beaten bloody were the most effective. It wasn't that Domino was afraid of Carlos being in pain. He was afraid that his brother was being forced to join the enemy against his will. He continually begged them to kill Carlos. He was willing to lose his brother to death. He was not, however, willing to concede him to America.

"We're done, Princess," Chance said. "I got a call from O'Connor and we're heading back stateside as soon as this fog lifts."

James quit chewing, "This is all crackin' open in a hurry."

"I'm keeping an eye on the radar. I think we should be able to take off in an hour or so. You all should pack up and get ready."

"The bird ready?" James asked after he swallowed his last bite of toast.

"Once this caffeine kicks in, I'll get the pre-flights done," Chance replied. "The plan is to fly the chopper to the Lublin airport. From there we'll board whatever O'Connor has waiting for us."

"Sounds good. You want Doms to be awake, or should I knock him out for the trip?" James asked as he stood and stretched.

"Knock him out."

"Copy that, Stones," James answered as he left to prepare for their departure.

"What will happen to him now?" Carlos piped up.

Chance held up his hands and said, "Not my problem anymore. Once I turn him over to the officials, I'm out of it."

Carlos almost asked another question, but then decided he didn't want to hear the answer. He'd probably find out soon enough. He felt Chance studying him closely. He looked up at him and the American seemed to understand.

"I could lie and tell you that your life will just go back to normal, whatever that is. But, it won't," Chance stated softly.

"But, I haven't done anything wrong."

Chance shrugged. "That's the breaks, Father. Can't choose your family, right?"

"Will I be free to go?"

"Yes, but you will be monitored indefinitely."

"I'll be watched?"

"Monitored."

"What's the difference?"

"There may not necessarily be eyes on the ground looking at you, but every time you make a digital footprint like sign onto a computer, make a phone call, write a check or use a credit card, it will be recorded. If you want details, ask my brother.

It'll creep you out when you find out just how intrusive they can be."

"They? Who's they?"

"Talk to James about it if you really want to know. My advice? Don't find out any more than you have to or it will make you paranoid. Plus, if you don't have anything to hide, why worry?"

"Would you let anyone do that to you?"

Chance laughed, "Nope. But, I've got a lot to hide."

"So, do you think it's over for us or will we be assigned to finish this out?" Anna asked as she slid onto a bar stool next to the island.

"I don't work in the States," Chance answered.

"Why?" Anna asked in surprise.

"Never have. Too risky for me."

"You've worked in some of the most dangerous places this world has to offer and you're telling me that you can't work in the States because it's too risky? Funny." Anna proclaimed with a laugh.

"Too many Justin Beiber fans. I might just lose control of myself and shoot some of them."

Anna rolled her eyes. These past few days she had found herself laughing, against her will, at Chance's dry wit, or even worse, almost involved in a conversation with him. Oddly enough, despite the incredible pressure to extract information from Domino, Chance didn't appear rattled or worried. He was a consummate professional, intensely focused on completing this operation.

"How come you can never answer a question?" Anna asked.

"Ask me the right question, and I'll answer it." Chance flashed a rare smile causing Anna to do a double take.

His smile transformed his face into someone she recognized from a previous life. When she first met him in Russia, he had smiled at her a lot. That image of him, smiling, perfect white teeth and twinkling blue eyes had been burned into her memory. Granted, he was pretending to be someone he wasn't, but it was someone she would never forget.

"Fog's lifting, Longshot. You better get things ready to fly. Are you sure you know how to fly that chopper?"

Chance only rolled his eyes.

"Fine. I'm gonna go pack up," Anna said as she stood up, drained the remainder of her coffee into the stainless steel sink and walked out.

Chance watched as she exited the room, then turned his attention to Carlos who had been silently listening to their exchange. "She's right. Better get your things together, Father."

"What does the image on your gun mean?" Carlos asked.

Chance smiled and pulled his gun out from his belt and ran his finger over the etching.

"I just thought it would look cool."

"You told me about the stars," Carlos replied. "Rigel and Betelgeuse. The brightest stars in Orion."

Chance's eyes widened. "I did, huh?"

"You go by the name Orion, so I understand the stars. What do the dice mean?"

Looking at the image on his gun, Chance paused, weighing the risks of revealing any more to the priest. Finally, he said, "The dice represent my true identity. See how the stars of Orion are partially hidden behind the dice? This image reminds me that my identity as Orion, my career, is never more important than who I really am. It's my daily struggle, to keep those stars behind the dice."

Carlos was stunned at the man's genuine revelation. In that moment, Carlos understood why he had wanted to trust this American from the moment he met him. Orion was doing his best to be a good man.

"Thank you. God bless you," Carlos held out his hand.

Chance hesitated as he looked at the priest's outstretched hand. Then he met the handshake in a firm grip. "I hope you find peace after all of this."

Carlos left the kitchen to prepare for departure. As he made his way down the hall he nearly ran into James as he rounded the corner.

"Excuse me, señor James," he said quickly.

James smiled and patted him on the back. "You okay, Father? You look tired."

"So do you."

"We all do," James agreed. "Are you ready for this?"

"Señor Orion explained things…how my life might be, once this is all over."

"He did? Huh. I wonder if his coffee was laced with something," James replied, surprised anytime Chance got chatty.

Carlos glanced back toward the kitchen. "He's not Shay tan, or evil. I believe underneath, he's a good man."

Now, James really looked shocked. "It was in *your* coffee, too!"

"He has you to thank for that," Carlos stated quietly. "I heard you talking to Anna, back in Iraq. How you remind him that he is human, how you didn't let his training turn him into a mindless killer. You didn't allow him to become a machine."

James was speechless.

Carlos stared down at the floor and whispered, "I failed Dominique. I couldn't do what you did, señor James. I let my brother turn into someone who kills innocent people."

James swallowed hard. This was a conversation he had no idea how to continue.

"Walk with me; we need to get packing," James said as he began walking down the hall.

Carlos matched his stride while James talked.

"This is the sort of shit I try not to let myself dwell on. The 'what-ifs'. What if I hadn't been there while my brother went through his training? What if I wasn't involved in most of his operations? What if he had never gotten captured and tortured?"

"And?"

"There's always going to be a lot of unanswerable "what-ifs," but there is one thing I'm absolutely certain about."

"What's that?" Carlos asked curiously.

"Regardless of my action, or inaction, my brother would have never become a terrorist."

"Oh."

"Now, it works the other way, too. There are some people who aren't capable of using their talents and abilities for good. There will always be people in this world convinced that terror is the only way to get their message across. You did not fail your brother, Carlos. There was nothing you could've ever done to stop him from becoming who is now."

The two of them walked the rest of the distance in silence. Before going their separate ways, James turned to Carlos and said, "I think next time we should all refrain from drinking castle coffee."

Carlos smiled. "Thanks, señor James. For everything."

"You're welcome."

Chance pulled on his lined leather coat and black stocking cap. The weather in Warsaw was blustery and snowflakes were skittering through the air. A full-fledged winter storm would be moving into the area later on tonight. The fog had lifted for the time being and they had a narrow window of relatively clear skies through which to navigate. He stomped his feet as he stood outside the Bell 222. The luxurious private helicopter was yet another perk bestowed upon him during this operation. He was seriously beginning to change his negative attitude about becoming a legitimate CIA agent. The bird would be about as much fun to fly as his Camaro was to drive. The last time he had the opportunity to fly a Bell was when he commandeered one in Belize in order escape a hostile environment that he may, or may not have caused. At any rate, Chance was looking forward to lifting off and enjoying the ride.

James pushed a heavily sedated Domino out onto the helipad in a wheelchair. They were followed by Anna and Carlos, toting their duffel bags.

"There are not enough seat belts in this thing to make me happy," James grumbled loudly as he strapped himself into one of the soft leather seats.

"Relax. No one's better at this than me," Chance stated as he revved up the rotor speed.

"Said the guy who once flew a plane into the side of a barn."

"I did that on purpose," Chance replied as he checked the gauges. "Check it out," he added pointing behind him. "A minibar."

James glanced to the rear of the cabin. "Now that's what I'm talkin' about. Finally, a tried and true method of coping with your piloting skills. Alcohol."

Chance only smiled as he throttled-up and pulled back on the lever. "Up, up and away," he commented to himself.

No one said a word as the Bell lifted off the helipad. Within seconds, the Kornik Castle was nothing but a memory as the turboprops kicked in, sending the powerful helicopter into top speed. Within an hour, Chance gently brought the bird down to earth at the small Lublin airport, where another luxury vehicle awaited them. This time it was Gabrielle's own private jet, a Bombardier Challenger.

James wasted no time transferring Domino into the jet. Anna, Carlos and Chance grabbed their luggage and ran onto the plane. A uniformed, armed pilot along with a similarly attired copilot met them at the entrance. After ID's and credentials were verified, everyone strapped down and prepared for takeoff. The runway and Poland gradually disappeared as the jet slowly rose above the heavy winter clouds. Exhaustion was beginning to show its effects. No one had had much rest since they had left the United States, almost two weeks ago. James popped in his ear buds and closed his eyes. Carlos stared blankly out the window. Chance leaned his head back and appeared lost in thought. Anna watched him. Her nagging curiosity prevented her from closing her eyes and drifting off. Glancing at James and Carlos, she decided to make her move. She quickly left her seat and slid across the narrow aisle to sit next to Chance. He showed zero reaction to Anna's change in proximity.

Finally, he softly said, "This isn't a good place to try to kill me sweetheart."

Anna sighed. "I'm not trying to kill you. Just drop it, ok?"

Without looking at her he replied, "I thought that was your grand plan."

"Maybe it is, but it's not happening now."

Chance smiled and nodded. "So what can I do you for? Gum? Pillow? Ice water perhaps?"

"What's the deal with you popping pills all the time?"

That question garnered an immediate reaction; Chance turned his head to stare directly at her. "What?"

"Don't give me that look," Anna snapped. "I've

seen you sneaking around swallowing a handful of pills every time you think no one's looking. You must know O'Connor's got zero tolerance for agents using anything."

Chance thought a moment, reflecting on the past few weeks, his headaches, the relief of the pain pills, and the anxiety he felt over the fact that he only had a couple left. Being dependent upon anything never crossed his mind before this. He simply didn't have an addictive personality. Even though these past few weeks required a bottle or two of Vicodin to manage some painful headaches, he still wasn't concerned about a blossoming addiction. The only change he underwent was to develop some understanding how an addiction could start. Not one to harbor much sympathy for people, much less an addict, Chance came to realize how the spiral into a dependency wasn't always controllable.

He grinned at Anna and shook his head.

"I guess I wasn't sneaky enough. You caught me. I'm hooked on crack. There, you have it. Happy?"

Anna nearly slapped him. Instead, she said, "How come I had to take over for you in Kuwait? You were in charge of catching Mario, yet at the last minute, after you'd already gone and done the hard part; I get a phone call that I'm needed to finish the job."

"So that was you? I bet your ego grew immensely knowing you were called in to finish up one of my jobs."

"My curiosity certainly did. What happened?"

Chance leaned in closer and said, "I know you're Russian, but you do know about that whole curiosity and the cat thing, right?"

Anna answered, "I'm not a cat."

"No. But you are a pest."

"I just want to know what's wrong with you."

Chance laughed softly as he leaned his head back and closed his eyes. "Jesus, Princess, you really don't wanna go there."

"Don't call me Princess."

"Don't ask me questions."

"Just answer something for once and I'll quit asking."

Chance inhaled deeply. He was beginning to understand the misery suffered by anyone unlucky enough to be interrogated by Anna.

"I couldn't do Kuwait because I was ordered to take a few days off to recover from being blown up."

"Blown up? Really?"

"More like blown out. I got knocked on the head, had a concussion, end of story. There. Was that worth all the effort?"

"So, the pills. They're for your head? Headaches?"

"Between the concussion and the company I've been forced to keep, yeah, I've got some serious headaches," Chance answered with a smile.

"So, O'Connor knows?"

"Of course," Chance lied.

Anna sat back and after a moment of thought and said, "You're an impressive liar."

"Quit flirting with me."

"Can anyone actually tell when you're telling the truth and when you're full of baloney?"

Chance smirked. "I love how you say "baloney." Sounds so serious with that Russian accent. By the way, Americans don't really use that expression much anymore."

Anna couldn't hold back the smile forming on her lips. She shook her head, irritated that she was allowing this man, whom she had hated for years, to somehow make her want to laugh.

"Seriously, is there anyone you don't lie to?" Anna asked. "And if you just turn this around and ask me the same thing, I'll shoot you."

"Ooookay. Isn't it…"

"No. No questions. Just answer mine."

"I thought you were only gonna ask me the pill question. See, you lie too."

"Yes or no. Simple."

Chance tapped his fingers on the arm of his chair. "Is there anyone I don't lie to? Hmmm, let me see. No." Chance grinned. "You're right. It was

283

simple."

"Even James?"

"You asked if there was anyone I didn't lie too. You didn't ask if everyone believed my lies."

"Ah, so James can see through your baloney."

Chance laughed, his chilly eyes holding an unusual twinkle. "Thanks for saying baloney again."

"You're impossible."

Chance closed his eyes and nodded. "I know."

Chapter Fifteen

Langley, Virginia

For the second time in his career, Chance stood within the confines of CIA headquarters in Langley, Virginia. Gabrielle O'Connor's office was spacious and sparsely decorated, yet Chance still felt an itch of claustrophobia just under the surface. At least this time he had James at his side. Having his brother with helped him ease the irritation of Anna's continuing presence. He couldn't give an exact reason why she bothered him so much. She was proving that she was capable of playing with the big boys. Her skills were top-notch. Still, Chance preferred to keep a safe distance from her.

After landing at Reagan International last night, Domino was handed over to heavily armed, CIA operatives and taken to an undisclosed location. Carlos was taken to a safe location and would be held until someone of authority deemed it proper to release him. Chance and James, thinking their jobs were done, headed to a familiar bar deep within the heart of the city, far from politicians and suits and lawyers. The combination of his pain meds and his adversity to losing an ounce of control, Chance abstained from indulging in any alcohol. He rarely drank booze anymore; instead, he sipped on a Coke while laughing at James who had no qualms about clearing his head with more than a few stout drinks. The loud music, the mindless chatter and laughter from the mostly collegiate crowd around them was a perfect decompression remedy. So one could imagine their reaction when they got a call at six in the morning telling them to report to an important meeting at Langley in two hours.

"You don't look good," Chance commented to James, whose red-rimmed eyes squinted in the bright light. He had shoved a baseball cap over the top of his disheveled hair and didn't feel the need to wear anything other than his jeans, boots and a wrinkled shirt from his suitcase.

"Yeah, well I feel just rosy," James answered dryly.

"Probably should've skipped that last drink, huh?"

"More like the last five."

Having the benefit of not suffering from a hangover, and also from having a closet full of pressed shirts and jackets at his small rental apartment near Langley, Chance look a little more polished and ready for business. Even though he rarely spent much time at his apartment, he did always keep a change of clothes and a few essentials just in case plans changed. In his experience, plans changed quickly and often.

"You look pretty," James grumbled at his little brother.

"Thanks, dude."

Anna shook her head as she kept her distance from the brothers. She truly believed she would never see them again after they went their separate ways at the airport last night. With only an awkward handshake and a "stay safe out there" comment from Chance, their goodbyes were brief. Now, for some reason, she felt even more uncomfortable around the Hughes brothers. What bothered her the most, she was coming to realize, was seeing them act normal, especially Chance. He was supposed to be a legendary killer. A machine with no emotions, no remorse, and most of all, no likeability. After spending a few days with him, Anna was discovering he wasn't quite what his reputation advertised.

"Where's the funeral?" James asked suddenly, looking over at Anna, who was doing her best to ignore them both.

"That's not that funny in this business," Chance interrupted, trying not to smile.

James shrugged and stated, "I'm just sayin', since she's always wearing black and looking less than happy."

Before Anna could respond, Chance jumped in once again and said softly, as if he was telling his brother a secret. "That's her spy suit, bro."

James cracked a small smile. He was about to vocalize another observation when the office door swung open and Gabrielle walked in carrying a thick file in one arm and her briefcase in the other. She quickly eyed her three operatives and paused as she studied James.

She walked up close to him, "Are you hung over?"

"I'm pretty sure I'm still drunk," James answered with all the sincerity he could muster.

"How dare you come into my office in that condition," Gabrielle scolded.

"You are the one who wanted me here, with all due respect," James replied.

Gabrielle sighed and shook her head as she walked over to her desk. Controlling either one of the Hughes men was next to impossible. Chance was constantly breaking rules and boundaries. She was used to his insubordination and tolerated it because he got the job done. James on the other hand, rarely blatantly locked horns with her. He was quietly stubborn. Doing his own thing no matter what she said. Fortunately, most of the time, James agreed with her plans and she could always count on him to protect her most valuable operative.

Because of that, she could look past a few flaws.

"Are you going to be able to remember anything discussed here? What I'm proposing needs your utmost attention."

"Relax, O'Connor. I've done a lot more in worse condition than this," James replied as he pulled up a chair.

"So, what's up Boss? Why are the three of us here?" Chance asked as he slowly paced the room.

Gabrielle placed the thick folder and brief case on her desk and leaned a hip against the corner.

"First of all, good work on not only capturing Domino but also on extracting information from him. Because of that and the results of the DNA tests done on those two prisoners found in the basement, we can say with almost 100% certainty that our Secret Service has been infiltrated with two of the enemy."

Chance stopped pacing and Anna stepped closer to the conversation.

"Presidential detail?" Chance asked.

"Doubtful, since those guys have all been in service for at least four years. But, that doesn't mean our imposters can't get close to the President, Vice President and their families. We are doing our best to narrow the search. Domino has orchestrated this and he is not dumb. This plan has been in the making for a long time. The two imposters have taken the ID's of the men you found and created two people that we would never suspect of terroristic acts."

"What were their names?" Chance asked.

"Jared Schmitz and Wyatt Jenners."

"Stupid question, I know, but why not just find two guys walking around with those names?" Chance asked.

"According to the IRS, MasterCard, Social Security, two banks and a couple of post offices, Jared Schmitz lives in California and Wyatt Jenners resides in Arizona."

"Oh. So, then who are the bad guys in the Secret Service?"

Gabrielle looked over at James and raised an eyebrow. "You probably know more on how someone can pull this off than me. Can you help explain?"

James cleared his throat and his fingers played with the zipper on his jacket while he thought a moment.

"Basically, Domino's guys swiped the two recruits from the training facility to harvest their physical identity. The names weren't important except to create the illusion that these men weren't missing at all. They set up these shell accounts and addresses and such in order to keep these two men "alive." Since they were both without much family, this scheme would work for quite a while. Not indefinitely, but Domino wasn't thinking long term.

They just needed a few years to pull this off. So, while Jared and Wyatt appeared to be alive and well, two of Domino's men used everything they could to create new identities. Even though the imposters have unique names, their pasts belong to Jared and Wyatt. All background checks or personal inquiries are automatically routed into the true Americans' histories. All medical records, training, schooling, and digital footprints belong to the dead guys. It took some decent computer hacking skills and digital manipulating to create what appears to be a foolproof identity.

I've dug into how they might have pulled off providing authentic ID markers, such as palm and fingerprints, retinal scans and blood work. Obviously, these physical traits were stolen from our victims, and from what I can tell, they used the real body parts to create true-to-life replicas. Special, ultra-thin latex gloves created with the exact hand prints are fairly easy to make but hard to detect. Retinal scans can also be fooled by a man-made device that has been coded with the same pattern as the actual eye. Costly? Yep. Runs about 10k per eye, but I don't think Domino is too concerned about a budget. Blood type can't be faked, so I think that problem was solved by simply finding two imposters that had the same blood type as the prisoners. You wanna know anything else?"

"God, no, please stop," Chance replied. "How

do you know all this stuff?"

"How do you know about the haunting of the White Lady in a painting hanging in a Polish castle?"

"Focus, please," Gabrielle stated firmly.

"So, what do you need me for?" Chance asked. "This is all interesting and stuff, but I don't work in the States."

"Right. Don't want him killing all those Justin Bieber fans," Anna huffed, drawing surprised looks from everyone in the room.

James looked over at Chance and then back at Anna. He laughed out loud as he proclaimed, "She made a funny! I didn't think it was possible!"

Chance grinned but remained quiet.

"What's wrong with all of you?" Gabrielle asked in frustration. "I'm about to assign you to the most important operation of your careers and you're all acting like this is a comedy."

James pulled himself together and both Chance and Anna perked up at the idea of another operation. Especially one described as "the most important of your career."

"Do I have your attention?" Gabrielle asked, getting nods. "Good. Yes, Chance, you are going to get your first job right here at home." Gabrielle noticed the questions flash across Chance's face. He knew this meant significant changes coming his way, yet she had no doubt he would do this job without a second thought.

"The three of you will be working undercover as Secret Service Agents," Gabrielle stated as she walked around to pull out her chair and sit behind her desk. She opened the thick folder and began pulling out individual files. "Each of you will find your specs in these files, along with all the proper forms of ID you will need."

Chance opened his folder to find a new name on a driver's license, birth certificate, credit cards, Secret Service badges, and all other forms a normal human being requires to prove that they exist.

"There's a lot of information there," Gabrielle motioned toward the folders. "Memorize all of it and destroy everything except the IDs." Gabrielle stood before adding, "You'll be joining me in a private meeting with President Dawkins at three this afternoon." She walked over to James, "Do whatever it takes in order to be sober and ready to work by then."

"Of course."

"And Chance," Gabrielle started as she walked up to him.

"Yes?"

"I need a word with you. Privately."

"I'm outta here. See you later, bro," James stated as he got up out of his chair. "Come on, Princess. That's our cue to disappear."

Anna rolled her eyes and reluctantly followed

James out the door, softly grumbling, "Please stop calling me Princess."

Once the door shut and Gabrielle was alone with Chance she asked, "How are you feeling?"

Not expecting the question, Chance merely shrugged it off and asked, "So, how is this going to play out, O'Connor. What if someone recognizes me? I know it's been a while, but still, there's a risk."

Gabrielle nodded. "Dawkins remembers you from Comanche Point, and I already told him you've been working for me."

"What? Since when?"

"After the so-called "Great Camera Glitch" that left everyone in the dark while you worked the operation in Fallujah. He knew something was up. I had no choice but to tell him."

"Are you in trouble?"

"Not if you can stop Domino's puppets from pulling off this attack."

"If I do, then you'll be okay?"

Gabrielle smiled, slightly surprised at Chance's concern for her own well-being rather than his own possible troubles resulting from being recognized.

"Yes, Chance, I'll be just fine. What about you? Sometimes coming out of the shadows is a little unnerving."

Chance grinned. "I have no idea what it feels like to be unnerved. Not possible. I'm solid."

Gabrielle walked over to her desk shaking her head. "Your surplus of arrogance has never ceased to amaze me."

"So, what happens after this operation? Does everything go back to normal or does the Prez start calling my shots?"

"Honestly, I don't know. If I'm reading Dawkins correctly, I believe he wants you to keep doing what you're doing, but obviously, something will have to change since you are no longer a secret. Our main concern is your protection and with our military backing, we can get you out of the most difficult situations."

"I don't need protection."

"Don't argue with me. You and I both know that your reputation is growing rapidly, along with your list of enemies. There will come a time when you need protection."

"Do whatever you have to do to keep your career on track. Don't worry about me." Chance suddenly snapped his fingers and said, "You know, I just thought of something."

"What?"

"We might have an issue with someone in the Secret Service."

Gabrielle stood straighter. "Out with it Chance. What did you do?"

Chance appeared offended. "I didn't *do* anything, per se. Not wrong, anyhow. Or at least I didn't think so at the time."

"I'm growing old. Quit playing games and just tell me."

"I went out a few times with Cole Silverman."

Gabrielle looked stunned. "Ms. Nicole Silverman, the young woman on presidential detail?"

"That would be her."

"You dated Nicole Silverman? You can't be serious."

"I don't date. We just went out a few times, and no, we certainly were never serious."

Gabrielle sat on the edge of her desk and looked at Chance incredulously.

"What? Why are you looking at me like that?" Chance asked. "I had a little down time last summer. Can't a guy ask a girl out?"

"Why can't 'a guy' go out with a girl who works at the gym, or library, or college, or just about *anywhere* other than the Secret Service?"

"I actually did meet her at the gym. She thought I was funny."

"Well, you're certainly not funny. Or charming. I have no idea how you could convince any woman to date you, especially one as smart as Ms. Silverman."

"I don't date. Like I said, we just went out a few times. Had a few drinks. That's all. No big deal."

"You don't drink."

"I pretended."

"What else did you pretend, since I'm assuming you weren't dumb enough to give her your real name."

"She thinks I'm an airline pilot, named Brian."

"Good God, Chance, why do you always make things so difficult?"

"How was I supposed to know that I'd be working undercover in the Secret Service? I was under the perception that I don't operate in the States."

"Well that was a misconception now, wasn't it?" Gabrielle stood up and sighed, thinking about how to smooth over yet another bump in the endless road. She walked up to Chance and pulled the folder out of his hands. "Well, I guess we'll have to redo all your IDs again. Did Brian-The-Pilot have a last name?"

"Wilson."

Gabrielle jotted down the name and then looked up and asked, "Like the Beach Boy, Brian Wilson?"

"I have no idea O'Connor. That was waaaay before my time."

Gabrielle jotted down a few more notes while she shook her head.

"You are something else, Hughes."

Chance only shrugged. He realized that when his boss resorted to calling him by his last name, he was rapidly on his way to landing on her shit list.

"How close were you two?" Gabrielle asked, as she closed the folder.

"I'm not close to anyone."

Gabrielle looked him in the eye and said, "Let me clarify, since you seem to be extra dense this morning. How close did she *think* you two were? Did you sleep with her?"

"Why in the world would that make any difference?"

"I'll take that as a yes," Gabrielle muttered. "It makes a difference because women tend to get their hearts involved when you take them to bed. What I need to know is, how much hatred is this woman going to have for you when she discovers you lied and took advantage of her? You already have one angry woman waiting in the wings to seek revenge. This operation can't handle any extra drama brought on by your jilted lovers. Does Ms. Silverman need to be removed from Presidential Detail during the duration of this operation?"

"I'm sure she'll be surprised that I'm not Pilot Brian, but after the shock wears off, I'm sure she'll be fine. She's a grown woman."

"Who also happens to be an excellent marksmen and carries at least one loaded weapon at all times." Gabrielle thought a moment and shook her head before saying, "You know, you shouldn't underestimate Nicole. She has some serious skills. There was a time when I was actually interested in her."

"Hey, great minds think alike."

"Except I was interested in *hiring* her, not in whatever the hell you thought you were doing with her."

"Ah, don't overreact. She'll be fine. I just thought I should tell you about her."

"How thoughtful of you."

"I never thought it would be a big deal. You want me to send you names of all my potential dates in the future?"

"Is there that many? You aren't really that good with women."

"Thanks."

Gabrielle paused a moment before saying, "I'll leave her alone for the time being, but if she distracts you in anyway, I'm pulling her out."

"How come you weren't worried about Anna distracting me?"

"Is she?"

"No."

"That's because she's trained to handle liars and jaded assassins."

"That's because she is one," Chance answered softly. "Thanks to you."

"Oh, enough of this. Now, back to my original question, how are you feeling?"

"Why? Do I look shitty?" Chance snapped, perturbed at the question.

"Not overly, but I think it's reasonable to inquire after someone's health after they sustained a serious head injury a short time ago."

"It was more than three weeks ago. I'm fine."

"Some head injuries take months to completely heal. I know the circumstances forced you to return to the field much sooner than you should have."

"Seriously? I've been banged up a lot worse before and you haven't been too worr—wait just a second," Chance said suddenly as an idea sprung to the surface. "Have you been talking to Anna?"

"Of course I talk to Anna. She is one of my employees."

"And I'm still pissed about that." Chance then smiled and pointed a finger at his boss. "Don't even try to deny that she told you I was popping pills the past few weeks."

"She may have brought up the fact that you were self-medicating on occasion."

"For the love of Pete," Chance said as he ran his hand through his long hair. "I took a few Tylenols whenever I felt a headache coming on. That's it."

"So, you're still having headaches?"

"I'm feeling one coming on right now," Chance answered sarcastically. "This is too stupid to even waste another moment on. Is there anything else? If not, I'm outta here."

"Fine. I trust you, Chance, but if there's a problem, you'd tell me, right?"

"Nope. Probably not."

Gabrielle looked at Chance, trying to figure out if she should let the subject matter go. She decided it was only her choice.

"I'll see you at three," Gabrielle stated, stuffing papers into her briefcase. "Oh, and get a haircut. A shave wouldn't kill you either. You look like a hippie."

"Thanks, ma. I promise to look and act civilized. No worries."

"I'm always worried."

Chance smirked and gave her a quick wink before he strolled out the door.

* * *

True to his word, by the time Chance was escorted to the Situation Room, in the basement beneath the West Wing of the White House, he had donned a well-tailored suit, a haircut and a fresh shave. He nodded as he passed the Secret Service agents standing guard outside the door and once inside immediately began taking inventory of his new surroundings. Neither the President, nor Gabrielle was present yet, so he moved around at ease. James and Anna were already inside, sitting at opposite ends of the long table.

"Sobered up?" Chance asked his brother, whose appearance did seem to have improved since this morning's meeting.

"I'm fine."

Chance's eyes passed over Anna, though aiming to be brief, he couldn't help it; his glance lingered a touch longer than he intended. She looked stunning in her navy blue pin stripe pantsuit -professional, dangerous, and completely unavailable. It was a hard combination for Chance to resist.

Turning his focus away from something as irrational as an attraction toward Anna, he walked around the room, noticing the innovational whisper walls, the privacy telephone booths and all the other bells and whistles that a room such as this required. Six flat-screened TVs lined the front wall, while a shelf held several keyboards, remote controls and other nifty devices used to illustrate plans, dissect maps and pin point locations.

Chance peeked into one of the two the smaller Watch rooms as well as the President's Briefing room, which were attached to the Situation Room, before walking to the head of the table, pausing at the President's chair.

"Welcome to the Woodshed," Chance stated softly.

"How did you know we called this room 'The Woodshed'?" Gabrielle asked as she entered the room.

Chance just shrugged and circled around the table.

Gabrielle eyed him carefully and nodded in approval. "Good job. You clean up nicely. I hardly recognize you." Then she looked at James, who had donned a sports coat and slacks that appeared to be somewhat less wrinkled than his morning's attire.

"Feeling better?" she asked.

He smiled and held up his coffee. "I'm good to go. But I do need to talk to you about something."

"Now?"

"Well, yeah. I happened to see that I have a new identity for this operation. Seems odd since I'll be outside, doing what I'm supposed to do which is tech support. No alias needed," James stated firmly.

"Before we go any further, I want to say that I had this room swept for surveillance a half an hour ago. All devices have been deactivated. Whatever is said in here is confidential," Gabrielle stated. "Including your real names. Once we step out of this room, however, only use the aliases given to you for this operation."

"Which brings me back to my issue, O'Connor," James spoke up. "My job description doesn't require an alias."

"Not this time. You'll be *inside* conducting surveillance."

"What the hell? I'm not trained for that shit."

"Please don't talk like that around me. I think you'll manage."

"I'm supposed to memorize that entire folder?"

James asked incredulously. "Remember, I'm not him," he added, pointing at his little brother.

Chance, finding the situation amusing, jumped in. "Yeah, he hardly remembers who I am half the time."

"Nobody knows who you are, ever," James shot back grumpily.

"I know. I'm good."

"Stop. Just stop, you two." Gabrielle sighed. "This is why I hardly ever meet with the two of you together." Gabrielle pointed at the brothers in turn. "James, you'll do fine. Chance, I spoke with Ms. Silverman and informed her of the situation. I wanted her to have time to process everything before she saw you."

"Okay," Chance replied. "When's Dawkins getting here?"

"Soon," Gabrielle answered as she settled into a chair.

"Who is Ms. Silverman and what is the situation?" James asked.

"Nothing," Chance replied quickly, only adding to James curiosity.

James laughed. "Oh, it's something, bro. What did you do?"

"Why does everyone assume I did something?"

"Because you have a history of doing things that lead to *situations*."

"Enough," Gabrielle interrupted.

Everyone stood up when the door opened. President Dawkins walked in and took a quick survey of the room. "Hello, everyone." Then he walked directly up to Chance and held out his hand.

"It's been a long time, Sergeant Hughes."

Chance met the President's firm grip and replied, "Yes, it has sir. And please, call me Chance."

"From what I hear, you've been busy keeping the enemy at bay. Once again, on behalf of this country, thank you. It's too bad people never get to know some of our most brave and heroic fighters out there keeping us safe."

"I think it's best if we remain in the shadows, sir."

Dawkins studied the young man in front of him. Unlike their first meeting, Chance was now healthy, strong, and even more guarded than he had been at Comanche Point. Dawkins clearly recalled the feeling he had when he first looked into the young Marine's eyes as he presented him with the prestigious Medal of Honor. There had been so much intensity, anger and turmoil brewing within them. Now, looking into those same grayish-blue eyes, the intensity was still obvious, but any emotion or clue to his thoughts was gone. Chance was no longer struggling with controlling the damage done to him in Afghanistan. Whatever mental scars he carried from his ordeal were secured and carefully guarded behind a thick sheet of icy control.

Turning to acknowledge the others in the room, Dawkins held out his hand to James saying, "I believe we met before, Mr. Hughes. Good to see you again."

"Call me James. Good to see you, too, Mr. President."

"It's unfortunate we have to meet under these circumstances," Dawkins stated. "Miss Petrova. I don't believe we've met before."

"No, sir, we have not," Anna replied as she shook his hand.

Turning to Gabrielle, Dawkins said, "Let's get down to business."

The five of them sat down at the long table. Gabrielle did a quick run-down of the situation.

"You mean to tell me that Domino planted two of his men in our Secret Service? That's impossible. The Secret Service has never had a breach of security," Dawkins said. "I've known most of the agents for years."

"I know this is difficult to hear, sir, but we are fairly certain there are two imposters posing as agents. This plan has been years in the making. The imposters could have been agents for as long as three years, since the disappearances of the two hostages."

Dawkins leaned back in his chair, trying to

visualize the many faces responsible for protecting him and his family.

"Do we have any idea who they may be?" he asked.

"We're looking at anyone who came into the agency within the last three years. That means everyone on your detail is safe, since they have all been in service for much longer than that."

"What about my wife? My children?"

"There are a few agents that fit the timeline, although, so far, their backgrounds are solid. We are looking closely at every agent that fits the timeline."

"How could this happen?" Dawkins asked, the seriousness of the matter weighing heavier with each passing moment. "All agents have such stringent training and guidelines. Plus, don't they all have to take a polygraph before they are accepted into the program?"

Gabrielle turned toward Chance and asked, "How many times have you taken a poly?"

He shrugged and said, "I don't know. Ten, fifteen maybe."

"How many times have you passed?"

"Every time."

"And how many times have you actually told the truth while taking them?"

"None," Chance answered.

Gabrielle turned back to the President and said, "Although not common, polys can be beaten. These imposters obviously received some of the same training Chance had regarding beating a polygraph."

"Still, there are so many variables that had to be overcome for them to break the system," Dawkins argued, unable to believe the solidity of the Secret Service could possibly be broken.

"The short story is that Domino's clan kidnapped two Americans who were recruits at the JJRTC. Their identities were stolen and two imposters took their spots. The long version is much more complex, and if you do want to hear the details, I recommend you talk to James. He would be able to explain it all much better than I."

Dawkins looked at the older Hughes and nodded. "I'd appreciate that. I know we are short on time right now, but I'd like to hear more about how the enemy could possibly infiltrate such a tight-knit organization. If there is any way to prevent from this ever happening again, I need to know so we can implement appropriate safeguards."

"Yes, sir."

"I will see if I can meet with you later on today."

James nodded.

"So, what is the plan?" Dawkins asked. "And why am I the only one being notified of this? Shouldn't the Vice President and the Secretary of Defense be notified immediately?"

"Sir, you and I will meet with them later, along with Homeland. I think it's best that you are the only one who knows the real identity of our operatives. Especially Chance. I am aware that this assignment will likely expose him, but I'd rather deal with that issue once the imposters have been flushed out."

"Okay, I agree we don't need any unnecessary attention," Dawkins replied.

"The imposters are obviously highly trained, by us and their own regime, and will sense any change of actions in the people they are guarding. The more people who act even the slightest suspicious, the more likely they will catch on and initiate their plans. We can't let this happen before we are able to detect who they are and prevent whatever attack they are planning. It's imperative we all go about our normal business. The moment we captured Domino and discovered those bodies, our enemies have been on high alert. They don't know if we've uncovered the identities of the dead prisoners, and will be vigilantly watching for any signs that we've figured out their plan."

"How are we utilizing these three?" Dawkins asked as he looked at Chance, James and Anna.

"They will be Secret Service Agents. Now, I know the other agents will wonder what is going on, and we will tell them that my agents are from the Secret Service Investigative Unit and they are conducting a routine security check. Under no circumstances will we tell the other agents what is really going on."

"How will they be deployed?"

"Chance will be on your detail. James will be assigned to Vice President Evans and Anna will be with your wife and children."

Dawkins looked at each of the agents who would be responsible for the most important people in his life.

"Don't worry, Mr. President," Chance suddenly spoke up. "We won't let anything happen to you or your family."

Dawkins met Chance's eyes that seemed to hold a laser-like focus, and zero self-doubt. His confidence was contagious. Dawkins nodded his head. "I know that I'm sitting in a room with the best operatives this country has to offer."

"You are, sir," Gabrielle agreed. "These three give us the best opportunity to stop this attack."

Dawkins asked, "How long do you expect this operation to last?"

"We don't know, but if our intelligence is accurate, our enemy appears to be preparing for the fall-out from this attack. There's been some chatter about an American economic crash and worldly disruption of trade and general chaos generated because of whatever is planned. If I had to guess, I would say the attack is scheduled to occur within the next couple of weeks. A month at most. We need to go over your schedule, Mr. President, and look at all the high-profile events you will be attending as well as any events taking place here at the White House. Anytime you, your family, the Vice President and other cabinet members are together in one location is a potential target."

"What about the meeting with the Prime Minister of Israel next week?"

"Yes, that is one event we will watch closely. It would be a perfect opportunity for an attack on the leaders of the two countries our enemy hates most," Gabrielle answered.

Chance leaned forward. "That's it. That's when it's going to happen."

"We haven't received any intelligence verifying that, Chance," Gabrielle argued. "Although the Israelis have stepped up their security, as well. They, too, are looking at this meeting as a possible target."

"Are they aware of the latest developments?" Dawkins asked.

"Enough of them to raise some concern," Gabrielle answered. "Earlier today I spoke with my contact in Moussad and Israeli Intelligence is incredibly up to speed on everything. I can only surmise that they have agents on the ground, imbedded in the Domino organization, in order for them to have gathered the information they have."

"Never underestimate Israeli Intelligence capabilities," Chance stated with a slight smile.

"Do the Israelis believe we should postpone the meeting?" President Dawkins asked.

"Absolutely not and neither do I. That move would tip our hand. No, everything must go on as planned," Gabrielle answered.

"There is a gala planned for after that meeting. My family will be there, as well as Vice President Evans and his family. We will all be in one location. Isn't that too risky?"

Chance spoke up. "You receive over thirty threats per day, sir. It comes with your job, right?"

"I understand that."

"My job is eliminating threats. You focus on doing your job, sir, and I *will* do mine."

Dawkins looked hard at Chance. The operative's attitude bordered on cocky, but there was no arguing with the fact that the guy wasn't familiar with failure. Chance Hughes would do his job, or die trying.

"When will you start?" Dawkins asked.

"As soon as this meeting is over," Gabrielle answered.

Dawkins stood up. "Okay, then." He looked at the three operatives standing before him. "I guess I'll be seeing more of you. Especially you, Chance. If you're half as good as your reputation, I should have nothing to worry about."

Chance shook the President's hand. "You have nothing to worry about, sir."

* * *

After using one of the smaller conference rooms to change into their new Brooks Brothers' suits, Chance and James strapped on their holsters, double checked they were carrying their new credentials and stepped out into the hallway. There they met up with Anna, who had also undergone a transformation. Gabrielle was also there, softly conversing with the attractive female Secret Service agent standing next to her.

The agent was of average height, but she held herself confidently, making herself appear taller than what she actually was. Her wavy blond hair, that bordered on unruly at times, was neatly controlled in a tight bun. With a hint of temper glowing in her hazel eyes, the woman's focus quickly left O'Connor and their conversation the moment the Hughes brothers entered the hallway. She briefly eyed James before pinning her gaze onto the man she thought she knew.

"Fancy meeting you here, *Brian*," Nicole stated without an ounce of friendliness.

Chance smiled and held out his hand, "Cole, good to see you again. I guess we'll be working together."

Caught off guard by the look in his eyes, she hesitated before she met his handshake with a firm grip. The man she had known was friendly, engaging, and genuinely seemed to care about her. She saw nothing resembling those traits in the frigid hardness glistening in Brian's eyes now. He almost looked a different man altogether.

"Call me Nicole. What am I supposed to call you, again?" she asked.

"Brian. I may not be a pilot, but I'm still just Brian."

Forgetting that she still gripped his hand, Cole studied him closely, trying to discern anything other than cool detachment in his manners. Her keen instincts told her that below his controlled exterior, something dangerous and wild was lurking.

"I think we're way past believing you're 'just Brian'," Nicole replied, suddenly pulling her hand away from his.

"Believe what you want, Cole."

"*Ni*cole, please."

What she wanted to believe was that this man was an airline pilot who grew up in New Jersey, played hockey and cheered on the Patriots. She really wanted to believe that he hadn't fooled her so completely. She thought she knew him, and even worse, she had trusted him.

The Brian she had met had been an immediate attraction. Newly separated from her husband of five years, Nicole hadn't been looking to date, or hook up with anyone. She just needed a break from drama. Her career in the Secret Service and her advancement into the Presidential Protection Detail was killing her marriage. She wanted to focus on her own life, her own career and have some much-needed solitude from an increasingly demanding husband.

She had always worked off her stress physically, either logging miles outside on trails, or in the gym lifting weights and treading the mill. That's when she had run into Brian. Literally. She had been walking out of the locker room when she bumped into a tall, shirtless blond man in gym shorts, with broad shoulders, ripped abs and mysterious scars. When she pulled her eyes upward, she found a pair of the most intriguing blue eyes smiling down at her.

It was as if Brian had his own gravitational pull. She had been quickly drawn into his orbit and before she knew what was happening, she caught herself developing strong feelings for him. He was quietly funny, with a subtle, dry wit that she found hilarious. He never spoke much about himself, claiming there wasn't much to tell. Her curiosity regarding his scars was never satisfied. She recognized more than a few of them as remnants from bullet wounds, but Brian never elaborated on his short explanation saying he had been shot a few times when he was deployed as a soldier in the National Guard. Wanting to respect his privacy, she never pushed for more information.

Being a strong, independent woman herself, Cole appreciated Brian's ability to go days, even weeks without seeing her, yet when they did meet up again; it was if no time elapsed. He didn't dwell on her failing marriage, and she was even more impressed that he wasn't intimidated by her career. He truly gave the impression that he only cared about who she was as a person and didn't give a damn about the extra drama. They just focused on each other and forgot about the grind of the real world for a while. Brian was fun, pure and simple.

Now, after shaking his hand and looking into those eyes, she still had to admit they were beautiful, she realized the truth. Brian was a lie. He didn't exist. When Brian disappeared after their few short weeks together last summer, Nicole was heartbroken. Somehow, she had developed a fairly strong addiction to the freedom and fun Brian offered her. He found the perfect balance of treating her like a precious gem while respecting her strong-as-steel personality. She had the sense that he was proud of her, and despite not knowing him for long, his opinion meant a lot to her. When he called her Cole, as only her closest friends were allowed to do, it sounded perfectly natural and right. Their relationship easily withstood a few weeks of Brian's absence, but once his absence grew into months, Nicole knew it was over. She assumed he went back to whatever life he didn't talk about.

At least she got that part right.

"Give him the five-cent tour and then get to work," Gabrielle instructed Nicole. "President Dawkins will need you both in an hour when he holds his weekly conference."

"Lead the way, Cole," Chance as he stepped aside. "I love tours."

Nicole glared at him, but he only smiled. He was fully aware that he no longer had the right to call her by her nickname, yet he refused to abide. Obviously, he was looking to get under her skin. *That's fine by me, jerk. Bring it on*, she thought as she briskly turned to walk down the hall.

"You two, follow me," Gabrielle commanded James and Anna, as she turned and walked the opposite way down the hall.

"How'd she know he was Brian?" James asked softly.

"I'll fill you in later," Gabrielle answered over her shoulder.

Anna glanced back at the sight of Chance and Nicole disappearing around the corner.

"She doesn't really seem his type," she mumbled.

"Sure she does," James answered unexpectedly. "Didn't you see that ring on her finger?"

"What? He's attracted to married women?"

"Unavailability. That's the key to getting my brother's attention. And of course, if she can handle a gun, that's a bonus."

"That seems a little dysfunctional."

James laughed and nodded. "You got that right, Princess."

* * *

"So, I have to say," Chance stated after following Nicole all the way to the location of the weekly press conference in complete silence, "that was the most informative tour I've been on. Ever."

Nicole spun around and snapped, ""I'm done giving you information, Brian. Or whatever your name is."

"Hey, I'm not asking for State Secrets here. I just thought it would be nice to know where the damn restrooms are. Maybe a fun fact thrown in here and there. Five cents sure don't buy much anymore."

Nicole almost convinced herself to remain silent, to not engage in any pointless arguing with a man who clearly had skills in the art of irritation. Almost.

"How did you do it?" she asked angrily.

"Do what?"

"Lie to me so easily? I'm trained to detect the

tiniest of lies. I can read facial tics and body language and know if a person is lying, or even thinking about lying. But you? Oh, hell no. Somehow you managed to fabricate everything, *everything*! And I had no clue."

Chance watched as a group of men in suits walked past them on their way inside the conference room before he responded.

"You didn't want to see the truth, Cole. If you had looked closer, you would've seen it."

"That's bullshit, Brian," Nicole shot back, her voice louder than what she had planned. She looked around to see if anyone had noticed her outburst before she continued. "No one played me like you did. No one."

"I'm not out trying to set any records," Chance replied evenly. "We're playing for the same team, sweetheart. How about we let the past be the past and focus on doing our jobs. Deal?"

"Fine. But to be perfectly clear, I think you're a complete asshole."

"Duly noted."

"And, if you ever call me 'sweetheart' again, I'll shoot you."

Chance smiled. "That's my girl."

Nicole's eyes flashed as she began reaching for her gun. Chance held up his hands, forcing himself not to make another abrasive comment. Instead, he said, "Sorry. I'll be quiet."

Nicole left her gun in its holster and took a deep, calming breath.

"Good to see that you and ole Deano made nice," Chance stated as he motioned toward her wedding ring.

"Brian, I swear to God, if you don't shut up—"

"Fine. I'm done."

"Somehow, I have a hard time believing anything you say," Nicole muttered as more reporters, staffers and presidential aids made their way into the conference room.

Finally, President Dawkins, along with four other protective agents approached the conference room. Dawkins made direct eye contact with Chance as he walked past. Chance and Nicole took up their posts, forming a protective barrier around the President as he prepared to make his weekly press conference, regarding the economy, unemployment rates and the increased violence occurring in Iraq, Syria and even in Russia. As he discussed all these topics in a calm, businesslike manner, the back of his mind constantly reminded him of the possibility that the most dangerous threat was not only in the United States, but also in this very building. He found himself eyeing each Secret Service agent he came into contact with, wondering if that particular agent was actually an imposter, an assassin just waiting for the opportunity to pull the trigger, flip the switch or push the button.

Just keep on doing your job. Chance Hughes' words drowned out the other thoughts in his head. Dawkins knew the operative's advice was the right advice. Still, it was impossible to feel calm about the situation. The magnitude of the danger he was in was proven by the fact that America's most deadly assassin was standing just a few feet away from him.

Chapter Sixteen

Washington, D.C.

The highly publicized meeting between President Dawkins and Israeli Prime Minister Yitzhak Olmert went off without a hitch earlier in the afternoon. Major media outlets, along with increased numbers of Secret Service agents filled the State dining room on the second floor of the White House's East Wing. The world watched as the two leaders exchanged smiles and pleasantries, pausing for photo ops and promising each other that their respective countries were dedicated to the safety of the other.

With the onset of evening, the Presidential gala was rapidly living up to its billing. The White House's largest room, the East Room, was decorated beautifully, and partygoers were dressed to the nines with men having donned tuxedos and the women wearing swanky gowns and cocktail dresses. Waiters dressed in their formal white uniforms kept the champagne flowing and the hors doeuvres plentiful. The seven-piece orchestra kept the mood light with airy classical arrangements by Beethoven and Bach. In between the orchestra music, a piano virtuoso sat behind the keys of the 1938 Steinway & Sons grand piano and filled the air with beautifully complex melodies.

The large crowd of dignitaries, the Israeli Prime Minister, presidential cabinet members, and of course, President Dawkins, his Vice President and their families was a security nightmare and the Secret Service agents working the event constantly scanned the area, looking for any drifting eye, nod of head or fingers slyly typing at cell phones.

For Chance, working in this environment tapped into most of his phobias. He was comfortable in chaotic gunfights, making split second decisions that could easily determine whether he lived or died, and living in complete isolation for weeks, even months while he stalked his prey, but standing in a crowded room, full of potential threats dressed in tuxedos, easily topped his list of most-hated situations.

He watched as Nicole Silverman maintained her position within a few feet of President Dawkins. It came as no surprise to him that after their initial confrontation, she remained completely professional and focused on her job. Other than an icy glare tossed in his direction here and there, Cole managed to work side by side with him without any drama. Chance's initial attraction to her was partly because of her mental toughness and dedication to her job. Too bad his own dedication to his career was to blame for the dirty looks shot his way from a woman he cared about. Chance's thoughts were interrupted when Nicole caught him staring at her. He gave her a quick smile and then turned away.

James and Anna held their posts as they stood watch on the other side of the room. James eyed his brother knowing full well how miserable he was. He made sure his frequency was turned to the private channel before he asked, "On a scale of one to ten, how much are you enjoying this?"

Chance's voice responded with a "I'm going with a negative one or two."

"Where would you rather be?" Anna questioned.

"Anywhere."

"Oh, take a pill. You'll be fine," Anna said.

"You're funny Princess. Hear that Cowboy? She's becoming a real comedian."

"Too bad we can't dance," James replied. "This tune is kind of jazzy."

"I don't wanna dance with you," Chance shot back.

"Not we, as in me and you, moron."

"I don't wanna dance with you either," Anna quickly stated.

"I happen to be a pretty damn good dancer,"

James argued.

"Hey Twinkle Toes, who's that guy talking to the First Lady?" Chance asked.

"I've been watching him," Anna jumped in. "He's had a lot to drink, so I think he's just stupid. I'll move in and check him out."

"He's harmless. Just boozed up," Anna stated after a few minutes. "You guys seeing anything?"

"A few dresses that should've remained in the closet." James replied.

"Did you see the Lansdowne Portrait," Chance asked while he scanned faces and registered movements.

"What's that?" Anna asked.

"1797 painting of George Washington. Martha Washington is hanging right next to him."

"What's with you and art lately, Stones? It's a little weird," James stated.

Chance checked his watch and noticed the wait staff were now preparing for a new round of drinks and hors deouvers. One waiter carefully pushed a large wheeled, stainless steel serving cart through the door and parked it near the wall. Chance immediately noticed a new face. One of the waiters, carefully placing several dainty glasses of champagne on his tray, hadn't been present before. Chance felt his heart rate slow and his senses sharpen. In a matter of seconds, all the irritations and discomforts of his environment melted away. A sense of calm and comfort eased over him and he casually made his way closer to the waiter.

"Close ranks," Chance said quietly into his bone mic, prompting Anna and James to move nonchalantly into defensive positions in front of the President, Vice President and their families.

Chance was thankful he had the benefit of hiding his eyes behind his mirrored shades. He closely studied the waiter, picking up subtle body language that may give away evil intentions. The waiter appeared relaxed; his hands didn't tremble nor did the tray that held the champagne. He moved smoothly, confidently and professionally, just like all the other wait-staff.

Chance took one step closer and the waiter paused at what he was doing and looked directly at the tall Secret Service Agent near him. In that one glance, Chance knew he had found one of the imposters. The waiter's pupils were dilated so dramatically that his eyes appeared black. Chance had seen this exaggerated state of calmness before.

Chance slowly walked away so as not to appear suspicious and cause the waiter any alarm. After double-checking he was on the private frequency, Chance spoke softly into his bone mic, "I've got a tango. Waiter by the south wall. I think he's wearing a vest. Get the A Team outta here, but don't cause a panic. Once you guys start moving, he'll focus his attention on you. I'll move around behind him so I can get a clear head shot."

James notified the other agents of the threat and Anna began evacuating the evening's dignitaries. Even though they did this without causing a spectacle, the quick exodus of all the high-profile targets was impossible to ignore.

As predicted, the waiter watched curiously, realizing his time-frame for action was being cut short. He would have to act immediately. He carefully laid down his tray of champagne and slipped his hand under his jacket. His fingers fumbled for the tiny switch.

Chance made his move, getting as close to the waiter as possible before taking his shot. He knew once his gun was drawn, pure pandemonium would break out. He had no doubt he'd hit his mark. The waiter had to be killed instantly in order to prevent any last second detonation of the suicide vest Chance suspected he was wearing.

In his periphery, Chance noticed James and Anna re-enter the room. In one fluid motion, he pulled his gun, aimed and fired. His silenced pistol only made a small "pop" and no one panicked. That is, until they saw a waiter fall over dead with half his skull blown off. Screaming party-goers stampeded to the doors. Agents quickly grabbed the dignitaries and cabinet members and pulled them to safety while trying to prevent the panicked mass from trampling each other as they raced for the exits.

While the world was spinning around him, Chance remained calm, searching for the second imposter. He watched for anyone who wasn't racing for a door. He stood guard over the dead waiter, gun drawn, watching and waiting. *Come on, make it obvious*, Chance thought as he studied the chaos. Yet, no one deviated from normal. Everyone looked scared and anxious to make it to the exit doors. Everyone, except the Secret Service Agents, of course. They all acted calm and professional, perfectly executing their jobs.

"I don't see anyone, Orion. Where is he?" Anna's voice asked in his earpiece.

"Princess, I think our missing tango is still undercover as an agent. Continue getting everyone out of here. Cowboy, you copy?"

"Loud and clear. No one has made a move yet, but I've got my eyes peeled," James answered.

"Look at every agent's eyes," Chance stated. "Check to see if they're dilated. Their eyes will appear nearly black. If you find dilated eyes, you've got your imposter. I'll secure the area in here and hold down the fort until the cavalry comes."

Chance knelt down next to the dead waiter and pulled open the terrorist's white shirt. Strapped to his chest was a bomb with enough C4 to kill everyone in the room and maybe even beyond.

"This one was loaded," Chance muttered to

himself. Then he noticed a tiny remote control wired to a gold ring on the dead man's right index finger. He searched for a connection to the vest and came up empty. A small red indicator light flashed at the tip of the control.

Oh boy, Chance thought. *Not good.* Then he eyed the food cart. *Shit.*

Part of him didn't want to open the compartment under the serving tray, but he had no choice. He quickly scanned the room to make sure everyone had gotten out. He needed to be alone before he proceeded. Seeing no one, he carefully pried open the storage compartment.

Chance felt a slight fleeting moment of fear, but he was not surprised with what he found hidden in the food cart. What appeared to be some sort of high-tech pipe bomb was packed tightly in the small space. He searched for, and quickly found the detonator and timer, which was designed for a remote override. Apparently, the fake waiter had already started the timer, as it was steadily ticking off seconds. He breathed deeply, clearing his head. He had worked a few bombs as a Marine, but that was a long time ago. Other than that, his only experience had been dealing with the aftermath of the explosions. Knowing there were no better options, Chance slipped out of his jacket, pulled off his tie and rolled up his sleeves. In just under ten minutes, the entire world would find out if Chance was successful or not.

James and Anna, along with about thirty other Secret Service agents formed a hard wall of protection as they escorted the high-profiles and their families through multiple vault-type doors with biometric access control systems. Those doors led to an elevator that would drop them six stories below ground into the President's Emergency Operations Center, the PEOC. The bunker was designed to withstand anything with the possible exception of a direct nuclear blast, and it was equipped with virtually all the same technology found in the West Wing's Situation Room.

One by one, James and Anna made a mental check-list of agents that were real and those that may be imposters. Luckily, all agents had removed their sunglasses as they made their way through the maze of doors. Desperately wanting to identify the mole before they were all locked together in the bunker, James moved steadily through the crowd of dignitaries, eyeing each agent carefully. Anna did the same, but to no avail.

Nicole Silverman maneuvered her way so that she was walking next to James. She peered up at him and asked quietly, "What's really going on here? Are you and Brian really Secret Service Agents?"

"We're agents, just doing our jobs, like you need to do. Focus and let's keep this crowd calm, okay?" James replied and sidestepped a bit to put some distance between them. "So far we're coming up empty. Orion, do you copy?" James spoke quietly, cupping his mouth with his hand to keep unwanted ears from prying. After a moment of static, he repeated, "Orion. You copy?"

James rechecked to make sure his radio was on the correct frequency before asking one more time, "Orion? You copy?"

Finally, Chance's calm, reassuring voice entered the airwaves. "Copy that Cowboy. I, uh, am dealing with a little issue of my own here."

"What's going on?" Anna asked softly, joining in the conversation.

"Nothing I can't handle. You must find our tango. He's gotta be with you guys. It doesn't make sense he'd be anywhere else. If his eyes aren't giving him away, search for anyone sweating excessively. The drugs keep them calm, but a possible side effect is profuse sweating."

The last doors leading to the bunker slid open and the agents with all the dignitaries stepped inside.

"Copy that Orion. We're inside PEOC," James said as he heard the last bullet and blast-proof door lock behind him. A surge of claustrophobia threatened to rattle his composure.

"Better find him," Chance voice stated evenly.

His brother's words forced him to regain his

focus and settle his emotions.

"We'll find him. You okay?" James asked, not because Chance's voice held any urgency or fear, but because of a nagging hunch that his brother was dealing with something big.

"Princess, you copy?" Chance responded. After hearing Anna's voice affirm her presence, Chance continued. "So, here's the deal. I've got an Aunt Martha here. But, no worries, I think I can deactivate it."

"You *think*? This is something you better fuckin' know," James replied, doing his best to keep his voice quiet, amid his spike in adrenaline.

"I'm thinkin' positive," Chance replied, still sounding as if he was doing nothing more than lounging on the beach sipping a Martini.

"What's an Aunt Martha," Anna asked, and James motioned for her to come closer so he could mouth the word *bomb* to her.

Anna's eyes widened but she immediately pulled out her phone and texted a message to O'Connor to send a bomb squad ASAP.

"Shit, Stoney, you aren't that great with Marthas. Just get the hell out of there."

"Thanks for your vote of confidence. I needed that."

James felt sweat beading up on his forehead. This was one of those times when he somehow simultaneously hated and loved his brother. He could kill him for having to be so damn heroic.

"Quit joking around, Stones. You need to get out. Now."

"Uh, no. I've got about ten minutes. You might have less time if you don't find the missing tango. Get to work."

James squeezed his eyes shut and understood that Chance was right. They both had very little time left on earth if they didn't execute their jobs perfectly. A little bit of luck wouldn't hurt either.

James opened his eyes and noticed Anna meticulously stalking through the agents. She paused briefly to reassure the vice president's wife and handed her a tissue. Despite being crowded and terrified, everyone in the bunker was quiet. Only an occasional whisper, or muffled sob, broke the silence.

Attempting to clear all thoughts of his little brother struggling to deactivate a bomb upstairs from his mind, James focused on walking around to try and flush out the mole. He glanced over at Anna, and that's when he noticed an agent stiffly pull his arms from her approach, as if he was protecting something inside his jacket.

"I think we got him, Orion," James whispered.

Chance's voice immediately responded, "Head shot only. Do not screw up and send a bullet into his chest."

"Copy that, bro. We've got this. Now you focus

on Aunt Martha."

Upstairs, Chance felt the sweat drip off his nose as he ever so slowly dismantled the outer casing making up the bomb's shell, exposing the cobweb of wires inside. All hopes that the bomb would be a simple IED dissipated as he studied the assembly. Complex arrangements of various colored wires attaching to the detonator, the timer and a canister firmly attached to the main body of the bomb, which was a pipe filled with explosive material. Chance had no idea if that explosive material was the more stable TNT or the extremely sensitive nitroglycerine that could explode with the slightest bump. To be safe, he kept his movements as gentle as possible. He softly cursed under his breath and tried not to let himself obsess on the blaring red numbers decreasing with every blink.

Somewhere in the periphery of his mind, he could hear the distant sirens, the chaos and even the condescending voice in his head telling him he wasn't that great at dismantling bombs, but he determinedly directed his entire focus on the network of wires. He had to kill this bomb.

Chance carefully pulled apart the wires, ignoring the red numbers that said he only had seven minutes left. He studied where each wire went, detaching them, one by one, as the seconds ticked by. He hastily pulled out his earpiece and shut off his radio, not wanting any distractions now that he was down to the wire.

Actually, he was down to two wires. Detaching the right one would mean success. Detaching the wrong one would mean a loud, fiery death. Taking a long slow breath, Chance steadied his hand and placed his fingers on the green wire. Just as he was about to give a firm tug, his eyes landed on the small silver canister attached to the bomb. At first he figured it was more explosive material, but now it dawned on him what that canister actually contained. This particular bomb was rigged up to kill in more ways than one. A dirty bomb. In all likelihood that little canister was filled with the lethal cocktail conjured up by the late Dr. Jafari. Dr. Death was at it again.

* * *

"You just walked by the tango," James whispered into his bone mic.

Without looking back, Anna began circling around.

"You sure?" she asked.

"Tell you in a second," James replied as he approached Agent Sullivan from his left side and brushed against him ever so slightly. That was all

James needed, as his hands that could've made him a decent income picking pockets, felt what he was looking for. "It's him, and he's wearing vest," he whispered. "Clear the area in front of him. I'm taking the shot."

Without hesitation, Anna shoved the group of people, including President Dawkins, aside at the same moment James drew his weapon and fired. The sight of a gun being drawn within the confines of the bunker brought about instant action. Three agents nearest James tackled him, aggressively pinning him on the ground and disarming him. More agents threw themselves in front of their charges, willing to take any ensuing bullets for the ones they promised to keep safe. Anna kept her focus on Agent Sullivan, who now lay dead in a growing pool of blood originating from the single shot to the back of his head.

She clawed her way through the chaos and approached the dead man. She pulled open his jacket to reveal the suicide vest strapped to his chest. She quickly detached wires ensuring it could no longer be detonated. She checked the dead man's hands to see if he held any remote detonating device. She thoroughly patted him down, not wanting to overlook any other possible deviant weapon he had planned to use against them.

"Why didn't I spot you earlier?" she asked angrily as she opened the dead man's eye lids.

"Contacts," she muttered angrily. She popped out one opaque contact lens that both changed the man's eye color, and hid the fact that his pupils were the size of dinner plates.

Anna tapped her earpiece and stated, "Orion, we got him. Tango is dead. You copy?"

Hearing only static she repeated her statement but was then interrupted by someone saying loudly, "Is that a bomb?"

She looked up to see one of the senators staring down at her, pale faced and in obvious shock over the current situation. Of course, upon hearing the word, bomb, the already chaotic atmosphere got worse. People began panicking and pounding on the door. The Secret Service Agents desperately tried to keep the situation under control but were quickly losing their handle.

Hating chaos, and noise, and the sounds of panic, Anna abruptly stood tall and yelled, "Hey!"

Not getting the silence or attention she needed, she spotted Nicole Silverman standing near her. "Shut everybody up!" she yelled at the woman.

Not fully understanding the scope of what had just happened, but realizing chaos could not be tolerated, Nicole snapped to action.

"Hey! Everybody shut up and listen for a second!"

Finally, all eyes were on her, pleading for an explanation.

"Everything is under control. The man who shot him," Nicole turned to look at James standing in handcuffs, pinned to the wall. "Yes, him. He saved our lives. He's one of us. Turn him loose."

Instead of uncuffing James, the agents merely stared blankly at Nicole.

"Uncuff him," a voice stated loudly from behind a wall of agents.

All eyes turned to see President Dawkins push his way through his agents, reassuring them he was fine.

"That man is working for me," Dawkins said. "Let him go so he can complete his job."

Within seconds, the cuffs were off and James had regained possession of his gun. He walked directly over to the President.

"Are you okay, sir?" James asked.

"Yes. Is he dead?" Dawkins asked, motioning toward the man lying prone in a puddle of blood.

"He is. Orion is still upstairs dealing with a situation. This isn't over yet."

"Are we safe down here?"

"I believe so, sir. Stay calm and we'll all get through this in one piece."

Dawkins nodded and proceeded to confidently reassure everyone. As Commander and Chief, he had extraordinary leadership skills, especially during times of turmoil.

"Have you had contact with Orion?" James

asked softly as he approached Anna.

"I've tried, but no response."

Suddenly the blast-proof door slid open to reveal an FBI Hostage and Rescue Team; six men, dressed in black fatigues and armed with assault rifles.

"Alright, everybody outta here," the leader demanded. "We'll be taking all of you to another secure location."

James stood up and approached the team leader. "I'm—"

The team leader held up his hand and shook his head. "I know who you are. I've spoken with O'Connor and she has filled me in with the situation. You and your partner have orders to remain here to secure the scene."

James glanced over his shoulder at Anna who held up her phone and nodded. "Just got those orders. Copy that."

As the H and R team gathered everyone and moved them out of the bunker, James and Anna could only wonder what in the world was happening upstairs in the East Room.

"Orion, please copy. What's going on?" Anna asked into her bone mic, feeling her heart thump through her chest. "Why isn't he answering?" she mumbled quietly. Then she asked, "Does he have much experience deactivating bombs?"

"Some. Not enough," James answered. "Maybe

the bomb squad is here and he's not even in there anymore."

"Wouldn't he tell us? Besides, there can't be much time left, right?"

James checked his watch. "A little over four minutes."

"What about us?"

"We're in a bunker, Princess. We'll be fine." James tapped his earpiece before demanding, "Orion, Goddammit, answer me."

* * *

Chance's focus switched from disabling the bomb, to detaching the canister. If he couldn't deactivate the bomb in time, or pulled the wrong wire and detonated the bomb himself, he had to make sure the deadly contents of the canister weren't released. At this point, his decision was all about choosing the lesser of two evils. His large hands barely fit into the tiny space as he felt for the point of attachment. When he found it, he swore under his breath, wishing he had some tools. He knew he could probably dig up something if he wandered around, especially if he searched the kitchen, but there was no time for that. The decreasing red numbers were brighter than ever as they mocked him with their blinking. He strained to grip the tiny nut and bolt that held the canister to the bomb. Between swearing and praying, he loosened the nut. Ever so carefully, he pulled the pop can-sized canister out from the serving cart. He wrapped it in several white linen towels, tucked it under his arm like a football and ran out into the vacant hall, directly over to the private dining room.

This dining room, otherwise known as the Family Dining room, was a small, formal area used by the President and his family to entertain smaller, more private meals than those served in the adjacent State Dining Room. Chance had briefly studied the floor plan of the White House after being assigned to this job. Quickly, he spotted what he was looking for and he darted across the room to the adjoined pantry, where he found a large walk-in freezer. He gently laid the white bundle inside, shut the door and sprinted back to the East Room. He dropped to his knees and slid to the serving cart, much like a baseball player sliding over home plate. Wiping the sweat from his face and catching his breath, Chance stared at the two remaining wires attached to the bomb. He placed his fingers on the green wired, once again prepared to give it a solid tug. Then self-doubt crept into his brain. *Maybe it's the red wire.* He released the green wire and looked at the timer. Four minutes happily blinked back at him.

* * *

James wanted to take his radio and throw it when he heard nothing but static fill the silence. He understood why Chance did what he did, but he hated it all the same. With some relief, James heard on Anna's radio that the D.C. Bomb Squad had arrived. He switched his radio frequency in order to communicate with the squadron leader.

"Give me all the information the agent inside has told you regarding the bomb," the squadron leader demanded.

"All he gave me was how much time he had, which was ten minutes. Now, we're down to under four. Actually," James checked his watch. "Three minutes two seconds.

"Is everyone secure?" asked the squadron leader.

"Yes," James answered.

"Are the bombs clean?"

"He didn't indicate otherwise," James replied hastily.

"The agent inside, he believes he can deactivate this bomb? Has he done this sort of thing before?"

"Yes he does, but that doesn't mean he will. We need to get him out before this thing goes off," James insisted.

The squadron leader looked over his team as they assembled their gear. He knew they didn't have enough time.

James recognized the silence on the radio. With

agonizing clarity, he realized what was happening. "No way. Leaving him in there is not an option!"

Not waiting for a response, James ran toward the door. Anna was right next to him, punching in the nine-digit code. James and Anna hurriedly made their way out of the bunker and began the frustrating process of passing through the vaulted security doors. Once through the doors, they sprinted down the hallway toward the stairs.

"They're leaving him in there," James yelled back at Anna.

"I know."

"That's bullshit. I'm going up there and yank him before this thing blows!"

"I'm right behind you!" Anna yelled. "How much time do we have?"

"About a min—"

James was abruptly cut off as a loud blast erupted from upstairs, causing the walls to shake and glass to shatter. They were too late.

Chapter Seventeen

Washington, D.C.

Gabrielle's phone had rung non-stop for the past thirty minutes as she received real-time updates of the events taking place at the White House. The moment after she received the text from Anna regarding the bomb in the East Room, Gabrielle informed her driver that she would be heading over to the White House. Anna's text was brief, but it did say that Orion was trying to disarm the bomb. Of course, he would evacuate everyone else while he stayed with the bomb. That was just Chance doing his best to keep everyone else alive while putting his own life in jeopardy. As she urged her driver to break whatever laws necessary to get her to the scene as quickly as possible, she said a quick prayer for a good outcome. She had been notified that one imposter had been killed in the bunker, but she had no idea what the status was the second imposter. Various reports were coming in regarding a shooting in the East Room that set off the

344

evacuation, but the information was spotty and sparse on confirmed facts. She could only hope that her agents would be able to put a stop to a national disaster.

A small amount of relief hit her when her driver made record time and skid to a stop near the White House lawn. However, as she took the first step out of her car, her worst fears became reality. A loud fiery explosion burst from a couple of the second story windows of the East Wing. Instinctively she ran toward the gathering of agents, law enforcement, SWAT teams, and Bomb Squads.

"Did you get him out?" she asked breathlessly. "The agent who was in there. Did you get him out?" she demanded more forcefully.

Gerald Finn, FBI's gritty tactical leader, grabbed her arm and pulled her aside.

"We can't confirm the status of that agent, O'Connor."

"Has anyone had contact with him? The Bomb Squad?" Gabrielle demanded loudly, her eyes unable to look away from the smoldering East Wing.

"Not that I'm aware of. Look, we're doing everything we can to figure out what's happening in there. Nobody knows anything at this point."

"What about the President?"

"He is safe. Everyone has been accounted for and are being held at a secure location," Finn answered.

"Everyone except my agent, that is."

"Hold on," Finn stated as he grabbed his radio and listened. He held the device close to his ear to hear over all the chaos.

Gabrielle could see the bad news reflected in the man's eyes as he listened to the voice on his radio. He turned away from her and said, "She's right here. I'll tell her." He clipped his radio back onto his belt and turned to face Gabrielle.

"Bomb Squad has entered the East Room and there is no sign of your agent. They have, however, found the bomb, which was located in one of the bathrooms."

Gabrielle paused a moment before saying, "The bathroom? But that's also a—"

"Blast room. I know. Either the bad guys made a tactical error or your agent knew about the bathroom's secret and moved the bomb there to minimize the damage."

"So, where is he?"

Finn hesitated a moment before saying, "They believe he was in the bathroom, still trying to deactivate the bomb when it went off. Nobody in proximity to the bomb could have survived."

Gabrielle's eyes filled with tears.

"I'm sorry, O'Connor. I wish he would've made it out, I really do. From what I gather, his actions were nothing short of heroic."

"I don't want a dead hero, Gerald. I wanted my agent out alive."

Finn nodded sympathetically before grabbing his radio and listening. After a moment he turned toward Gabrielle and stated, "I'm needed inside. Please excuse me."

"Yes, of course. Go," Gabrielle answered quickly as she tried to blink back the tears. She knew that Chance wouldn't have changed a thing. He had done his job and saved many lives. Except this time, he couldn't manage to save his own.

"Dammit, Chance," Gabrielle whispered. She looked at the White House; it was now being swarmed by every sort of agent possible along with firefighters who were putting out the smoldering portion of the East Wing.

She wondered how Chance knew about the recently renovated bathrooms. The ability of those rooms to withstand substantial blasts and armor-piercing rifle rounds was a well-kept secret. Nonetheless, somehow he knew, and because of that, he probably saved the East Wing or even the White House. Certainly, after the experts dissect and study the remains of the bomb, everyone would know what could've happened if Chance hadn't moved the bomb into the bathroom.

Gabrielle wiped her tears, pulling herself together as much as possible. She shifted her focus to James and Anna, certain she would have a whole new set of issues to deal with now. With Chance's death, James would no longer be a reliable ally. Truthfully, James would likely become an enemy if he blamed her for his brother's death. And Anna? She was a wild card. Gabrielle held no illusions about Anna's mixed feelings toward Chance. Now that he was gone, Anna could go rogue, as well. She needed to track them down and control them until she could assess whether she could trust either one

Gabrielle turned and looked at the front doors. They were supposed to wait in the bunker, until receiving further instructions from her. Then she realized that the explosion changed everything. Once James and Anna found out that Chance was dead, Gabrielle may never lay eyes on them again. Gabrielle kicked off her heels and started running.

* * *

"Why did it go off early?" Anna yelled struggling to keep up with James as he hurdled over fallen chunks of ceiling plaster.

"He cut the wrong wire!" James yelled back rounding the corner. Then he slammed on the breaks. Anna nearly ran full speed into his back before she realized he had stopped. Then she saw the reason. Walking toward them with a blackened face and a bright white smile was Chance. He had a slight limp, his suit was in tatters, and he cradled his left arm. He was the most beautiful sight she had ever seen. If James hadn't beaten her to it, she would have run up to him and hugged the hell out of him.

"Son of a bitch," James said after he released his brother. "You, stupid son of a bitch," he repeated surveying the damage.

Anna walked up to him, feeling oddly shy, as she asked, "How did you get out?"

"I pulled the wrong wire," Chance said with a cough. "Which sped up the timer. I figured my only shot was to move the whole thing into the bathroom."

"You put the bomb in the bathroom? I don't follow," James replied, the relief of not having to face his worst fear, sinking in.

"I'll tell ya later. I just wanna get outta here."

"That puts a whole new spin on the idea of dropping a bomb in the bathroom," James said with a grin.

"It's a blast room, isn't it," Anna stated, solving the puzzle.

Chance looked over at her and smiled. "You're catchin' on, rookie."

"It didn't contain the blast, though," she replied, motioning with her hand toward the obvious damage.

"Not completely, but it did pretty good. That was a big-ass bomb. A couple of weeks and the East

Room will be ready to entertain foreign dignitaries again. Hell, I bet even ole George and Martha escaped unscathed," Chance replied, wiping at a small stream of blood dripping down from his hairline.

"Hit your head again?" James asked.

"Of course."

"Great. I think the last bump on the noggin turned you into some sort of art expert. What's this one gonna do to you?"

"Turn me into a nice guy."

James pointed at his brother's shoulder. "Dislocated?"

"Yep. Can you get it back in?"

James gently took hold of Chance's arm, lifted it horizontally, pulled and then pushed, popping his arm back into its socket. Chance winced and then let out the breath he had been holding. He gingerly moved his arm.

"Better?" James asked.

"I remember that being less painful the last time you did that to me. Have a nice time in the bunker?"

"Lovely time. Only one person died," James replied. "Come on, let's get out of here."

"Why are you limping?" Anna asked as she walked beside him.

"To get a little more sympathy," Chance answered with a crooked grin. "Is it working?"

Anna tried not to smile back at him as she shook

her head.

When they rounded the corner, they spotted Gabrielle running down the hallway.

"Oh boy, here starts the ass–chewing," Chance mumbled.

When Gabrielle saw that the two agents she was hoping to find were standing next to the agent she believed to be dead, she stopped and stared. Then, without trying to hide her tears, she walked directly up to Chance, hesitated a brief moment, then grabbed him and held him in a tight embrace. With his uninjured arm, Chance awkwardly patted her on the back.

When they parted, Chance smiled, "I've known you for over six years and that's the first time we've ever done that."

Gabrielle quickly wiped the tears streaming down her face, "And it'll probably be the last time, too."

"I kind of like this softer, less 'administrative' version of you," Chance added.

"Don't get used to it."

"Does this mean you're not mad at me?"

"Why would I be mad at you?" Gabrielle asked incredulously. "You identified the imposters, got everyone out safely and probably prevented the complete demolition of the White House."

"We had a little bit to do with all that, too," James stated as he motioned toward himself and

Anna.

"I pulled the wrong wire," Chance said.

"Oh, Chance, please, don't be stupid."

Chance shrugged but then added, "You need to tell the Bomb Squad to retrieve a canister wrapped in white towels. It's in the walk-in freezer in the pantry by the private dining room."

James, Anna and Gabrielle stepped back and looked directly at Chance.

"Where did you get the canister?" Gabrielle asked, her mind already connecting the dots.

"Off the bomb."

"Oh my God, it was dirty," Gabrielle gasped.

"By the time I detached that damn canister, I was running out of time. That's why I screwed it up. I didn't have time to try and figure out which wire to yank. I shoulda pulled the green wire. Sorry."

Gabrielle turned away to hide a resurgence of tears. James and Anna only stared in stunned silence.

After taking a moment to gather herself, Gabrielle turned back. "My dear Chance, you have so many things you should apologize for, but tonight is certainly not one of them. Now, get yourself out of here and directly to an ambulance. If I find that you skipped out on a medical eval, you truly will be in trouble," Gabrielle ordered, unable to hold back a grateful smile.

She looked up at James and over at Anna and

added, "Yes, I am fully aware that you two are as much a reason for this success as anyone. Job well done."

Gabrielle tucked in the wisps of hair that had fallen loose and straightened her jacket. Emotions under control, she now had more business to attend to. First and foremost, she had to see that the canister was retrieved and sent to the lab for analysis. An operation like this would need endless reports filed, debriefings prepared, statements made, and summaries completed.

James stuck to Chance like glue to ensure that his brother did indeed proceed directly to one of the several ambulances parked on the front lawn. Anna stuck with the brothers, realizing she felt the safest in their midst. The three of them emerged from the White House to a barrage of questions and interruptions that basically trapped them in the crowd of emergency workers and security personnel. Finally, James pulled out his Secret Service badge and a path to an ambulance opened up.

As Chance sat with his feet swinging out the back of an open ambulance, he was suddenly approached by an unfamiliar group of people. Reporters. He eyed them suspiciously as they lifted cameras and microphones in his direction.

"Are you the agent who shot a man in the East Room?"

"Did you kill the terrorists responsible for this attack?"

"Are you a Secret Service agent?"

"Who is responsible for this attack?"

"How did the bomb get into the White House?

The questions flew, each one louder than the last.

Chance, looked over at the EMT who was preparing to stitch up the gash on his head. She only smiled back as if to say, "You're on your own with this buddy." He tried to ignore the persistent group, but he began feeling more and more claustrophobic as they closed in on him. The cameras were flashing and microphones were shoved into his face. He was considering taking matters into his own hands when he heard a sharp command given by a voice he recognized.

"He will not be answering any of your questions. This man requires medical treatment so please, give him some space. The White House will be issuing an official statement within the next few minutes."

"Aren't you Gabrielle O'Connor of the CIA?"

"Is this man one of your agents?"

"Was he working undercover?"

"Were you aware of an impending attack?"

Gabrielle held up her hand to silence the unending questions. "Again, the White House will be issuing an official statement within the next few minutes. Please, give us the room necessary to treat all incoming injuries."

The reporters finally relented and backed off. Some even shut off their cameras and prepared to look for another interview. Then, from a few feet away, a voice shouted a question that got everyone's attention.

"I heard a rumor that you're Sergeant Chance Hughes, the Marine who was taken hostage seven years ago. Is this true? Are you Chance Hughes?"

Silence draped over the small crowd that had gathered. Gabrielle, James, and Anna were the only ones who were staring at the reporter in disbelief. Everybody else's eyes were fixated on the lanky, blond-haired man swinging his legs out of the ambulance. Gabrielle suddenly looked over at Chance, worried he'd be tempted to pull out his gun and permanently shut the reporter up. When he reached behind and pulled out his favorite pistol, a shocked collective gasp reverberated through the watchful gathering. Chance, thankfully, appeared calm.

He thoughtfully brushed his fingers over the image of the stars and dice etched on the slide. He had to keep those stars in their rightful place. Behind the dice. Orion couldn't take over Chance. When he looked up, he noticed Gabrielle studying him with concern. Chance smiled.

Then he slowly stood up, looked directly at the

reporter and said, "Yes I am. I'm Gunnery Sergeant Chance Hughes."

Chapter Eighteen

Langley, Virginia

The consequences of revealing his real identity
to those reporters were beginning to arise for
Chance. The first hints of change were when he
arrived at CIA Headquarters. Before, he had merely
flashed the security clearance badge Gabrielle had
given him, and he could walk the halls unimpeded
and completely unknown. He'd meander his way to
Gabrielle's office with hardly a second glance. This
time, he didn't even make it out of his vehicle. The
moment he parked his car, he was swarmed with
reporters who had staked out all night taking their
chances that the now famous, resurrected Marine
hero would show up. Their patience appeared to pay
off big time when they spotted their target drive in,
sitting behind the wheel of his powerful black
muscle car. Instead of getting out, Chance dialed his
boss.

"Someone sent the Welcome Wagon. If you
don't find a way for me to avoid these maniacs, I

will. Blood will be shed. It won't be mine."

"For heaven's sake, drive up to the main gate. I'll notify the guards it's you, and they'll let you in. Park on Level B and come in Door 15. I'll meet you there."

As he followed Gabrielle into her office, he saw that James and Anna were already there.

"Since when are you early?" Chance commented to his brother.

"I'm not. You're late."

"Yeah, well, there's a bunch of crazies down there looking for Elvis."

"You look nothing like Elvis," Anna commented seriously, as she pulled up a chair.

"Oh, but you should see him dance, Princess. The man moves like the King," James stated.

Anna huffed and tried not to smile, which seemed to be harder and harder to do while in the presence of the Hughes brothers.

"What? You have a problem with dancing?" Chance teased.

"She has a problem with fun," James interjected.

"Oh. Well, fun can be a little risky. Better to stay safe than be sorry right?" Chance asked.

Anna pointed her finger at him and replied, "I don't have a problem with fun or risk. Now, fun with you? That's a chance not worth taking."

Chance immediately turned away and shook his

head. "Oh man, you did *not* just say that."

"What?" Anna asked, wondering what she had said that was so wrong.

James cleared his throat and said, "I think that one is my new favorite: 'not a chance worth taking'. Every woman should have those words tattooed on their forehead. I'm still really partial to 'half a chance'. And of course, 'fat chance' is always good, although not that applicable. 'Slim chance' is more believable. 'Good chance' is completely unbelievable. 'Bad chance' is true, but not that funny. 'Not a chance' is a little sad. 'Chances are' is way too open-ended and could have horrible results. My biggest fear involves the possibility of a 'second chance'."

Chance only looked back at Anna and shrugged helplessly as if to say, "See what you've started?"

Gabrielle grinned and sat behind her desk. "Are you done James? Or is there a 'chance' you have more to say?"

"Oh, not you, too!" Chance gasped.

James nodded his head seriously. "Oh, I almost forgot the 'is there a chance' dilemma. Truthfully, no one really knows if there actually is a 'chance'."

"Ok, ok, already," Chance said holding up his hands in defeat.

"Oh, come on," Anna stated. "Give them a 'chance' to speak."

James laughed out loud, and even Gabrielle

laughed softly at the unexpected comment from Anna. Chance turned and stared at the woman.

"You, too? Really?"

"Okay, now seriously. Let's talk business for just few minutes and I'll let you be on your way," Gabrielle stated in a firm voice. "First of all, how are you?" she asked, looking at Chance. "Shouldn't you be wearing a sling?"

"Nah. I've dislocated my shoulder a few times before. It's not that big of a deal."

"I've heard you say that exact same thing about concussions, stab wounds and bullet holes."

"What's your point?"

"Moving on. Both of the imposters have been ID'd as Rahid Mohammad and Al'johar Aleed. Both Islamic radicals. Both long time loyalists to Dominique Rodriquez."

"They didn't look like Arabs," Anna commented.

"They weren't," Gabrielle replied. "They were both born in the Czech Republic. They converted to Islam as teenagers, changed their names by the time they were twenty five, and were bona fide terrorists by the age of thirty."

"And dead by age thirty-five," Chance added. "So, give me the low-down."

"These men were pros. They've been on the Secret Service payroll and have impeccable work history. Neither one ever raised a red flag.

Obviously, there's still information coming in but here's what I believe; they were planning on detonating three separate explosions. The imposter acting as a waiter would begin implementing the plan by pretending to discover a bomb in the service cart. This of course, would create immediate evacuations. Civilians and White House staffers would be escorted to a separate location, while the President and the dignitaries would be taken to the bunker."

"Ah, so that explains the remote device I found on his finger," Chance interrupted. "I'm connecting the dots now. The waiter would have been herded off with the other staffers and civilians, while the second imposter, still perceived as a Secret Service Agent, would be holed up in the bunker with the President and company. Waiter remotely detonates the service cart bomb, and then himself, to ensure maximum destruction. In the meantime, knowing the bunker is blast proof, the fake agent detonates his vest and blows everyone inside to smithereens."

James shook his head in disbelief as he said, "And just like that, the White House, all of our political leaders, along with the Israeli Prime Minister, and a few hundred civilians are dead. Wow. That's quite a plan."

"And they almost succeeded," Gabrielle added, "if it weren't for your actions. The three of you saved a lot of lives."

"That was about as close as it comes," Chance commented softly.

"Be that as it may, it's over. We'll take this experience, study everything and hopefully learn how to never let it happen again."

"What about the canister?" Anna asked.

Gabrielle nodded. "Preliminary results indicate that the contents, although close to Dr. Jafari's recipe, are not an exact match."

"Domino couldn't find anyone to replicate it after Jafari's untimely death," Chance stated. Then he looked over at Anna. "Good job with that, by the way."

Anna nodded.

Gabrielle watched the notable change in the dynamics between her best agents. Were they actually getting along with each other?

"I'm curious," Chance said, his steady gaze interrupting Gabrielle's thoughts. "What corner of the earth did you stuff the priest?"

Gabrielle was momentarily caught off guard. Chance's voice sounded dismissive and cold, yet she could clearly see the concern in his eyes. Displays of warmth and caring were so rare with Chance, yet on occasion those close to him could occasionally glimpse a side of Chance he carefully guarded. Despite his ability to separate emotion from his lethal actions and make cruel decisions, Chance actually cared about people.

"I'm in the process of finding a safe location for Father Sanchez. If everything goes as planned, he will be released from his holding cell and on a flight out of the country tomorrow."

"Did you find him another parish?" Chance asked.

"He'll be safe, Chance. That's my main priority."

Something dangerous flashed in Chance's eyes. "Does that mean he'll soon be working for you?" he asked as he glanced briefly at Anna.

Gabrielle took a slow breath, not allowing Chance to drag her back into an argument over Anna.

"I'm hoping to place Sanchez in a small church near Calgary," Gabrielle said after realizing the only way to satisfy Chance's curiosity was to tell him the truth.

"Canada? Really?"

"Yes. He should be able to lead a quiet life there."

"While under constant surveillance and heavily monitored," Chance remarked.

"Of course. That's for his own safety as well as our own. We can never forget that Carlos's brother wanted to decimate the United States," Gabrielle replied.

James suddenly spoke up saying, "Hey, a guy shouldn't be punished merely because he has a brother that's a menace to society."

Chance rolled his eyes. "I'm not a menace to society, bro."

"That depends on who you ask," Anna quickly added, bringing a look of surprise from Chance.

"You're sure quick with the jabs today, Princess," Chance said with a grin.

Gabrielle checked her watch. Her life didn't allow much time for idle chit chat, and today was certainly no exception.

"Let's discuss the next order of business, shall we?" Gabrielle spoke loudly, reining in everyone's focus once again. "I'm sure you've all seen the news and are aware of the fact that Chance is no longer a secret. Obviously, this changes things."

"Do we still have jobs or are we fired?" Chance asked bluntly.

"No one is getting fired," Gabrielle replied quickly. "Anna, we've been reviewing video footage, and I believe we can keep your identity confidential. You will be reassigned to a new operation within the week. I think it's in our best interest to get you out of the country as soon as possible. Do you feel fit to work?"

"Of course. Why wouldn't I?"

"Good. Now, James and Chance. We have some decisions to make, but before we do, the President wants to have a talk with Chance, privately. After that, we'll go over our options. Deal?"

"I'm feeling left out," James said, sounding perfectly pitiful.

"The President asked to see you, too, but I told him you'd rather avoid any more 'suit and tie' affairs, conference rooms and drives across town. I could call him and tell him you're coming."

"Nope. I just remembered I had someone to see about a guy who knows a guy."

"That's what I figured," Gabrielle answered with a grin. "Chance, suit up and you'll come with me over to the Capital to meet with the President."

"Yes, ma'am," Chance answered.

Anna quickly stood and grabbed her black leather jacket and headed for the door.

"Hey, Princess," Chance said.

Anna stopped mid stride and turned around. Chance walked up to her and held out his hand. "Thanks for not trying to kill me."

Anna smiled as she shook his hand and replied, "There'll be a better time."

"Truthfully," Chance said slowly. "I think you missed your chance."

James snorted with laughter behind him and Anna only rolled her eyes as she let go of his big hand.

"See ya, Princess!" James called out after her.

"Don't call me that!" she answered as she walked out of the room and shut the door behind her.

"Good one, bro," James said as he high-fived his little brother.

"Thanks. Ready, O'Connor? I wanna get this over with."

Gabrielle nodded as she grabbed her coat and briefcase and led the way.

* * *

Chance fidgeted with the glove box, the window controls, the pens he found in the console and everything he else could get his hands on. Sitting in the passenger seat was not one of his favorite things to do. He rarely allowed someone else to be in control of his actions and sitting quietly while someone else drove certainly violated his comfort zone.

"I'm trying to be patient Chance, but it's getting difficult," Gabrielle stated as she signaled to turn off the freeway.

"You should've let me drive."

"It's my car."

"So?"

"I think you're getting worse."

"With what?

"Everything. I'm making an appointment for you to spend some time talking with Reinholt. He is about the only one who can help you with your issues."

Chance rolled his eyes and sighed. "I'm worse because for the past few weeks I've been forced to work in extremely difficult and uncomfortable situations."

"You mean civilization?" Gabrielle asked.

"Yes! Release me back into the wild and I'll be fine."

"You're not an animal, Chance. Don't act like one," Gabrielle replied, instantly regretting the motherly tone she heard in her own voice.

Chance glared over at her. "Most of the 'human' was trained out of me," he stated evenly.

Gabrielle pulled her car into the private drive leading to the secure rear entry of the Capitol building. They drove slowly past a fleet of limos and SUV's with smoked-out windows parked nearby. After finding a spot to park, Gabrielle switched off the engine and turned to face Chance.

"After this meeting with the President, regardless of the discussion, I'm requiring you to take some time off. Away from here. Go to Montana and decompress. I think a minimum of two months would be beneficial."

"Two months? Are you kidding me? Not happening, O'Connor. I don't do well with time off. I need a job."

"You will take the time off to heal. I don't want to hear from you or see you until your injuries are healed and you're off the pills. Don't believe for an instant I bought your story about taking a few Tylenols to ward of a headache or two. I know I pushed you to get back to work before your symptoms were gone. You did whatever you had to do to function, and I respect that, but starting today, no more pills. I don't want to see your face until you're fully rested and ready to work again. Am I clear?"

"Why do I think there is an 'and'?"

"And, I want you to listen to what Dawkins has to say today. Think about his offer and don't make any rash decisions. For once in your life, don't let your instincts rule your actions, okay?"

"Offer? What sort of offer would the President make to someone like me?" Chance asked, genuinely confused.

Gabrielle placed her hand on his knee, "Just tell me you will hear him out."

"You've certainly tickled my curiosity, that's for sure."

"Tell me."

"Okay, okay," Chance replied with a laugh. "I'm all ears. I'll carefully consider all offers thrown my way."

"Good. Now, get going. The guards are waiting to escort you inside."

Chance glanced out his window and spotted Nicole Silverman, standing quietly beside two other agents he didn't recognize.

368

"I think I should have my gun," Chance stated seriously.

"Go before I kick you out myself. I have a meeting I must get to in a few minutes."

Chance groaned softly as he opened the car door. He noticed a small gathering of reporters had congregated near one of the "staff only" entries of the Capital.

"Why is the media here?" Chance asked his boss before exiting the car.

"They're going to be everywhere you are, at least for a while. You'll be fine. Just try not to kill any of them."

Chance slipped on his shades and walked over to the agents. Nicole met him halfway and stopped him.

"Oh, come on Cole, I'm not in the mood to lock horns with you right now. Besides, I'm already gonna be late."

Instead of the verbal attack he was expecting, she stepped closer and slowly extended her hand as a peace offering.

"I just wanted to thank you, Chance," she said softly. "I knew your name wasn't Brian."

Chance studied her a moment to ensure she wasn't joking before he reached over and grabbed her hand.

"What you did was phenomenal. A lot of people owe you their lives and gratitude," she stated seriously.

Feeling far more uncomfortable in this situation than he would have had she stuck with her usual behavior, he pulled his hand away and felt his heart rate speed up a tick. He couldn't help but notice a couple of camera flashes going off. His heart rate jumped another tick.

"You would've done the same thing," he replied quickly. "Besides, it wasn't just me. Everyone did their part."

Nicole pulled off her shades and smiled up at him. It was the first smile she sent his way since last summer.

"Humility? That's about the last thing I ever expected from you," she replied in exaggerated shock. "Is this your real personality finally shining through?"

Standing exposed to the photographers felt similar to discovering that you were dead center in a sniper's crosshairs. Chance needed to escape.

"There's very little about me that's real or shiny," he shot back. "Now, if you don't mind, could you please get me inside? I've got a meeting with the President."

Nicole's smile disappeared, and as she slipped on her sunglasses she said, "You're really messed up, aren't you?" Getting no response, she turned her back and added, "Follow me."

Chance ignored the camera flashes and

questions as he was quickly escorted through the back entrance doors into the Capital. He wondered what sort of circus he would have had to endure if Gabrielle had dropped him off at the front doors. He walked in silence, suddenly realizing that he had Secret Service Agents guarding *him.* The three agents held a hard line around him as they made their way to the presidential office at the end of the hall. Chance shook his head thinking that in all likelihood, if he had to, he had the skills to take out all three of the highly trained agents. He wondered if they realized that and quickly surmised that they didn't. They oozed confidence in their mannerisms, in the way they walked, communicated and portrayed a typical cool detachment.

"Here you are, Sergeant Hughes," Nicole stated without an ounce of warmth. "Go on in, the President is expecting you."

"Thanks, Cole," Chance replied, feeling a tiny trickle of guilt over how he had talked to her outside. He knew it was pointless to remedy his actions. He would only say or do something else that would eventually piss her off again.

Chance walked inside and heard the door click shut behind him. President Dawkins rose from behind his desk and quickly circled around to greet Chance with a broad smile and outstretched hand.

"There aren't enough words to express my gratitude for what you have done, Chance. All I can say is thank you, but I know that is not nearly enough."

"Oh, that's plenty, Mr. President. I don't usually get so much attention after an operation has been completed. I have to say, this is all a little weird for me," Chance shook the President's hand.

"I'm sure it is. Please, have a seat," Dawkins said motioning toward the chairs near a small library along the east wall of his office. Dawkins sat in the chair facing Chance and crossed his legs. "How are your injuries? I understand you dislocated your shoulder?"

Chance shook his head. "I'm fine. Ready to go back to work."

Dawkins sat back and smiled. "O'Connor told me you'd probably say that. She also said that you're ordered to take some time off to rest and heal up."

Chance scanned the walls and décor of the office, subconsciously noting points of entry, exits, hiding places and perfect places to stash weapons.

"There are times that Miss O'Connor and I disagree about my schedule," Chance replied evenly.

Dawkins grinned. "She cares a lot about you. I've known Gabrielle for many years, and I've seen how she handles her agents. She doesn't treat any of them carelessly, but I'm seeing a different side of her when it comes to dealing with you."

"I'll bet."

"She doesn't want you to be left hanging in a bad situation without backup. You've been operating without support or protection for a long time. Even though I don't necessarily agree with what she did, I do understand why Gabrielle kept you off the grid, even from me. Now, obviously, the secret is out. You have some decisions to make, Chance."

"I need to know my options, first."

Dawkins nodded as he replied, "The sky is the limit for you. You are an American hero with an amazing story to tell, if you want to. Best-selling books, movies, speaking engagements, political office, you name it, you've got it."

Chance felt his stomach tighten and the walls close in. He felt the blood drain from his face.

Dawkins noticed Chance's complexion pale, prompting him to ask, "Are you feeling ok, Chance? Would you like some water?"

"Water would be good, thanks."

Dawkins stood and walked over to the small sink and counter across the room and poured a glass of water. He handed it to Chance and sat back down.

Chance gulped down the water and stated, "I'm hoping you have some other option for me. I don't really fit the mold of a public figure. I work best in the shadows."

Dawkins clasped his hands and paused. He planned to word the next option perfectly in order to get the answer he wanted.

"The way you took charge as an agent in my protection detail was remarkable. You commanded respect and handled yourself as though you were a veteran of the Secret Service. Because of this attack, and your actions to protect me, your cover was blown sky high. The least I can do to repay you is to offer you a job."

"A job, sir?"

"I would be honored, and well-protected, I might add, if you would join my protection detail for the duration of my presidency. I would also ensure that you maintain a top position within the Secret Service for as long as you wish, after my term is up. The options are endless. You could be station chief, or an Investigative Agent, or one of the many special agents out there making a positive difference in our world."

Chance was at a loss. He didn't see this one coming. Him? A Secret Service Agent? Somewhere from the corners of his mind, he heard Gabrielle's voice pleading with him not to make any fast decisions and to hear the President out.

"I'm both honored and extremely surprised at your offer, sir," Chance finally replied.

"You shouldn't be surprised. You have the talent and the mentality to make a superb agent in the Secret Service."

"I'm not all that accustomed to working within boundaries and –"

"Rules? I know. But I'm fully confident that you could adjust. Everything I've read and learned about you suggests that there is very little you can't do, Chance."

It's the stuff that wasn't written down and recorded you should worry about, Chance thought to himself.

"I'm just not sure I can give you an answer right now."

"Oh, I certainly wasn't expecting an answer from you today. This is a decision you need to think about. I would like a response by the end of the week, however."

"Of course. Just out of curiosity, what is left for me if I choose neither option?"

Dawkins hesitated. Then he walked over to his desk and pulled out a file.

"You get back to work, doing what you were doing," Dawkins answered. "But this time, you'll have the full resources of the CIA and military at your disposal. You would officially become an agent of the CIA."

Chance sat a little straighter. "How much would I have to change my tactics?"

"Gabrielle and I have already had a long discussion about this scenario. Basically, what we decided is that the best way to handle you is to keep you as far below the radar as possible. Now, this is just between me, you and Gabrielle."

"Of course."

"You and your missions would be off the books. Gabrielle informs me of an operation, I'm the one who gives it a red or green light. You're responsible for doing your job without creating an international incident, nothing changes from what you've been doing already, and it's my job to protect you with support and backup from the military and Special Forces, if needed."

Gabrielle's words reminding him of patience and listening were quickly overruled. Chance hated wasting time when he already knew what his decision was.

"Sir, I really appreciate the time you've take to talk to me about these options. I'm truly honored that you have asked me to serve on your protection detail, but I'd just be delaying the inevitable to wait a week to give you an answer. I'm sorry, but I just don't belong in the Secret Service. I'm not a defensive player. I can't wait for the enemy to come to me. I prefer to be on the offensive side of things. I have to go find the enemy before they find us."

Dawkins truly wanted Chance Hughes on his detail for two reasons. Not only would Chance keep him and his family safe, but by keeping him in America as a Secret Service agent, he would ultimately be keeping Chance safe, as well. He figured the young man was due to have someone finally looking out for his best interests. Although disappointed with Chance's decision, Dawkins nodded his head; it wasn't meant to be and he understood and accepted Chance's answer graciously.

"You are an exceptional young man," Dawkins proclaimed as he stood up.

Chance rose from his chair and grasped the President's hand. "Thank you, sir, but I'm just a guy who does his job."

The President laughed, "So am I. You know, I do have one question I want to ask you. How on earth did you know that the waiter was an imposter?"

"His eyes sir. They were dilated."

"I don't understand."

"He was drugged up, sir. See, due to the fact that nerves screw up more operations than anything else, individuals often dose up on chemicals that dramatically relax their nerves without dulling their senses."

"I had no idea. You've seen this before?"

"More than a few times, sir."

Dawkins looked into the eyes of one of America's most important security systems.

"Thank you, Chance. If you ever need anything, I'm there."

Chance grinned. "That's good to know, Mr. President."

Chapter Nineteen

Washington, D.C

"How the hell did you ever find this place?"
James asked as he sat down at the small table with a
fresh pitcher of beer.

"Seems like I'm always cooling my heels in this
town, waiting to be debriefed, or getting a new
assignment, blah, blah blah. I was wandering
around one night, and I stumbled upon this dive.
Beer's cheap, crowd's small, and everyone seems to
mind their own business. My kind of joint," Chance
leaned back in the chair and stared out the small
dingy window over the dimly lit, concrete alleyway.

"Nice view, too," James added sarcastically.

"Yeah, on a good night there's even some
criminal activity down there for entertainment."

"Don't your hero tendencies give you the urge
to intervene?"

"Nah, I don't work in the States."

"A little late for that to be true. Oh, how things
change. How's it feel to be a rock star, Stones?"

James asked with a laugh.

"Hate it. Can't wait to disappear for awhile."

"Comin' home, right?"

"I think I'll give you a little space so you can rekindle whatever you've got going on with that hot vet. What's her name again?"

"Casey, and I don't have anything 'going on' with her."

"Then I'll come home. She seemed to be my type. Maybe I'll ask her out," Chance replied, unable to meet his brother's glare.

"She is a normal, well-adjusted single woman who has never killed anyone. I'm fairly certain she's not trained in hand-to-hand combat, nor does she carry a loaded weapon at all times. She's not even close to your type."

"Hey, I try to keep an open mind about people. She might be more dangerous than you think," Chance grinned.

"You are one of the least open-minded people I've ever known," James grumbled. "Stay away from Casey."

Chance sat back and stretched. "I think I've made my point. I'll give you two some space. I'll show up in a few weeks or so."

"What are you gonna do in the meantime?"

"I promised Sean the next time I had a few days to spare I'd let him take my car for a cruise."

"Whoa, that's risky. A nineteen-year-old behind

the wheel of four-hundred horses is a recipe for disaster. If anything happens, O'Connor will mount your head on her living room wall."

"If anything happens, O'Connor will be buying me a new car," Chance shot back with a grin. "Ah, nothing will happen. Sean's a pretty level-headed kid. Besides, I'll be in the passenger seat, strictly enforcing the speed limit."

"Good luck with that."

Chance leaned forward on his elbows. "I know O'Connor told us Carlos was going somewhere near Calgary, but can you find out exactly where he ended up?"

"I had a feeling you'd want that information," James replied with a smile. "I've already located him. Are you planning on doing what I think you're going to do?"

Chance turned his gaze out the dingy window to watch a small group angry-looking kids strutting down the alley. Finally, he said, "Nobody wants to live under constant monitoring. He didn't do anything wrong, there's no reason he should be punished."

"Sometimes you're almost a good guy, Stones."

"Almost."

"Don't worry, you hide it well."

"Thanks. I might need your techie geek skills to pull it off."

"Might need? You couldn't pull off half your

crazy-ass stunts if it wasn't for my skills you little punk," James shot back angrily.

"Think what you want," Chance said with a shrug. "So you'll help?"

"I always do. Besides, I don't think Carlos likes cold climates. Let's find him someplace warmer."

Chance smiled and nodded.

"I hate to admit it," James said, "I do agree with O'Connor about one thing. You need a break. You look tired."

"Maybe. After I help Carlos disappear, I'm gonna fuel up the Camaro and drive wherever the open road takes me."

"Almost sounds peaceful."

"I'm all about peace."

James focused on not laughing until he swallowed the big gulp of beer in his mouth.

"You sure you don't want some?" he asked as he poured himself another frothy mug of ale.

"Nah."

"Man, you used to be able to drink men twice your size under the table. You've changed little, bro."

Chance shrugged. He had changed. Gradually, little by little, he had lost whatever youthful tendencies he had once had, and now he gripped tightly onto controlling everything he possibly could, because in his world, the only thing he could actually control was himself.

"One beer won't turn you into a raging drunk."

"It might. I don't have much tolerance built up, anymore."

"That's for sure. But, you don't make a very cool spy if you don't have any vices."

"Oh, trust me, bro. I have my share."

"Speaking of vices, I see one sneaking up on you, now," James said quietly.

"I saw her the moment she stepped through the door."

James smiled at the woman approaching their booth. When she was near enough to hear, he said, "I guess she's not that sneaky."

"I wasn't sneaking," she grumbled.

"Did you change your mind about killing me?" Chance asked nonchalantly.

"What's a vice?" she asked.

"A vice? Oh, ah, zamestitel," Chance quickly translated the unfamiliar English word into Russian for her.

"Zamestitel? I don't even want to know about your zamestitels," Anna quickly replied.

"Wise choice, Princess," James answered as he toasted her with his beer glass. "How the hell did you know what we were talking about?"

Before she could answer, Chance said, "She reads lips."

Anna looked at Chance in surprise. "How'd you know?"

"I've noticed you doing it from time to time."

"Not much gets by you, Longshot."

"Except the reason why you're here."

"I need a moment with you."

James grabbed his pitcher of beer, "I'm outta here," he said and headed for the bar.

Anna slid into James' seat.

"I thought you'd be half way around the world by now," Chance stated, studying her closely, wondering what on earth she was doing sitting in this shitty bar, talking to the one person she claimed to hate with all her heart and soul.

"Wheels up tomorrow."

"Lucky you. Is there something wrong?"

"No," she answered quickly. "I mean, yes, well no, not really," she stuttered. "This was stupid. I shouldn't have come."

"Okay. Goodbye," Chance replied.

Anna sighed and asked, "Do you like this job? Your life, doing this…whatever this is?"

Without hesitation, Chance answered, "Yes. Do you?"

"Really? I mean do you actually enjoy all the killing, the exposure to the worst the world has to offer day in and day out?"

"Gosh, Princess, don't glamorize it so much," Chance replied dryly. "It's a job. Don't over-think it."

"I hate it when you call me that. I want to hear

you say my fucking name, just once, okay?"

Chance smiled and leaned forward, "I love it when you swear. That Russian accent of yours is so damn sexy."

Anna held his gaze a moment before she slammed her hand on the table and stood up.

"You're an impossible pig. Good riddance."

Anna quickly strode toward the door. Chance took one more sip of his Coke before he slid out of his seat and easily caught up with her before she walked out the door. He followed her out onto the sidewalk.

"Hold up there, Prin—Anna," Chance corrected himself as he grabbed her arm and spun her around. "Why in the holy hell did you track me all the way to this shit hole? Talk to me."

Anna felt shaky with anger and adrenaline. She wasn't even sure herself why she was standing in front of the man she had sworn eternal hatred for.

"I did want to kill you, you know. I had dreamt of it often. I thought working for O'Connor would get me closer to you, so I could gun you down and watch you die. I wanted to watch as that arrogant light in your eyes faded into nothing," Anna spat.

"Wow, you did put a little thought into it, didn't you. What's stopping you? I'm not saying you'll be successful, but hey, everyone has a lucky day here and there." Chance reached under his jacket and pulled out his gun and handed it to her. "Here, I'll even give you my gun to try and even the odds a bit."

Anna backed up as if repulsed by the thought of taking his weapon. Then she walked in a small circle kicking at rocks. Finally, she faced Chance and looked up at his face. "I read your file. I know what happened to yo—"

"Stop, Anna." Chance's voice was deadly serious. "I'm going inside now. Have a nice trip."

"Wait!"

Chance stopped in mid-stride and turned back to face her.

In a near whisper, her voice unsteady, Anna spoke. "I guess I just wanted to tell you that I don't want to kill you, anymore."

He saw the mixture of defeat, sadness and confusion in her eyes. If he was truthful, he felt more than a little confusion himself. He was comfortable with the idea that she hated him. He expected it. If she went and changed that scenario, his comfort level would vanish. That irritating little voice in his head piped up enthusiastically, telling him it was in his best interest to remain as detached as possible. Something in her troubled blue eyes threatened to make him teeter towards stupid.

"Good to know," Chance replied softly. "That's one less name in a long list of people to look out for."

"I know why you had to kill my father," Anna's

voice wavered.

Chance took a step back. "Hold on. I'm not a fan of Memory Lane. Let's not go there. If you need to talk out your issues, I know a great shrink. I'll give you his number." He had absolutely zero desire to revisit the bloody shootout that had taken place in that dingy warehouse in Moscow.

"I understand that you were doing your job and lying to me was just a way for you to complete the operation," Anna continued, ignoring Chance's remark. "You're a professional, and I respect that. I just don't want to waste time being angry at you, anymore," Anna added. "That's all. That's what I wanted to tell you."

Chance swallowed and felt his throat tighten. He ran his fingers through his hair as he scanned the area for any creepers.

"I'm not okay with that," he finally said.

Anna's eyes widened. "What are you talking about?"

"I mean, that whole not wanting to kill me part, that's a good decision. But a healthy dose of hatred for me is smart."

Anna stepped closer to him, wondering if her somewhat limited English comprehension skills were causing a misunderstanding. Chance took a step back keeping a distance between them.

"You are a cagey bugger, aren't you?" Anna commented. "I'm sick of hating you. Deal with it. I think you should dial that number you were going to give me. A little time on the couch might help."

Chance couldn't help but smile. She reacted exactly how he would have reacted if the roles were reversed. A little of his smart-ass had rubbed off on her. He allowed himself to look back into those blue eyes. The sooner he faced up to the fact that she had the potential to expose a weakness in him, the sooner he could fix the problem. Even Superman had to deal with Kryptonite.

"Not everything that happened back then was a lie. You should know that," Chance spoke deliberately, treading on unfamiliar ground as he cracked open the door to the truth just a tiny bit.

Anna held up her hand. "Stop. Just stop. I don't need placating. I don't need any more of your lies. Working with you, I see now what you are. Nothing about you is true."

"I don't lie all the time, Anna."

"Really? How can anyone tell? Even the polygraph doesn't know, right?"

"I guess you just have to trust me."

Anna laughed. "Have you forgotten who we are, Chance? We're spies. Trust doesn't exist in any language."

"Everyone needs one person they can trust."

"You have James."

"I do. Who do you have?"

Anna looked away, shaking her head. "I don't

need anyone."

"Good luck with that."

Anna checked her watch. "I need to get back and start packing. Sorry I interrupted your evening. Take care."

Anna turned to leave and Chance nodded as he stuffed his hands in his pockets. Then Anna stopped and turned around to look at him once more.

"If I did happen to need someone, down the road, hypothetically of course, wou—"

"I'd come running," Chance answered before Anna could finish.

She smiled a true, genuine smile and their eyes locked for a long moment before she said, "Thanks, Chance."

"Take care, Anna."

With that, Anna turned and disappeared into the shadows. Chance watched until he could no longer make out her silhouette. Then he turned to walk back inside the bar.

Epilogue

Calgary, Canada

"Bless me Father, for I have sinned."

Father Carlos Sanchez felt his blood run cold as he heard the familiar soft voice speaking to him from across the confessional curtain. He did his best to control the fear from affecting his response as he said, "Go on, my son."

"My last confession was about two months ago, but it didn't turn out that great since the church blew up and nearly killed me."

Sanchez felt his fear drift away as a smile crept onto his lips. He reached up and pushed the curtain aside to reveal the American he knew only as Orion. The man's icy light-colored eyes held a spark of humor in them as he smiled.

"Hello, Carlos," Chance said softly.

"Why are you here? Am I in danger again?" Sanchez asked, nervously looking toward the door of the small confessional.

"I doubt it. Do you like it here?" Chance asked,

quickly scanning the tiny room for cameras or recording devices.

"It's clean," Sanchez said, noticing Chance's glances. "I insisted that the confessionals remain confidential."

"Good. I knew you would. That's why I'm here."

Sanchez smiled and asked, "Not to confess?"

Chance laughed softly.

"Then why are you here?" Sanchez asked again.

"To make you disappear."

Sanchez's eyes widened as the fear rushed into his system again.

However, Chance only smiled back and said, "Not from existence, just from the watchful eyes of the CIA. Sound good?"

Sanchez let his mind ponder briefly about the constant knowledge of being followed, watched and monitored. The price he paid for betraying his brother was the complete loss of privacy. He looked directly back at Orion and nodded.

"You can help me?" Sanchez asked softly.

"If you trust me, yes, I can help you live off the grid, in peace."

Sanchez felt the heaviness lift from his chest as he took a deep breath. Freedom was within reach. All he had to do was decide if he trusted this mysterious American.

"Well?" Chance asked. "This is a one-time

offer. If you tell me, no, you will never see me again. You can stay here, safe and sound under the watchful eyes of the CIA."

"I'll go. I trust you," Sanchez said quickly before doubts changed his answer. "When do we leave?"

"Now. You can't bring anything with you," Chance replied as he stood up and opened the door.

Sanchez stood and started to follow the tall man through the doorway when suddenly he stopped and turned.

"By the way," he said as he held out his hand. "I've never properly introduced myself."

Sanchez cautiously raised his own hand and placed it into the man's firm grip.

Chance shook the priest's hand and smiled. "I'm Chance Hughes."

#

ABOUT THE AUTHORS

Lora Moore lives on a farm in southern
Minnesota with her husband, Dan, and children,
Jessica and Travis.
Julie Zuehlke lives on a ranch in northern South
Dakota with her husband, Darin, and sons Jake and
Luke.

www.brokenbranchpublishing.com

www.amazon.com

www.barnesandnoble.com

www.smashwords.com

Books by Lora Moore and Julie Zuelke

THE SECOND OPTION (Chance Hughes Series#1)

AMERICAN SHADOWS (Chance Hughes Series #2)

Made in the USA
San Bernardino, CA
31 May 2014